THE LEGEND OF
HALLIE ELAINE THOMPSON
AND THE
DEMON OF MORELAND HILL

The Legend of Hallie Elaine Thompson and the Demon of Moreland Hill

Ormine Thompson

The Legend of Hallie Elain Thompson and the Demon of Moreland Hill

Copyright © 2018 by Ormine Thompson. All Rights Reserved.

Cover designed by Esther Beentjes

The final edit by speedy876

Ormine Thompson

http://orminethompson.com

aswainsen@yahoo.com

Printed in the United States of America

First Printing: December 2019

Oogoobe Tree Publishing

Revised printing 2022

ISBN-978-1-7328803-1-3

DISCLAIMER

For the sake of characters, period, and their locales authenticity, some characters may switch from English to Patwa in the same sentence. While the grammar may differ from your mama's, it doesn't mean they're suffering from a grammar deficiency.

*Dedicated to the cultivators of peace and to those
who sow and nourishes empathy.*

ABOUT THE AUTHOR

Mr. Ormine Thompson was born in Western Jamaica and has worked as a police officer, in public relations, and as a lyricist and music producer before migrating to the USA to further his writing. He's the father of one daughter, four sons, and grandfather to six. He presently resides in North Carolina.

In addition to writing, his hobbies include reading, listening to music, watching TV and movies, and taking long walks.

*Evil never leaves. It is and ever was
The craft of those who spilled blood.
It may very well copy from creation
While masquerading in the light
To hide the darkness within us.*
                    -Ormine Thompson

Prologue

In 1834, the October rains came a month early in Western Jamaica, and the welcome precipitation made the countryside lush by the second week of September. A two-thousand-year-old demon disguised as a fifty-year-old man trudged leisurely through a guinea grass field in a valley; his locks were white like egrets' feathers, and his skin black as burnt coal. A leather string tied his calico britches, wet from morning dew around his slender waist, and the ends hung down to his knees.

The sun climbed above the eastern hills behind him, and two thin, horizontal, spear-shaped, gray clouds marched across the crimson sky in attack mode.

Flocks of mosquitoes and flies followed a yard above his head, but none attacked, as if he had an invisible shield of protection around him.

He jumped a creek, exhibited a nimbleness well below his age, and trudged through a marigold field on the other side of the gutter. A cave mouth yawned at him a hundred yards ahead in the hillside as yellow butterflies, dragonflies and honeybees cleared a path in front of his lanky frame.

Smoke rose five hundred yards to his left from the first few huts of a new village. He had instructed the formerly-enslaved people to name the place Moreland Hill, after the she-demon's plantation where they had slaved upon. Dense bushes and low trees hid the huts from the valley.

England had abolished slavery over a month back, and some former slaves had hacked through the wilderness, staking their claims on small plots.

The old man sat on a rock a few yards inside the cavern as the first sunray muscled through tree branches and danced on the dull front walls. The cavernous darkness stood like a foreboding barrier behind him.

He had protected the slaves belonging to the Ashanti out of Western Africa from the she-demon's abuses for two hundred years on the Moreland Hill plantation. Although he couldn't free them outright, he had made sure their lives were comfortable in his unique way.

His ebony eyes gleamed golden flames from a pang of regret, but his leathery face remained impassive. The abolishment of slavery had nullified the pact between himself and the she-demon.

He transported Kabba, the old bookkeeper prince from Jamaica, back to Africa and reinstalled him in his house in a few days. He had not gone back to Africa for two hundred years himself but, before he left, he had to protect his beloved Ashanti's new village against the planters and the powers of the day. The deal between him and the demon plantation owner Tilly Whitelock did not include an indentured period for his people—they were through fucking slaving.

The old man sighed as he jumped off the rock like a young man in his prime vigor, and flames danced in his eyes. The sounds of bass drums reverberated from the holes and crevices in the cave, to which the old man danced. The pounding sounds followed his stomping feet as his arms reached out and his fingers twirled the air. As his body twisted in a mystical dance like a serpent on its tail mocking time something stirred.

The infectious occult rhythm captured his being, and he hummed in a deep bass voice. The air vibrated, as loosened rocks ascended and danced around him.

A fissure opened six yards from his twining fingers and expanded into a churning black hole, deep as time. Demonic howls echoed like a thunderous force from the maw of the abyss. The old man pulled, twisted and danced until a black, four-footed animal sprang from the pit. It dropped on its feet, scampered into the dark recess and flaming red lights illuminated the cave's walls from the beast's eyes. A large chain, six feet in length, levitated into the old man's hand. His long talon fingers zapped it, and consuming flames ran along the chain-like an animated entity. The flaming six-yard metal zipped from his hand and wrapped itself around the animal's neck in the dark.

"Rolling Calf, I command you to protect Moreland Hill until the end of time from man, demons and beasts."

The Rolling Calf spoke telepathically from the dark, *"Free me, free me. Return me to my status as a boy."*

"I cannot undo what a powerful dimension god as Kaang did," the old man replied.

"Who are you, and what can you do?" the beast questioned.

"I am Sanga, and I have stolen you from Kaang's foul dimension," he answered.

"You could learn from me. I came from the first tribe, eons before the gods and Kaang came."

"Beast, they created me before time began," the old man asserted.

The chain rattled for an answer in the crimson crevice as if the calf acknowledged the man's dominance over it.

Chapter 1

In the 1970s, the Cuban secret police the DGI inserted an intelligence officer under cover as a medical doctor named Garcia Santiago, in Jamaica. The Jamaican Health Ministry assigned him to the Savanna La Mar Hospital. Aside from his medical duties, he supervised thirty Brigadistas: Jamaicans sent on training missions to Cuba by the government of the day. The Opposition claimed they were terrorists trained to inflict mayhem on the Jamaican people. Garcia, a Black man, had fit in perfectly in western Jamaican nooks and lawless crannies, picking up tidbits.

He hailed from a large Santeria family in Cuba, and did not find Tilly Whitelock's gold legend as far-fetched as many people did when told. When the government changed in 1980, the new regime gave the Cubans forty-eight hours to leave Jamaica. However, Garcia landed in Miami on a bogus Jamaican passport and visa a day after the elections.

Garcia found he could not practice medicine in America and struggled in Miami doing odd jobs. As bad juju would have it, he met Ten-Cent a stocky Jamaican small-time hustler touching thirty in a Caribbean restaurant on 3rd Street and North Miami Avenue in downtown Miami in 1986, and they became friends. When Ten-Cent mentioned Moreland Hill, Garcia quizzed him about Tilly's gold and asked if he believed the story. Ten-Cent told him yes, like everyone else in Moreland Hill. Tilly Whitelock was not a legend, but a fact he grew up believing in until the story grew into the fibers of his being. Although he couldn't take anyone to the exact spot where Tilly buried her treasure, he could guide them to the general area.

"It's over there under those towering trees, people usually said."

Thousands of large trees were in the area they pointed, though. Garcia informed him he had an interest in exploring the story, but they had taken no further action.

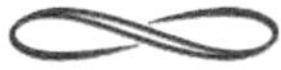

Many people claimed it happened in 1987, but folks around Miami Gardens placed it as late as the summer of 1990. Although stretched, punched and punctured, the story evolved into an urban legend in Miami's Jamaican community anyway.

Ten-Cent had robbed a DEA agent as the story went. Folks said it happened in the 183rd Street Flea Market in Miami Gardens. He took the agent's briefcase containing thirty thousand US dollars, his gun, and badge in minutes. The details remained foggy, but the agent had marked Ten-Cent on the Miami docks for a sting operation several weeks earlier. Karma labeled it a case of bad intentions and deceit from birth. The agent had Ten-Cent as a quick ten years of Federal time on his resume, and Ten-Cent fingered him as a Federal Agent he would offer to sell two keys of coke and robbed instead. If the DEA had read the FBI dossier on Jamaican criminals at the time, the operation would have gone in a different direction.

It played out amid a hundred people in the Flea Market's aisle. The two men walked side by side at 12:08 p.m. Ten-Cent intentionally missed a step, placing the agent a foot ahead, and delivered a hammer fist to the agent's neck, flooring him. He sprinted through a rear exit, lugging the agent's briefcase to his car parked on NW 179 Street. He drove to MIA, purchased a one-way ticket and by 4:00 p.m., he landed at the Sangster's International Airport in Montego Bay, on his way to Negril.

It hadn't taken Ten-Cent but three months to blow through the government's $30,000 partying in Negril. Desperation soon dogged him to a point where he would try anything except return to America so early. One evening, while searching for a-hustle in the local bar, he overheard a loud conversation between two elderly drunks about Tilly Whitelock and her gold.

Garcia's old scheme popped in his head. He ran to the payphone on the wall and poured in coins like water going into a sinkhole.

Weeks after, six men barged through the Moreland Hill bushes, hacking a path as noisy as a parade of wild elephants. Ten-Cent led the pack, cutting and slashing. Garcia led Jose, a Santeria priest; Toussaint and Loubens, voodoo masters from Haiti, followed.

Brother Teekus, a Jamaican Obeah Man extraordinaire, brought up the rear. The men carried heavy backpacks, and occult oils stained the air. The mid-afternoon sun rays speared through the leaves and branches of the tall trees like solid golden beams. Birds' songs came from everywhere, and a flock of chattering parakeets flew madly away from above the men's heads. After some time, Ten-Cent sat on a dead tree trunk and mopped his face while the men wet their parched throats from water bottles.

"Are we going in circles?" Jose asked.

"No, we are searching for a pile of animal bones," Garcia replied.

Loubens and Teekus felt the crunching of bones under their boots in the robust underbrush minutes later. They stopped and made hands signaled. Loubens pointed in a circle, placed a finger to his lips and lifted his foot to backtrack. Within seconds, supernatural machetes blurred and hacked Loubens' body in two halves. The four other men glimpsed forty ghostly machetes descended on Teekus and made mincemeat of him. They shouted and bolted in different directions, as elongated ethereal blades slashed. The supernatural machetes sliced through small trees and bodies in a fast second before a deadly silence reigned over the windless woods. A woodpecker subsequently nailed a tree as if it drove the nails into another expedition for Tilly Whitelock's gold.

Chapter 2

Tilta Brown one of the most wanted men in Western Jamaica, drove a new BMW X6 along a muddy, potholed, dirt road between rusty zinc fences and the powerful headlight beams cut the darkness illuminating stark indigence.

Chasing dogs uttered a cacophonous chorus even before the vehicle's horn honked three times. It pulled under a sizable guinep tree and cut the lights. Two men melted from the shadows as the driver flew his door and illuminated a six-yard patch of light.

"What a gwan, Tilta Brown?" Bukky asked as he slinked from the darkness.

Tilta Brown, a light-skinned baby-faced youth, stepped from the car, flexing his twenty-two-year-old muscles. He had tucked his dreads under a black wool hat, and his tight black T-shirt pushed into his black jeans, showing every iron-hard muscle in his upper body.

He lit a joint, sucked and blew smoke in the night's face.

"Mi have a work."

"De car ready fe roll," Bukky said.

"Mek mi seet," Tilta Brown said.

Feather Pee exited the car, also wearing full black. He was a tall, lanky youth, and he wore a perpetual poisonous smile on his lips. A scar ran from his left ear to his nostril and made him seemed older than his twenty-five years.

Bukky was thirty-five, sported a chunky body and strong working arms, but the two younger men were taller than him. He led Tilta Brown, Feather Pee and his sidekick Big Lion, a massive late-teens youth wearing lion's mane dreads, through a zinc gate.

Tilta Brown turned at the gate, beckoned, and Lisa, twenty-one, stepped from the front passenger's seat. She wore a short, black evening dress, fighting to cover her essentials.

The men stood under a tarpaulin-covered shed around an early model car, painted muddy gray and throttling low and sweet. Lisa sat on a verandah facing the men.

"Where's the food?" Bukky asked.

"Moreland Hill, mi a tun over Sammy Fray's place tonight," Tilta Brown said.

"Yu boodclaat crazy, Tilta Brown? The supernatural protected Moreland Hill from its creation," Bukky replied.

"I'm protected by the best Haitian voodoo masters and Jamaican Obeah Men," Tilta Brown pressed.

He held up his left hand, showing off each finger clad in two rainbow-colored ring stones.

"Yu a ride or wat, dog?" Tilta Brown continued.

"No, Iyah, mi and Big Lion a sit out dis one. We're not protected," Bukky announced.

"A more food for Feather and me then," Tilta Brown remarked.

Feather Pee slapped Tilta Brown's hand.

"Lisa, hold tight till we forward."

"Left the key in case we have to move de Beemer, Tilta" Bukky said.

"I never remove the keys."

Tilta Brown bent for a kiss, and Lisa kissed him.

Her eyes might as well have flashed dollar signs in the dark.

Sammy Fray's Place boasted quaint thatched-hut gazebos scattered in front of the main building perched on a rock above the sea. The crashes of light waves attacking the cliff added to the night's ambiance. His jubilant patrons were a mix of locals and tourists on shellfish night and the waitstaff ran back and forth, serving crabs, lobster, conch, crayfish, shrimps and cockle treats. Tour buses and other vehicles lined the narrow road.

Tilta Brown drove by, searching for a parking spot.

"I haven't seen a single security guard," Feather Pee said.

"Dem nuh have no security," Tilta Brown uttered.

"What a piece of cake."

Tilta parked under a tree two hundred yards up the street in the darkness. The men tucked handguns in their waistbands, took two AR-15s from a bag on the backseat and selected rounds in the chambers.

"Maybe we should do a walk-through, Feather," Tilta Brown said.

"Yeah, it couldn't hurt." They returned the rifles to the bag and toted it between them.

The animal stalking Tilta Brown and Feather Pee could pass for a big, black dog in the dark. Its head hung low as it followed the men ten yards back on the Moreland Hill main road. The men stopped and watched a 2020 Grammy Winners' acceptance speech on a fifty-inch TV through an open front door. The animal had maneuvered around the light shaft and reappeared in the next shadow, three feet taller.

Tilta Brown's right hand subconsciously touched the Glock in his waistband. His left hand carried one bag strap containing the two AR-15s between him and Feather Pee. He stopped suddenly, and the bag dropped from Feather Pee's hand to the ground.

"What, did you hear something?" Feather Pee asked.

"More like I felt something crawling up my spine."

"Bukky's Duppy stories get to yu, mon," Feather Pee teased.

Tilta Brown sneered at him.

"What do they say? Moreland Hill protected its own, nuh? I'm killing five local and five tourists tonight to prove them wrong," Tilta Brown said.

"Yeah, show them who's top shotta and who ran Westmorland."

They peeked into the dark, picked the bag up and hurried away.

The animal had grown as large as a nine-month-old calf, but broader.

Flames ignited around its head, as a door slammed shut on the left and got the men's attention. Chain-links rattled in the dark behind them, and it was as loud as a ringing bell. The lights in the houses along the street went dark. The beast lit a six-yard-wide hellfire from the rusty chain around its neck and leaped on the men. The rotating flames illuminated two shiny vertical horns above blood-red eyes and a third polished horn on its snout above an extra ocean-color eye. Its dark face resembled a mix between a bulldog from Hell and an angry unknown demonic creature from the same neighborhood.

Both Tilta Brown and Feather Pee's mouths opened wide, but neither their shouts nor yells escaped as the creature burned them to dust. The flaring fire subdued back to black night. It left nothing where the men had stood. A fireball spun fifty yards down the road, and Moreland Hill's country ambiance reclaimed the night.

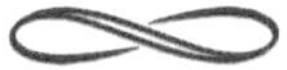

Meanwhile, Bukky gave Lisa a beer in his living room. His eyes had a mischievous glint as he guzzled a Guinness. Big Lion rolled a joint two yards from a monster TV playing music videos on the wall as Lisa returned to the couch, sipping her beer and two pair of eyes helped her cover herself in her mini dress. Bukky managed to see around curves as his invading eyes dug under her skimpy dress. Thick tension hung in the room and curled like an invisible fog between Big Lion and Bukky, but Lisa had not noticed it. The men had grown up in Moreland Hill's vicinity and had the district's reputation locked in their DNA. Based on their job descriptions, a working visit to Moreland Hill was off the table for them. Tilta Brown and Feather Pee weren't coming back. Lisa and the BMW hung in the air like suffocating objects, as Lisa's restless eyes strayed to the clock on the wall.

Ten minutes after Tilta Brown and Feather Pee died, a restless Lisa stretched her tightened muscles and sighed. Impatience and alcohol mixed a nice anxiety punch and wound her tight.

"My girl, they're not coming back," Bukky said.

"What do you mean? Tilta Brown is the toughest shotta alive."

"He's not alive anymore," Big Lion said.

A troubled Lisa glanced at both men; her eyes conveyed a flash of anxiety and anger.

"What's in Moreland Hill?" Lisa asked.

"Good and evil, supernatural protection."

"The only thing left is de sharing of de spoils," Bukky said.

Fear clouded Lisa's brow. *Fuck, Tilta Brown could be dead. Otherwise, these men wouldn't dare disrespect me. I dropped out of school for him, and my actions had left me dead to my parents. I cannot go back to 'ordinary, broke, dropped-out-of-college' Lisa.*

Bukky stared at Lisa and back at Big Lion.

"Girl, as fine as yu is, I'm holding the BMW," Bukky said.

Lisa gawked in shock at Big Lion.

"If what you say is true, I'm with whoever gets the Beemer. I ride in class," Lisa said.

Big Lion seethed. "You can't hold everything, Bukky."

"Mi holds de Beemer, and she wanna ride, nuh blame mi."

"It nah go so," Big Lion asserted.

"Wat yu mean, Lion?" his tone conveyed a sting.

"Si wat mi mean, yah, pussy."

Big Lion fired a shot at Bukky and missed by inches. Bukky dove behind the couch and returned fire. Two guns echoed, and when the smoke cleared, three bloody bodies lay motionless on the floor.

Chapter 3

Two years ago, on a warm evening in Bath Mountain a sleepy little village in mountainous North Central Westmoreland. Gem a brilliant seven-year-old and her two older friends next door played *Read the Verse*. They had sat around Sister Gina's dining table, and Gem read Matthew Chapter 19 fluently in a commanding voice. She finished the chapter and pushed the Bible across the table to Milda, two years older.

Milda fumbled her way through Matthew 20. She was a year older than her sister Pauline, who took the Bible and continued where Milda had stopped.

She, too, struggled to read the chapter. Sister Gina, the older girls' mother, considered herself righteousness on high, took in the drama through her deceitful, envious forty-year-old eyes from the doorway.

She had every identifiable sacred Christian image jumbled on her living room walls and breakfront, as if she accounted for all the saints and angels in Heaven, in attendance admiring her.

She fumed and sweat under her high-collared long sleeves floral dress from her neck to her ankles.

"Milda and Pauline, you've chores to do. Gem, you can come back tomorrow."

"Goodbye, Sister Gina. Goodbye, Milda and Pauline. See you at school tomorrow," Gem announced.

"Goodbye, Gem."

Sister Gina parted the curtain as Gem entered through her front door next door. Her envious eyes shone ill will, and she wheeled around to face her daughters, a slipper held high.

The girls cringed, and she clobbered them over their shoulders.

"Not a sound, do not make a sound."

The girls covered their mouths, and Sister Gina hit them until her fury abated. The children buried their heads in their arms on the table, and their bodies jerked hard enough to dislodge organs inside of their bodies.

Sister Gina stood over them, puffing like a broken motor.

"How could Gem read more fluently than you? Her mother is not even a true Christian. Answer me."

She expected no answers and had never sat her children down after school and helped them with their schoolwork. In her sphere of holiness, she commissioned God to cover her household.

The sobbing children had their heads hung in living fear as their stiffened shoulders braced for more beating. Sister Gina puffed away into her bedroom, dropped her backside on her bed and parted the curtain. She stared at Gem's parents' beautiful house next door, and envy twisted her face.

Monica raked leaves between the two houses and lifted her eyes as if she felt a presence. Sister Gina pulled away from the window, bit a knuckle and folded her arms.

"Monica dropped a hand on my girls. Her daughter cannot out-read my girls."

Her chest puffed like a heifer ready to charge.

"She's a sinful woman who grew up in an evil Pocomania church. She envied my girls and did evil things to them."

She folded her arms, dropped them to akimbo in the exact second, and pouted her lips in Monica's direction.

"I can play the game too. I hope you can manage return blows, Miss Pocomania."

The next morning dew wetted Sister Gina's purple and yellow trumpet-flowers ankle-length dress tail on a well-beaten bushed lined foot track. Mist curled from the ravine on her right, although it was after 7:00 a.m. A spring ran under the greenery and a breadfruit tree, burdened under huge fruits, hung low over the path. The Blue Quit's distinctive calls pulled her eyes into the ackee trees to her right. They'd always given her a thrill as a child, and she used to sit under fig trees to imitate their calls.

The steep track leveled out to a flat area, and zinc roofs shone through the trees in the morning sun. Occult oils and sulfur rode the wind, and Sister Gina rapid-fire sneezed as she got closer to the ranch-style board house painted gold, with decorated white shutters. Chicken wire fence surrounded the property and met at the high gate posts. A metal lift-up lock fastened the gate, and an ugly goat's skull hung by its horns in the center of the arch.

As usual for evil clandestine shenanigans, the meeting between Sister Gina and the Obeah Man was informally warm. She appeared well-rehearsed and comfortable in her skin in the presence of the diminutive Necromancer. The man had squeezed past fifty years a long time ago and wore a Kangol hat pulled over a missing left ear.

He possessed a weather-beaten, old tobacco brown face, dark eyes and cunning lines around his mouth. Sister Gina relaxed by his side on the verandah on white plastic chairs.

"Sister Gina, when you're a Christian, evil people take it as a habit to hurt you and your family," The Obeah Man said.

"My girls were doing so well in school before she dropped a hand on them," Sister Gina said.

"She's new to your church, huh? The Obeah Man asked"

"Oh, yes sir. She grew up in in a Pocomania church."

"Another evil nest right there, I tell you."

Pots and pans banged in the kitchen; a strong coffee aroma activated Sister Gina's taste buds, and she swallowed her saliva.

"Milli, bring us two cups of coffee, please," he instructed.

Sister Gina swallowed her saliva again.

"She intended to blind your children, but your Christian faith saved them. Instead, she only stunted them," The Obeah Man said.

Sister Gina's bosom puffed up to explosion point, and her eyes narrowed into slits.

"I'll lift the spell for twenty thousand dollars. For forty, I'll return the blow. If you wanted to make it slow and painful, it would cost you fifty thousand dollars."

"I'll do the fifty, Sir."

"Wise choice. Doctors will run them into the ground searching for a cure."

Sister Gina nodded her head, and a faint smile danced across her lips. The Obeah Man knew her children needed self-confidence and tutoring. However, the woman she envied had done nothing but show love to her children, but people do not pay Obeah Men for advice. They pay to inflict pain.

Monica had borrowed her husband's car to run an errand. On her way back, she and Gem sang along to Jah Bouks' "Angola" on the radio.

"De music sweet, Gem."

Gem giggled and played drums on the console.

Sister Gina had a rough day on her journey back home from the Obeah Man's place. Rain drenched the countryside for two hours, and her minibus had a fender bender. After waiting another two hours for a bus at Locus Tree, she hit the road, hefting two shopping bags.

By the time she reached Red Pond, her shoes had soaked to the soles and long evening shadows Criss-crossed the pot-holed road when she heard the vehicle approaching.

"Thank you, Lord," she mumbled.

The car came around the corner.

"Mamma, don't drive by Sister Gina," Gem remarked.

Monica cut the radio as she pulled up.

"Sister Gina, you're wet," Monica said.

"Wet and tired, my dear," Gina replied.

"If it wasn't for Gem. I'd have passed you by, Sister Gina."

"She is a smart little girl. God bless you, my dear," Gina commented.

"Thank you, Sister Gina."

"She is a fluent reader, way above her age, Sister Gina said."

"I try my best, ma'am," Monica said.

That night, Monica, gazed out of her daughter's bedroom window on the warm, moonlit night. A gentle wind distributed sweet night jasmine fragrances, and she filled her lungs before closing the window and blinds. Gem, her seven-year-old pride and joy, sat on the bed. Monica considered herself, her wonderful husband and gorgeous, intelligent daughter blessed. She beamed inside, and her inner joy flooded her face in a delightful smile. Monica hoped she could conceive after Gem's birth. Her mom had six children, and her older sister had four, but why complain when she had more time to love Gem? She glanced through the door; Religion had its place, but she didn't see it as something she should lose herself in when the world rotated on technology. Gem's future lay in math, science and technology. If she hadn't conceived again by age thirty, as she told Dave, she intended to adopt two orphans.

Monica tucked Gem into bed and propped a pillow under her head.

"When are we going riding again and playing some more reggae music, mommy?"

Monica whipped her head toward the open bedroom door.

"Shh, Gem. Beating reggae music in the car is a mother-and-daughter secret thingy."

Gem giggled.

"Husband and father shouldn't know everything."

Gem nodded her head, excited to share a daughter and mother's secret. Dave's church banned secular music. Monica loved using heavy bass and drums to blow dust from the speakers behind Dave's back.

"Please, read me something, mommy, but no fairy tales."

"Wait." Monica left and returned, carrying a magazine.

"The San People of Southern Africa carried the oldest human Y chromosome…" Monica paused: "The Y chromosome is present in males," She clarified.

She resumed reading: "Mitochondrial DNA studies—"

"Mitochondrial came from women, right?" Gem asked.

Monica high-fived her.

Midnight found Gem sleeping on her side. A low-watt bulb burned in the lamp. In the form of a smoky-white circular fog, a ghost seeped under the window. It hovered no larger than a soccer ball over Gem's head as she stirred and rolled on her back; her eyes fluttered in a dream. The apparition darted over her head, formed a full-moon-like face, glassy eyes and a clown's smile. It lingered a foot over Gem's face, compensating as her head turned in the restless dream. It made a rounded mouth, sucked in a mouthful of air, and blew back an icy blast into the child's fluttering eyes. It watched for another second and darted back through the window.

The next morning aroma of frying plantains invaded Gem's room. She woke up rubbing her eyes and stumbled from her bedroom. She picked up her dad's dirty breakfast dishes off the dining table on her way to the kitchen. A frying pan sizzled on the stove as Monica stirred a saucepan. Gem rubbed an eye and placed the dishes on the counter.

"Mommy, my eyes hurt."

"Remove your hand."

Monica stooped and inspected Gem's pinkish eyes.

"Oh, God, you've caught the pink eye, come."

Monica led her into the bathroom.

Chapter 4

Two arduous years had passed since Gem lost her sight from Obeah, and church elders including Sister Gina visited Monica's home at 8:00 p.m. on Tuesday nights to pray for her. Monica had made plans for the Wednesday, but Dave announced he had a rare midweek day off from his job as an assistant loan manager at the bank, and she wavered.

Sister Gina had arrived earlier and gone into Gem's room, not for Monica's sake but for Dave's the ardent Christian and member of her church. She clutched her life-size five feet tall cutout of Jesus affixed to an easel as if was the Holy Grail. Dave helped her place the tripod alongside Gem's bed, decked in white for visitors. Gem sat on the edge, bubbly as usual, her legs hanging over the side.

The radiation-protective glasses a quack doctor prescribed for her sagged on her nine-year-old face and kept sliding. Dave stood tall and handsome until Gem's illness sucked his spirit away. Hauled it over an ugly grave and buried it in a deep hole his thirty years spirit trying to climb from. He crossed himself in front of the image enthusiastically. He may have lost weight and physical strength, but never his faith.

Four church elders arrived, and Monica served them fresh carrot, ginger and beet juice, in the living room while they small talked. She served it cold from the refrigerator, with little ice for fear the ice may melt and steal the nutrients.

Monica wore the usual front for the elders. They've prayed over Gem on Tuesday nights for the past two years, and she was yet to see results.

Monica took the glasses to the kitchen, exhaled over the kitchen sink, and her hard, skeptical face dropped as if it burned through the civil mask she wore for visitors. A glance over her shoulder said she had enough. *Dave's day off or not. Tomorrow morning, she's gonna do it her way, and any man standing in her way better be standing taller than a mountain, aho.*

Chapter 5

It was two nights after the death of Tilta Brown and Feather Pee by the Rolling Calf and as Monica planned her clandestine trip in Bath Mountain for the next day. A blanket of low, dark clouds had ganged up on and hid the stars and the moon over the Moreland Hill's woods. Their actions left the night and countryside dark— the only exception was an eerie wild intensity flame burning in a contained spot in a wooded valley. The surreal fire raged in a fifteen-yard circle as if it burned in a transparent sphere. The tongues of the flame leaped and clung to shrubberies, but didn't scorch a leaf. Beyond the fire, the pitch-darkness stretched away as if the illumination had forbidden boundaries. A dark ridge outline rose tall, not far away.

Moreland Hill Village experienced victim and benefactor status of the supernatural from conception and mystical shenanigans had woven into everyday life for over a hundred and eighty years.

Its mantra remained from conception. *"If you encountered the supernatural. Cut yu eyes, be on your way, and mind yu own business."*

Back in the old days, Moreland Hill's denizens closed their doors, put out their lamps and if they slept, kept one eye open and an ear cocked on high alert. However, for its modern tech-savvy generation, it was different.

If they encountered the supernatural, they uploaded live feeds to social media on the spot. These were free souls, even during their physical enslavement.

They enjoyed occult protection up to this day from modern scourges, crimes in their ugly forms and evil trickeries from Hell or anywhere else.

Two women who were soon to play a significant role in Gem and Monica's lives stood in the center of the mysterious flames, and the vividness obscured their features. Six yards in front of them, the forty callous slave-era ghosts in tattered clothes stood guard, shoulder to shoulder in a circle. The ghosts had their heads bowed akin to sleeping sentinels waiting for visitors to invade their space. They held wicked, curved machetes gleaming in their hands as if they'd sharpened them a minute back and had not used them yet. The women spoke in Twi for a minute and changed to English. One sounded much younger than the other.

"So, what is this, Amazon?" the older woman asked.

"A store as large as the world, grandma where people can buy anything from a ship to an old lady's magic diary."

The older woman unwrapped an old book from black and white dried goatskin. She flipped a few pages and closed the book.

"How do we get the diary in your world store?" the older woman asked.

"I'll use a phone or a computer to open an account," the younger woman said.

"Okay, use your phone."

"It's a piece of junk, grandma. It struggles to call someone two miles away."

The ghosts wore war faces, bound by a spell over three hundred years old. The skeletal remains of people and animals littered the grounds around the ghosts' feet. Decapitated heads, shoulders hacked away, a cow's head split between the horns, torsos chopped in half, showed the cruel fate they'd met.

"If we do ugly acquired magic once, though, grandma and we could awaken Tilly Whitelock ourselves?"

"Once you go blood or black—"

"Grandmother, I'm a child."

"Around me, you are, but rumors said, at school, you were a raging sixteen-year-old."

The girl giggled, and the ghosts' heads snapped upright. Fiery eyes searched their lanes as forty heads swiveled 360 degrees and locked on the burning sphere. The women were not in the least troubled by the ghosts, as the girl picked up a human rib bone.

"The ghosts scattered bones all over. I didn't know they could kill outside the circle?" the young woman uttered.

Her fingers generated a white electric-like current, and it traversed the bone.

"A Cuban man's bone," she confirmed.

"Dear gunzey girl, when Cuban people rot in bushes, they also leave bones," the elder said.

"But see here."

"Place the book and list it as Sanga's Diary on your Amazon wrapped in a magic marker. I want people who acquired their powers to recognize it."

"I'll borrow a phone and do it in the morning at school. I'm gonna need to snap a photo of it also."

"Why do you need a phone to do something so simple?" the elder asked.

"I need a guidebook to tell me when to use my powers and when not to use them."

The older woman headed out of the light into the dark woods.

Her granddaughter followed. The light faded, and total darkness covered the forest.

"Are you saying I am not a good grandmother?"

"Let's walk through the logwood forest on our way home. If you slip and slide, you can grab onto a tree for support, the younger woman joked.

"Do you think logwood maka (thorns) dare fe prick mi, eh, pickney?"

The girl laughed and placed an arm around her grandmother's waist as they melted into the darkness.

Chapter 6

Beautiful morning rays raced across dew-wet sugarcane leaves, dancing in a light breeze and fighting off a silvery mist hung over the fields. Rainbow spectrum danced and sparkled, simulating variegated cobwebs above the fray. School children dressed in colorful uniforms rambled to nearby schools on the Little London to Moreland Hill main road at 7:00 a.m.

A local passenger bus, which people affectionately called a country bus sped around the corner, and the driver kept his hand on the horn. The children scattered, made faces, shouted and raced after the vehicle in jest. The passengers consisted of working people, schoolchildren and two tourists. Custom speakers pumped reggae music, and the ringtones of cell phones mimicked the universe in sounds and vibrations. Laughter and obnoxiously loud chatter represented Earth well.

Tourists were not a standard fixture on country buses speeding along the Jamaican countryside early in the mornings, but Albert and Wilma Allen, a middle-aged couple, sat on the bus as part of Albert's bucket trip. His prostate cancer had returned bearing vengeance a month back and the day of the shocking news.

Wilma had sat in a sad emotionless state in Dr. Levy's office, a lissome forty-year-old. After the word *terminal,* Wilma had not heard another word.

Albert focused on the verdict, like a prisoner in the docks. The doctor showed him his bone scan results and diagrams on a tablet. While the doc went through his presentation, Albert made plans in his head, and none included radiation or chemo. He would give naturopathic medicine a try, but he would not wait for death. Albert shook the doctor's hand and skipped away, never to return to his office.

Wilma and Albert had plans to visit the countries they had missed while living to work and had landed in Jamaica the previous day. Running on limited time, they woke at 5:00 a.m. to ride a country bus to wherever it went.

Last week, Monica touched twenty-eight, but she could easily pass for forty as Gem's two years old supernatural induced blindness has drained her mentally and physically. Doctors had wiped out their savings, and the piece of property her parents sold, every penny went to the doctors and more. Monica sat by a window on the bus. Gem's face glowed sitting on Monica's lap, as her radiation-protective glasses sagged down her nose. Monica wore a mother's pain, and her concern poured down the aisle like raw fear and anxiety. The little strength Monica exhibited at times she had siphoned from Gem's infectious personality. How could a child show such resilience in the face of adversity at her age? She fidgeted in her seat, stuck her head through the window, trying to search the road behind the bus.

"What're you doing, Mommy?"

"Hush, Gem."

She took a last fearful glimpse out the window and gathered her things; she had never opposed her husband, and her breath rushed through her nostrils in fear.

"Can I have a U.S. penny, please?" Monica asked.

Her voice lacked self-confidence and the words came out parched as if she'd dropped them from a furnace. The surrounding din had shredded her question and she wet her lips. Gem stood on the seat and shouted, "My mommy needs a United States penny."

"Si one here, mi pickney," an old woman said. She dug in her pocketbook for an eternity, mumbling, "Wat a shame, we nuh mek pennies anymore. Wat wrong wid de little one, dear?"

"She's suffering from retinitis pigmentosa."

"Oh, my, mi sorry fe true, dear."

"Driver, the Moreland Hill crossroad, please," Monica shouted.

The bus slowed to a stop. She shouldered Gem and labored to her feet, unsure; but from the directions she'd received, her destination was not too far from the main road.

Wilma and Albert sat across from the old woman. They had watched from across the aisle, and their curiosity grew as Monica lifted Gem and struggled off the bus. The old woman observed Albert's pale patchy skin and figured he had health issues.

"Sir, I suppose you could use Mother Penny's help. Follow the lady and the sick child."

"Where's she going?" Wilma asked.

"She's visiting a healer, for believers and nonbelievers, and she only charges one penny."

Wilma had hoped to find a healer somewhere on their travels, where the FDA and Congress had no authority or influence on rubber-stamp products. She had no plans to pass on the opportunity, hoax or not. She got to her feet and met Albert's cynical eye.

"We're going," she asserted.

"Ole up, driver," someone cried.

Monica led Gem by her at a brisk walk along the Moreland Hill main road, and her busy eyes darted over her shoulders every few yards exhibiting dark, desperate anxiety. The car needed repairs. Dave would've suspected where she went if she had driven and it broke, but if Mother Penny healed Gem's eyes, he could not undo them.

She stopped a group of school children.

"Are we nearing Mother Penny's church children?"

"Yes, ma'am," a girl said.

She held Monica's hand and pointed ahead. Another little girl held Gem's hand.

"Nuh worry, mi friend, Mother Penny a go fix yu eyes."

Monica glanced at the girl. *I sure hope so.* She felt guilty leaving the two tourists so far back, but the man could not keep pace, and they lagged fifty yards behind her. She sighed and slowed to a crawl under a tree.

"I could not live with myself if something happened to them."

"Who, Mommy?" Gem asked.

Brushie Brissett, a fit eighty-year-old, tended his flower garden in his front yard. Birds' songs filled the morning. Gem inhaled the fresh morning air and leaned her head, listening to the birds trying to oust each other. Brushie eyed Wilma and Albert laboring up the road and stood facing Monica.

"If those people drop a wallet on the road, they'd find it sitting where it fell when they returned, my child. You're in Moreland Hill."

"Sorry, sir, I didn't mean—"

"I know you meant no harm, dear. It's not far now. It's the little church on the right."

"Thank you so much."

Albert and Wilma had closed the distance to ten yards. Monica glanced at her phone. *Damn, he's awake by now.* Dave slept until after eight on his day off, give or take. Last evening, Monica had feigned tiredness when he reached for her. She lay sleepless through the night, as Gem's illness had affected their sex life, but the Tuesday night prayers usually lightened his load. She aroused him at 4:00 a.m. and did a job on him. Dave was already snoring when she slipped from the bed to the bathroom.

Monica glanced behind as a guilty shudder ran through her body, and Gem felt the tremor in her hand.

"Mommy, you trembled," Gem said.

"I did a terrible thing."

"Mommy is going to get a spanking?" Gem dug in.

"I spanked myself."

"I don't believe you," Gem remarked.

"Damn, suppose he figured out where I took you?" Monica uttered.

"Are you talking about Daddy?"

"Come, I think we've reached the place."

They stopped in front of a quaint Pocomania church adjoining an unfinished house. The upper floor windows and door had Plywood barricades as if they expected a hurricane, and the roughcast walls were a blight to the eyes. The white painted ground floor was beautifully finished and had expansive Casement windows.

A low picket fence surrounded the property and stretched to a second house twenty-five yards away from the unfinished one. The Jamaican flag and a white flag bearing a black inverted cross fluttered from a bamboo flagpole in the wind. A mango tree stood between the two houses, and the ripened fruits hung like red ornaments in the sky.

Wilma and Albert joined Monica and Gem, admiring the well-kept flower garden along the fence. The rose bushes and hibiscus were polychrome from grafting and splicing.

"My God, the roses are the most stunning I've ever seen," Wilma said.

Monica smiled at Wilma. *A sweet lady, I wish I had met her on a different occasion.* She took another fearful peek up the road. Wilma threw an arm around Albert's waist. His freight-train wheezing slowed and quieted, and Wilma tapped his back. Two schoolgirls bolted through the gate carrying fruit and vegetable baskets. They placed them inside the church and rushed away, burdened under their book bags.

"Children, is this Mother Penny's church?" Monica asked.

"Yes, ma'am."

Monica cast a quick eye down the road and led Gem into the church.

Chapter 7

Gem sat on Monica's lap as Wilma and Albert sat two rows back in the quaint little church. Red, black, green and yellow candles burned in polished mahogany candleholders, covered by Sweet Home shades. Wilma strained her head to admire the unique designs on the walls. Albert raised a skeptic's eye at her.

"Shush. What do you have to lose?"

Albert eyed the two horseshoes nailed high on the wall above the pulpit and a large black cross painted under them. He glanced at Wilma and pondered how the Hell he ended up in a church.

Hallie Elaine Thompson, a tall, elegant girl sporting long dreadlocks hanging on her back, sashayed from behind the curtain, wearing her school uniform. She moved gracefully, displaying power and confidence as if they had stamped them on her face at birth. Her complexion shone under the lighting like a mixture of rich red wine and cool polished gold in the perfect amount. She smiled, showing milk-white teeth and had a cute teenagers' swagger.

"Good morning. Can I have your pennies, please?"

Monica handed her the coin. Wilma fished in her purse and stretched a hand to Hallie.

"Give it to the gentleman," Hallie said.

Wilma gave the penny to Albert, and he extended the coin to Hallie. She held his fingers and fumbled the coin between them. Albert could not figure out if the girl did it intentionally.

"I'm sorry for my clumsiness, sir. My grandmother will be here in a minute."

Hallie placed the pennies on a dais. Roy, the fisherman, waved two strings of yellowtail snappers outside the window to get Hallie's attention.

"Round de back, Roy."

Hallie disappeared behind the curtain, lugging her infectious smile.

Mother Penny parted the curtains, and her wise dark eyes surveyed her clients as she strode to the pulpit. She was a slight, slim-built woman, a head shorter than the six-foot Hallie and somewhere in her early fifties. She wore a welcoming smile, and her expression screamed to the world; *I am honored to serve you.* A red cord tied her long white cotton dress around her waist, and ends swung six inches off the knees. A traditional white headwrap donned her head and a yellow lead pencil stuck under it above her right eye.

"Good morning. I am Mother Penny."

"Good morning, Mother Penny," Monica replied.

"Albert, you can go," Mother Penny said.

A shocked Wilma and Albert stared at each other.

"We didn't tell anyone our names."

"Albert, your prostate is back, healed and your testosterone chopping at the bit. Wilma, brace yourself. He will try to make up for time lost."

"You did nothing," Albert said.

"You came here, did you not? Monica, bring Gem, and please follow me to my office."

Mother Penny wheeled away. Monica grinned in jubilation for the first time in two years. If Mother Penny plucked their names from thin air, she could heal Gem's eyes.

The office doubled as a seamstress's workshop. Cluttered sewn women's clothes hung on strings. Three electric sewing machines fought for space. Hallie sat around the

Serger, and there were style diagrams posted on the walls above and colorful cloth piled on a cutting table.

Monica led Gem to a chair. Mother Penny inspected Gem's red, teary eyes.

"Wait for her outside, Monica."

"Yes, Mother Penny." Monica kissed Gem's cheeks and hurried away.

"Gem, mi a go blindfolds yu. Don't be scared."

"It a go hurt?"

"No, mon."

"But, mi blindness is already like a blindfold, mi caan si, and mommy don't want me talk Patwa to strangers."

"Dis a fe wi little secret den, and yu right about de blindfold, yu nuh. But, mine have in de gud medicine."

Gem giggled, well-relaxed.

Hallie observed how her grandmother had made the child comfortable. Mother Penny fanned a hand at Hallie and blindfolded Gem.

Hallie stepped forward quietly, outstretched her arms and stood behind Gem. She placed her hands over the child's eyes, and white light emitted from her hands, bathing the child's eyes under the blindfold. Hallie backed away to her seat, and Mother Penny removed the blindfold.

CHAPTER 8

Albert and Wilma remained seated as he felt his strength returning and his breathing normalized. Monica paced the aisle biting nails, and maternal anxiety maxed to a sharp edge. An angry Dave rushed into the church frothing at the mouth, and his burning eyes cut through Monica searching for Gem at nuclear fire intensity.

"Dave, please."

"Where's my daughter?"

Monica's eyes hit the curtained door, and Dave raced to the door.

"Dave, no."

"I warned you not to bring my child to an Obeah Woman. Monica, I'm a devoted Christian. I do not indulge in the devil's work."

"Please, Dave, don't."

Dave kicked in the door and barged into the office in a rage. Gem raced and hugged him around his waist.

"Daddy, I regained my sight. I can see," Gem announced.

"Do you see me, Gem?" Dave asked.

"Yes, Daddy, yu wearing a red shirt, mi eyes dem better."

Monica screamed for joy in the doorway and stomped her feet in ecstasy as Albert and Wilma joined her.

Dave lifted Gem and kissed her.

"I'm so sorry, Mother Penny. I'll fix the door. I'll fix it, ma'am."

"Do not worry about it, my son. Take your family and go."

Dave set Gem on her feet, hugged Mother Penny, and cried.

"Oh, thank you, Mother Penny. Thank you so much."

Mother Penny escorted them into the church. Gem ran to the window, squealing.

"Mother Penny, your flowers are so beautiful, the red, the white, the yellow—"

"We've seen a miracle," Wilma said.

"Let's hurry back to the hotel," Albert said, and a sparkle lit in his eyes.

"Where are you staying, Albert? We can give you a ride back," Monica said.

"Are you sure, dear?" Wilma asked.

"Yes, ma'am," Dave said.

Gem didn't remember her dad was so tall and handsome either. He had shaved his beard, too. It used to tickle her face and made her giggle.

Two muscular and pleasant young men entered the church.

"Good morning, Mother. Good morning, people," Ron said.

"Morning, boys."

"We're off from work today, Mother Penny. Do you have any chores for us?" Ron asked.

"No, Ron, today has been a wonderful day."

"Okay, den, Mother, wi a go hit de beach."

"Tek it easy on those fragile throbbing hearts now, boys."

Hallie's robust giggle reverberated from the office into the church.

Chapter 9

Hallie ate her oatmeal, buttered hard-dough bread, and avocado, as she sat at a sewing machine in the office. Mother Penny sat across from her, hemming a dress.

"Do the dishes and use your hands in soapy water," Mother Penny said.

Hallie held her nails up to the light and rolled her eyes.

"What about the fishes?" Mother Penny asked.

"In the freezer, they're cleaned too. I left four in the fridge. I want steamed snapper, okra, yellow yam, and dumplings for my dinner," Hallie remarked.

"Do you have a maid here?" Mother Penny asked.

She winked and got up.

"Fix the door before you leave the room," Mother Penny instructed.

"Grandma, I'm not a carpenter." She giggled, fired a light beam from her finger, zapped the broken door and repaired it.

Hallie wore an apron over her school uniform and washed the dishes in the kitchen sink.

A shriveled facial skin ghost slithered through the closed back door and danced up to Hallie.

Its white, bony cheekbones, two dark holes for nostrils and full-bodied, long black hair bobbed on her old cut calico dress shoulders gave her an incredible presence. She chewed on the stalk of an old chalk pipe, blackened on the side from fire in the right side of her mouth.

Hallie glanced at her and scrubbed a pot.

"Damn, you got up early, Miss Sitira."

"When I lay in my coffin for too long. I developed back pain."

"Yu know something, you are far too much, and your coffin must rot by now," Hallie continued.

"Yu must be crazy, child, a careless duppy mek dem coffin rot. Mine still has the mahogany stain sheen on it," Miss Sitira replied.

"I don't believe yu, from 1934 till now?"

"Come and check if I'm lying?"

"No, no, no, I'm good."

"Mek mi do de plate dem fe yu."

"Mi got dem, Grandma lady said I should do them by hand."

"If she mek yu bruk a fingernail, mek mi slap her a couple of times fe yu."

"We're cool, mon, but you can clean my room for me today. Do the whole house when Miss Grandma lady left gone a gossip road."

Sitira broke into a ghastly grin.

"Nuh over shine de floor. I don't want her to slide and bust her backside as she did last time. And do not enter her room," Hallie whispered.

"Mi, missis? Mi nah go near dat black cross deh, it nuh love dead people."

"Don't even mention the evil ones."

"How yu define evil, mi nuh kill nobody fe ten long months."

"Dem probably keep a party in Heaven."

"A dat pissed me off, but I went to the beach and missed two shottas the other night."

"Where was that?"

"Dem did come fe rob Sammy Fray's and by de time mi get a whiff, the Rolling Calf did dem already. Yu want to talk about pissed mi gal."

"What were you doing on the beach?"

"I visited the nude beach many times a week. I never saw a man ting I didn't like during my time."

"Hallie, your education should come from textbooks in a classroom, not from an evil duppy gal weh Heaven and Hell nuh want." Mother Penny shouted.

Hallie and Sitira doubled over laughing.

"Do not transform and fly into the bushes behind the school. There are buses and taxis on the road."

"But si yah. Grandma, a dollar saved here and there—"
Hallie grinned silly.

Lightning killed thirty-year-old Sitira in her kitchen in nineteen-thirty-four. Her tiny house was on the same spot as Mother Penny's home. For years, she had haunted the neighborhood as an angry, vengeance-filled ghost who held a mean grudge against Heaven and Hell. Sitira tried to haunt away Mother Penny and her family after they moved there ten years ago. When Mother Penny rebuked her, she turned to six-year-old Hallie, and they became friends.

Chapter 10

High school soccer remained the second most popular sport in Jamaica. It came in a slender shade below Champs. Check the eyes of the beholder before saying it, though. Moreland Hill High School played Frome High in a drizzle on an overcast evening. Hallie and her two friends Faith and Irene pushed through the crowd to the touchline. Their eyes on Moreland Hill Number 10, Steve Barnes, as he dribbled toward the goal. Faith climbed on Hallie's back in her excitement.

"He gonna score, Hallie. He's gonna score," Faith screamed.

The Moreland Hill supporters erupted in jubilation and loaded the word *goal* on their lips, ready to cast forth.

Hallie raced along the touchline, her face in euphoric love, her arms poised to celebrate. Steve shifted one defender, dummied a second and stared into the goalie's eyes. The stadium cocked in anticipation. A thunderous right-foot shot lodged in the net.

"Goooooooal!!!" echoed from the stadium, like rumbling thunder from the ground up.

After the game, Hallie, wrapped in a towel, tiptoed to Steve, covered in suds, and turned the water off in the shower. Steve turned and bumped into her, and his grin kept growing to clown's size. The towel fell from around Hallie, and Steve embraced her.

"Yes, at last," Steve said.

Their lips met.

Hallie jumped from her bed. Her wet nightdress clung to her body and she sucked air into her lungs. She gawked around the darkened room and rubbed her eyes.

"Damn, I hope grandmother didn't smell the burning. Something had to flame from the heat."

She peeked through the blinds on a hot night.

"What a dream. I might as well use more damns."

Her mind drifted back to Steve, the goal he scored yesterday and the dream. His implicit sexual pressures had become overt in the past few weeks. Her subconscious had begun to cook X-rated steamy little shower scenes. She sat back on the bed, her face warmed and mellowed as her mind touched Steve, her life and her love. *Why must things get worse before they get better on every damn thing in life?*

She held her phone but did not dial it. Instead, she displayed Steve's photo, pressed it against her bosom as she curled on her side.

Chapter 11

1645 was an awful year for enslaved people, as were the previous years and those that followed, but they were excellent years for most enslavers. The exception was, the unlucky ones who had turned their backs on the stubborn slaves who had stuffed cotton balls in their ears during the forced Sunday morning services.

Uncanny things unfolded in unique fashions and consistently above the paygrade of mortals. As usual, Tilly Whitelock, a gorgeous, olive-complexioned slave mistress, wore long, black hair and had the greenest eyes. She galloped nude in the afternoon sun on her demonic, black, three-footed, fire-breathing horse. As she raced around a bend into a giant fallen tree across the track, the horse turned off the beaten path into the woods.

She exited the woods at the cliff's edge, where Rick's Café sits today at about 4:00 p.m., in time to catch a passing Spanish galleon out at sea. She shielded her eyes under a broad brim straw hat, and for a thirty-year-old woman, her face was flawless like a baby's. The ship rode low in the water, and the sunlight-reflected sails appeared as if they rode the waves.

Tilly stood tall in the saddle and stretched her curvaceous, hard, tanned body to its full five-ten height. She had used the best designs from Heaven and Hell and incorporated them into a masterpiece of a body sculptured beyond human standards. The horse jumped over the cliff and galloped on the water out to sea at high speed. From the rocks, the animal's wake resembled a modern-day speedboat.

Tilly spurred her horse and encircled the sailing ship several times, leaving a stir as the fearful, curious crew bellowed in Spanish. Men ran from starboard to port and bow to stern. The lookout fell from the mainmast, dropped on a cannon and bounced on the deck. Sailors knelt and crossed themselves in fear. The raw fear from the shouting men induced an ecstatic shudder through Tilly's body, and a darting red tongue licked her lips. The horse jumped over the bow from a galloping position, firing blowtorch-type flames. In seconds, the unholy fire burned through the sails, leaving blackened masts and spars.

From the air, Tilly swung a magical rope and lassoed the bow. As the beast hit the water, she slapped its neck twice, and the massive ship turned toward shore behind the demonic beast.

The sailors fired muskets and booming cannonballs, splashing water, left, right and behind her. Panicked men scampered back and forth, shouting on the deck. The ship hit the reef and tossed many overboard. The remaining crew members jumped as the vessel listed on its side fifty yards from the beach. Tilly galloped onto the beach and disappeared into thick bushes.

The sailors swam and waded ashore in the shallow water, praying and swearing in Spanish. Tired, petrified men sprawled on the beach, and a hundred machete-wielding slaves attacked the men from the woods. The seasoned ship crew fought bravely, but did not match Tilly's ferocious, magic-enhanced, vengeful men.

Tilly sat astride her horse as the butchered sailors' blood turned the white sands red, and not one of the slaves had a significant injury to show for their effort.

"We bloody the beach," a man shouted.

Ever since, they called the spot Bloody Bay up to this day. Tilly waved a hand, and her spell rose like mist from the spellbound horde.

"All they had possessed is now yours," Tilly said.

They stripped the sailors and tossed their bodies in the water.

The sunset's dying rays shone on a human chain from the ship to the shore as slaves carried cases on their heads. Blood splattered from the ferocious battle spotted Tilly's nude body as she had lorded over the fighting from her horse's back. Women and children moved provisions into the bushes as the men stockpiled heavy wooden cases on the beach.

Fireflies and mosquitoes buzzed the workers as the beautiful sunset passed, minus a single admirer. Tilly perched on the demonic animal's rump and drew her knees to her breasts as the horse's nostrils flared and lit the area for the laboring men and women. She could have levitated the loot from the ship, but when one has three hundred slaves, one needs to put them to work and satiate their bloodlust while at it.

Many slaves sported the Ashanti tribal marks and carried themselves more freely. They daringly gawked at Tilly's nakedness and showed their manly attitudes. Sanga had told them their demonic boss could not harm them if they performed their duties.

A gaunt light-skin man without facial markings, dressed in a sailor's outfit, stumbled under his burden and sprawled on his face, as gold bullions scattered in the sand. The horse fired a stream of flames from its nostrils and burned the man to black dust.

"Anyone else who drops a bar shall receive the same. Get busy, maggots." Tilly announced.

The men scampered in fear.

Later, under a starry, moonless sky in one of Tilly's sugarcane fields, she perched on her fire-breathing beast ten feet above forty spell-induced workers as they shoveled dirt on the gold in a massive hole. The beast had turned on its flames bright as a searchlight and highlighted sweat on the workers' brows. They had no tribal markings, but each worked and kept a fearful eye on the demonic horse. They all shared Tilly's complexions, especially the women who bear an uncanny resemblance to her.

The magic-induced slaves refilled the hole in minutes, made rows and replanted sugarcane over the spot. Tilly waved a hand, froze everyone in place and her horse incinerated them to black dust.

"My children, you shall guard my gold for eternity."

The blackened remains came back to life, howled and formed a circle around the buried gold. Tilly zapped a supernatural machete in each ghost's hand.

Chapter 12

The Moreland Hill Great House was a grand 'Tudor period' white stone building two miles from the ocean on a high hill. Its walls reflected morning sunlight like a monument in the sky.

The well-kept grounds rolled downhill under groomed trees, blooming rose and hibiscus bushes. An array of blooming flowers dotted the front of the house, and a verandah ran the length of the second floor. Rainbow-colored orchids hung in coconut-husk nests every few feet.

In 1822, Tilly's plantation flourished at its zenith and owned over five hundred enslaved Africans, churning out sugar and rum in the hundreds of tons per year. The fields stretched for miles from the Great House, and sugarcane danced in the wind.

The lean, muscular cutters swung machetes, singing lewd working songs in the sugarcane fields, and women loaded the sugarcane on ox carts behind them. The hardy women lifted from the ground to their shoulders and into the wagon in one swift well-oiled motion.

Slaves, from eight-year-old children to seventy-year-old men and women, worked in the mill yard under Tilly's watchful eyes. She sat topless on her demonic horse, used a finger to lift her broad straw hat rim, and revealed a face that did not age a day in two hundred years. The more robust of the slaves carried the Ashanti mark, and they were in the majority by far. Tilly's brow wrinkled like the abolishment wind blew back and forth from England to Jamaica; fanning freedom flames in the enslaved' bosoms irked her. Based on the pact she and Sanga had drawn, she could not keep an Ashanti bloodline in her service after August 1, 1834. She cracked her whip in anger, and a fire trail lingered in the air as she galloped away. Tilly did not flog her 'heard or use' overseers, and not one child ever slacked off behind her back. Words came down from their grandparents that Tilly could see them from anywhere on her vast plantation.

The slaves' quarters were wood cabins and sugarcane-thatched-roofs facing each other in a circle, three hundred yards from the Great House, in a valley. The barracks shared a common, large, dirt courtyard, logs for seating and several fire pits in the center.

Slaves crowded the communal area under a moonless sky, eating boiled crabs and roasted yams. By 9:00 p.m., tired, yawing men and women left in twos and threes until only a handful remained.

Sanga, the tall, striking demon in disguised unkempt white hair, strung his face around the massive fire, and those remaining drew closer to him. He lifted a yabba pot of rum to his mouth and drank until rum wet his shirtfront. Wilba, a slave boy, added fresh wood to the fire, and as Sanga finished the rum, he squatted in front of him.

"Grandpa Sanga, yu two thousand' ears old as dem seh?"

Sanga, mellowed from telling stories and drinking the harsh liquor, grinned at Wilba.

Darkness covered beyond the fire like a wall. Tilly's Great House blended into the gloom like a dark blob on the hill. Fireflies had long patrolled and gone back home to wherever they lived. Toads, crickets and frogs had the night's stage, but no audiences.

Redebo, a handsome, well-built, light-skinned slave of twenty, tossed more wood on the fire.

"Grandpa Sanga, why yu nuh use yu powers pon de witch?"

Kabba, Sanga's sixty-year-old bookkeeper, unwrapped a red leather-bound book from sun-dried black-and-white goatskin. He dipped a feather in a homemade ink jar made from the logwood tree and poised to write. Sanga's natural speech was low to a growl but relaxed, intense and confident, like, if the world went under, it would not affect him.

"Two hundred and fifty years ago, I and the she-demon made a deal for my queen's love and honor. I cannot break it."

"Bruk it fe yu people," the boy suggested.

"Breaking my word will cause doom to my people."

"She was a great woman, eh Grandpa?"

"Your great-great-grandmother was a beauty and a queen. I went away for a year, and when I returned to the Gold Coast, they had sold her into slavery. The pact I made saved you from the demon's wrath."

"Wi still inna slavery, wen wi sufferings ago end?"

"Freedom is coming on yonder wind… and one day, the demon will slip, never to rise again."

Kabba wrote Sanga's words.

A blazing, spinning fire sped to the pinnacle of a dark ridge above the slave barracks. The flames flared and illuminated Tilly, in the nude, astride her snorting horse under a tree.

She gazed at the barracks' fire below emotionless. Rumors around the plantation were that Tilly rode night and day for no real purpose other than to haunt and instill fear. Sanga once told his flock that Tilly's vast untold wealth and power had not brought her peace.

Sanga also was a heaven-rejected beast who had magical abilities equal to Tilly's. Yet he had found some harmony and peaceful coexistence, even if it was a facade. He had loved countless women over the centuries and had adopted the Ashanti Tribe; his people numbered in the thousands, but he had never forced his will upon them. He existed more like a romantic wanderer than a demon-god-king holding a throne. If there were such a thing as a cool demon, Sanga epitomized it.

The cleaning department made a blunder and left essences of goodness in him. An iota from his former glorious life, but still precious. Higher-ups hated sexual deviancy, and he and Tilly still possessed dominant traits.

Tilly's horse raced downhill at tremendous speed.

Kabba's pen poised over his book, waiting for Sanga to speak as he gulped rum. The unfinished page read: *The slaves buried the gold in a sugarcane field…*

"She a cum. She a cum inna ball a fire," Wilba shouted.

The slaves raced inside the barracks. Redebo and four other muscular young men ran into an upscale shack instead of the other dilapidated buildings. Kabba stood anxious as if he were ready to bolt from great danger.

"Stay, bookkeeper," Sanga said.

Kabba's joints popped as he sat back on his wooden stool, and Sanga's hand waved him into invisibility.

Tilly galloped into the compound in a cloud of brown dust and pulled the reins yards in from of the sitting Sanga.

"Are you keeping my slaves from their bunks, old thing? You should keep your vain hope and long stories to yourself."

"My blood spilled on thorns," Sanga replied.

Tilly chuckled, dismounted and stood nude yards from Sanga.

"Don't forget the man who claimed the sea because he once sailed."

"Time was not his friend," Sanga said.

Tilly turned and strode away to Redebo's shack. Sanga watched her backside as she waltzed along.

"You took everything we had, even our women's backsides," Sanga shouted at Tilly.

"They are no more yours than mine," Tilly said.

Chapter 13

The slavery abolition act of 1833 placed a dent in the plantocracy expectations and bottom lines. Many farmers were already reeling on August 1, 1834, especially Tilly, who had lost all her Ashanti slaves. By 1858, logwood forests and other tropical bushes reclaimed the Great House's rolling lawn. Tilly's prosperous sugarcane plantation lay in ruin and wilderness.

On a sunny June morning, the Great House's exterior shone in pure splendor. The white walls competed and outdid the most exquisite, grounded mirrors. Rumor had it that Tilly's magic maintained the house and kept it alive.

Lazy, indentured Indian and Chinese laborers shuffled about, dragging their legs and hunched shoulders in the rundown mill yard. Their giant straw hats resembled dwarfs wearing roofs between broken wagons and rotted sugarcane.

The sugarcane fields had long lost the battle of the guinea grass and other bushes. Most barracks were roofless and in further structural disrepair.

Tilly sipped steaming coffee on the verandah and appeared more stunning than she had hundreds of years back. The long-gone orchid pots left rusty wire tails swinging in the wind. Her icy eyes surveyed her once-thriving plantation. If she had regrets, they did not reflect in her expression.

Tilly galloped through the dark woods on her demonic horse at midnight, propelled by whirling fire around its three feet.

They ripped the limbs from trees as they barreled into a valley. The horse hovered over a spot above the trees and lit up the ground as bright as sunlight.

The guard ghosts howled pitifully from the circle, pleading to Tilly as ten gold bars floated from underground into Tilly's saddlebags, and the horse chomped fire on the bit.

"Mother Tilly, Mother Tilly, release us," the ghosts moaned.

Their elongated hands reached out to her, and the haunting utterances sounded like distressed children wailing for salvation.

"Keep watching, my children. Why moan now? You are better off here than wailing in pits of Hell."

Tilly slapped her horse's neck. Fire whirled around its feet, and it zoomed away from a standing position.

"I believe the Spaniards were much better people than the bloody English," Tilly said.

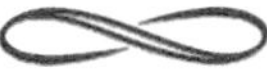

Many planters had pulled up stakes and returned to Britain or moved to America by 1840.

The Westmoreland Planters' Association had planned a meeting in Savanna La Mar for June 10, 1858. Flying rumors said the Fosters from Green Island and Little London's John Sygree were eager to sell and leave Jamaica.

Tilly had planned to buy out everyone. She harbored no fear of finding farmhands. In most cases, the formerly enslaved people had refused to work for their old masters, but, she had a plan ripe and ready for service.

Sanga went missing for years after the abolishment and their deal dissolved. His proud adopted Ashanti strutted around as if they owned the island, refusing to work for Tilly or the other planters.

Tomorrow's plan would bring back Sanga and evaluate his idea on the issue. If the wind blew Tilly's plans south, she had prepared herself for blood and fire. For she shall enslave the former slaves in Westmoreland and Hanover parishes, Ashanti included. If anyone objected, they should have God standing on their right.

Tilly planned to build an army and march on Kingston. She had staked a claim to the Island years before the British arrived.

Chapter 14

By 10:00 a.m., the sun had gathered enough strength to drive people indoors in Savanna La Mar. Surprised by the boisterous crowd around the courthouse earlier, the sun kept a close eye on the area.

From 7:00 a.m., a crowd of riotous former slaves gathered at the courthouse under the watchful eyes of mounted troops.

Rowdy men filled the stuffy main hall until people spilled outside on St. Georges Street. Tilly, adorned in a beautiful flowing red dress and matching accessories, bulldozed her way through the crowd. Her demonic horse, disguised as a regular stallion, followed. A stableman took the horse, and bustling people made way for Tilly up the steps. She pushed her way through the rowdy planters to the podium and crashed the meeting in progress.

"What is the bloody meaning of this, woman?" a man bellowed.

Angry men rushed forward. Only, Tilly's fearsome reputation held them in check.

"Those objecting to my intrusion and presence can see me outside later."

She stomped a foot hard enough to shake the building, dug in her purse and brought out a bag of gold nuggets.

"Who wants to sell? I am buying out any man on any property."

"Where are you going to get workers?"

"What do you care? You will be in England."

"I am selling Little London," shouted John Sygree.

"Name your price."

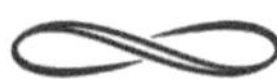

The battalion kept a watchful eye on the boisterous mob on St. Georges Street. They surrounded the courthouse, but concentrated most of their steel in the back and were thin in the front.

Rumors had raced through the ex-slaves' community until everyone had heard the stories. The planters had met to reenact slavery in Westmoreland. Every person had a hidden weapon, and a mob formed inside the nosier crowd. Six hard men squatted in a circle, surrounded by the hard-faced men and women. Longas, a tall, massive, jet-black ex-slave, led the gang. He hunched his massive shoulders, and his knife drew attack lines on the ground.

His bulging muscles, imitating large tree roots, were visible through a rip in his dirty flower bag shirt.

"The Backra Massa dem hab thread bags full a money pon dem," Longas said.

"Yeah, mon, dem thread bags full a gold," another man said.

"Dem expect trouble in de back, yu si how tin dem be in the front?" Longas asked.

He drew a line in the dry, brown soil.

"De pickney dem should stay six yards from the soulja, so wen wi jump ova dem head wi nuh hurt dem," Longas said.

"Gallie, cum listen dis and tell de pickney dem wat wi seh," a man said.

A kind moon-faced slender yellow woman, squatted on strong working legs, and her rough hands could strangle a bull. The machete stuck inside her long skirt reached below her knees.

"Wi a sen de pickney go beg de soulja food, den wi jump ova dem and chop up de souja dem. Tell dem fe stan' three yards away from the soulja and stoop when wi a come," Longas said.

"Mi practice dem all night," Gallie said.

She cast a dark eye on the soldiers.

Maudy, tall and fit, wearing meanness to match her forty-five years, pushed her way through the crowd, a good head taller than most men. Her right hand gripped a long, sharp knife tucked in her waistband. Her giant index finger wiped the sweat from her troubled forehead and dried it on her backside.

Out of breath, she reached the inner circle and dropped to her knees beside the men. Her bosom heaved and expanded as if it would never retract. Her nostrils flared, and her full mouth twisted in disappointment. Maudy grip tightened on her knife handle as if to crush it, and Longas gave her a questioning eye.

"Mi si Tilly Whitelock in deh."

The men's eyes bulged in surprise.

"Yu sure, Maudy?" Longas asked.

"Mi si de bitch wid mi two yie dressed inna red."

"De demon bitch only wears red or nuttin," Butty said.

"She have a front deh boy…" Felix Samuel said.

"A dead trap, no man enter dat and survive," Maudy said.

Longas sighed and stood dejected. One after the other, the long-faced men drifted away, their spirits wet mushy and their shoulders hunched. Longas placed a comforting touch on Maudy's knife hand, pried her fingers from the handle and slowly released her hold.

"Wi cut dem another day, Maudy."

She wetted her dry disappointed lips and managed a nod. They had left their huts to either die or get paid. Soldiers did not scare them, but Tilly Whitelock was Hell herself.

Longas led Maudy under a breadfruit tree and fed her water from a shetpan.

"Longas, I need fe cut a planter yu nuh."

Longas threw an arm around her shoulders as tears fell from Maudy's eyes at her disappointment.

Chapter 15

Tilly's hijacked meeting had turned into a joyous drinking affair. She shook hands and slapped shoulders between downing rum by the quart. The planters bellowed and roared boastful toasts as if it were a Christmas party instead of their death sentence party.

Tilly had made purchases until her gold was exhausted. The men had asked for exorbitant prices, and she paid them happily. She planned to take back every ounce in a few days.

She signed four promissory notes for Gordon from Delveland, a wiry, balding man. James- the Mount Pleasant lord, a handsome, graying man who loved his broad, attractive smiles, also signed his death warrant.

The other properties were as far away as Mint Estate and Broughton Farm. The men and Tilly downed enough rum to exhaust a brewery and continued well into the evening.

Felix's voice boomed, pausing his large mug inches from his lips. "Enjoy, boys. My next rounds will be in the Black Lion in Epsom a month from now."

"You are a bloody lucky bastard," a bloke said.

"The family and I are boarding the first sugar ship out of Savlamar," Browne said.

"Hear, hear." roared the house.

Tilly shook John Sygree's hand enthusiastically, and she marked his soft, bloated ass for death after she retrieved all her gold.

"How is your ailing mother doing, Tilly?" John Sygree asked.

"She passed a few months back, John."

"Bloody hell, where was I?"

"We had a quiet funeral service. You know how we Whitelocks treasure our legendary privacy."

"Your brother and I had a drink—in Lucea—back in 'forty-four," John said.

A sly smile formed on Tilly's lips as she gulped the rum faster than a thirsty camel at an oasis. She wanted to tell him it was her *son*, sired by another son. Tilly made a promise not to let him leave this Earth uninformed.

Although Tilly's mystical legends were common knowledge and her shenanigans witnessed by slaves, civilized men, as they called themselves, associated the stories to the superstitious rantings of primitives animals. They refuted the supernatural to preserve their refined sensibilities. The polite conversation in the Great Houses said Tilly was another daughter in a weird, secretive family who kept to themselves and interbred. This was acceptable behavior for many ruling families on the island for over two hundred years.

The meeting broke after dark. Soldiers escorted the planters through the thinned crowd on their way home. Tilly rode through the mob solo, and the Red Sea parted for her. Her horse appeared ordinary, but her former slaves knew the demonic beast and kept their distance. She rode north alone on St. Georges Street in the gathering darkness. Tilly's legend over the years had grown life, and not one man going in her direction traveled alongside her.

At the top of St. Georges Street, Maudy stepped from under a towering cotton tree in front of Tilly's horse.

"Tilly Whitelock, yu memba Maudy? Mi did a go cut yu fe mi son. But yu did 'fraid fe fight mi without yu magic."

Tilly laughed and reined in her horse.

"A de deal mi mek wid Sanga save yu, weh yu dutty puppa deh."

"Tilly, yu caan beat mi without magic. A woulda carve up yu front like wild hog meat."

"So, wah yu want, Maudy?"

"Mek mi tek back de gold from de Backra Massa dem and get sumting fe mi self."

"No, I can tek back mi own gold," Tilly shut her down.

"Yu greedy two-thousand-year-old bitch."

Tilly laughed and tossed Maudy her flaccid gold bag.

"Two nuggets left in deh. Yu and Longas lef mi blasted gold alone, nuh mek mi get mad."

"Sanga show mi where yu gold bury from mi yie dem was at mi knees."

"Gwan go dig it up nuh, Maudy."

Tilly cackled, spurred her horse, transformed it into its demonic form, reared on its hind legs, and fire sparked in its nostrils. Maudy held her ground.

"Loan mi Longas fe de night, nuh?" Tilly said.

"Go to hell from mi, a mi long tone man yu waan cum devowa?"

The horse sped away, leaving a fiery comet tail in its wake for a few seconds. Tilly's laughter echoed for a long minute.

Maudy hurried back along the street and ran into four teens. They giggled and broke into a song: *"Maudy rub it dung deh, Maudy rub dung Tilly's wiregrass wid her front, Maudy rub it dung deh…"*

Maudy shouted back: "A mi backside mi did use. But mi hab a place fe mi self now, onnue son of fucking 'horing slave bitches."

The kids ran, and their laughter rang up the street.

Chapter 16

On a hot, humid, lazy afternoon, Songeeta, a stunning seventeen-year-old girl, scrubbed herself in waist-deep water in a Moreland Hill stream. It was about a year before Tilly's courthouse land purchases. The water appeared dark under overhanging rose apple trees on the high bank, unlike Songeeta's elated feeling. Tilly had hired her to work at the Great House that morning. Her eager eyes strayed to the well-trodden trail ten yards away every few seconds.

An impatient leering impression took over her face, and her tongue unconsciously played on her open lips. Inch-long tiki-tiki swam around her in the crystal-clear water. An inquisitive fish nipped her on the leg, and she beat the water around her.

A wooden tub of washed clothes sat on a rock beside a large water gourd, wrapped in brown tree bark like a spider's web. Local people carried the tricky gourd by the bark traps like a bucket. Her plain calico dress hung on a broken limb.

Songeeta's cupped hands poured water between her breasts, and her anticipation grew. Her aroused nipples stood erect as her eager eyes wandered to the trail impatiently. Two birds buzzed each other in the trees above her head. They screeched, tumbled in a circle and flew away before hitting the water a few feet away from her.

Zekel, a tall, muscular eighteen-year-old, sat in a mango tree eating mangoes on a green hillside. Trees lined both sides of the river half a mile away from him. He cradled four large gift mangoes in his lap for his lover, Songeeta.

He sniffed the mangoes, smiling as the sweet aroma tickled his senses. Songeeta had told him to meet her by the river and based on the pieces of clothes he saw in her tub.

"She finished washing and bathing, mon," Zekel said gleefully.

Zekel reread the sun, and Songeeta waiting for him nude in the water evoked a king's smirk. Better not keep an impatient and aggressive girl waiting. He licked his lips, jumped to the ground and ran through the bush holding his four large, red mangoes.

The rose apple trees grew thick on the riverbank opposite where Songeeta stood in the stream, and Sanga's lustful eyes watched her from between two tree trunks. He bit his lips as Songeeta dropped her hand into the water between her legs. Sanga deflated his lungs, and his parched breath whistled through his mouth.

He had returned from Africa directly to Songeeta mom's shack by mystical means, and her scent led him to the river. Songeeta occupied favorite-daughter status amongst his thousands of offspring past and present. He had planned to make her his beneficence and give her the small celestial dust left in him as an eternal gift to run from generation to generation, he hoped.

A long whistle echoed from his left. Songeeta placed her fingers in her mouth and tried to answer, but only air escaped from her happy grin. On her second attempt, she managed a whistle to another call.

Sanga withdrew from behind the trees in a magical streak.

Zekel raced around a bend in the track and pulled up in front of Sanga, surprised but not too troubled. Sanga was a jovial man despite his formidable reputation. He joked around and played games alongside children like a big kid. Zekel could not remove the grin on his face, even if he tried. *Backside, Sanga had not aged in ten years.*

Sanga pointed a finger, zapped the boy and froze him. He lifted Zekel's 170-pound body, blew flames from his mouth into the boy's mouth and exposed a bright golden aura around his body. Fire streamed from the boy's nostrils into Sanga's until his life essence faded, and his young body withered into dust. Sanga tossed the remains in the wind, transformed into the boy's likeness, picked up the mangoes and ran the remaining twenty-five yards to the river, wiping his sweaty brow.

CHAPTER 17

Naana Meg, a frail, sick woman in her sixties, rested on her back on a wooden bed in her one-room shack. A three-month-old baby slept on the second bed under a patchwork, with a large blue and red letters' sheet made from flour sacks. A rickety wooden table and two chairs rested their tired frames against the bamboo wattle wall while the mahogany-stained wood floor gleamed and held a dark mirror sheen.

Women's clothes made from calico and flour sacks hung on nails over the beds, as a foot-long polished cross made from black padauk wood swung from a string over Naana Meg's bed. It had mysterious type-hieroglyphs engravings the length of its shaft and arms and a deep plus sign carved in the middle where the arms met.

Songeeta pushed the door open, carrying a wooden tray in her hands, and early morning sunlight rushed inside. She placed three roasted bananas and herbal tea on the table in a tin can.

"Mamma, de egg nuh good."

Meg stared at the ceiling and did not shift her gaze, lost in regrets and hoping she was going to a better place when she died.

"What dem a seh bout yu puppa?" Meg asked.

"Dem seh de east wind spirit tek way Puppa Sanga on his way back to Africa."

"No, he will ride back pon de west wind soon."

A smiling Songeeta squatted beside the bed, rubbing Naana Meg's cheeks.

"Rahtid den, Mamma, 'em caan heal yu."

"No, Song, Fe mi healer deh near."

Naana Meg stared at the cross.

"Yu betta drink de cerassee before it gets cold. Mi a left fe de great' 'ouse."

The baby rolled over on its back, kicked its legs, and cooed. Songeeta lifted and kissed her on both cheeks. An intense bittersweet emotion rocked her body and tears welled up in her eyes. Her lover had disappeared the day he impregnated her in the river. She swallowed a mouthful of grief and pivoted under the cross. The baby grabbed the cross, and it jumped from her hand.

"Mamma, how come mi nuh have magic like mi Puppa, Sanga?"

"Maybe yu daughter will have magic."

Naana Meg tried to sit, but her illness had weakened her frail body. As Songeeta whirled around, the baby's hand knocked the cross. It jiggled and suspended inverted, defying gravity as it swung back and forth.

The child's eyes glowed white fire over Songeeta's shoulder, and the grooves on the cross glowed red. Naana Meg jumped to her feet. The color came back to her cheeks, and she stood unassisted.

"A wah 'appened, Mamma? Yu betta? Yu foot dem strong?"

"Yes, Song, Jeezas answered mi prayer."

The cross swung and righted itself. Songeeta embraced Naana Meg, the baby between them.

"Mamma, mi hafi go."

Songeeta handed the baby to Naana Meg, but the baby held onto Songeeta's blouse collar and refused to let go.

"Gwan, Penny. Mummy a-go a her job up a Tilly Whitelock's Greathouse."

The baby cried in a deep, fearful, heart-wrenching voice. Naana Meg held her, but Penny's tiny hands grabbed Songeeta's blouse front strong like a ten-year-old child. Songeeta pried her tiny fingers from her shirt one at a time. The child clenched fists, bawled and kicked like a mule.

"A wat do her? She neva behave dis terrible. Hush, Baby Penny, hush," Songeeta cooed.

"Gwan, mi wi quiet her," Naana Meg said.

Songeeta ducked and ran. Penny cried and clawed the air calling her mother back from some terrible fate.

Water erosion had cut gutters on the road leading up to the Great House. Songeeta's bare feet skipped the stagnant water potholes and sharp, exposed rocks and she bent under the thick, overgrown bushes on the once-wide lavish carriageway. A mongoose chased a cackling hen across her path, and the hen flew into a tree.

Songeeta noted to sic Tilly's two hellhounds on the mongooses later.

Songeeta had an easy time by herself a day ago while Tilly visited Savanna La Mar, but the Mistress was home now, and she had a kettle singing on the fire as she grated the last piece of coconut. Minutes later, she squeezed coconut milk into Tilly's large white enamel coffee mug.

By 10:00 a.m., Songeeta had washed clothes in a tub, used a gallon of mahogany dye to polish the wooden floor and her coconut brush attacked it until her white teeth sparkled back at her. Barely catching her breath, she stood in the backyard, shielded her eyes and read the afternoon sun. She sprinkled the grated coconut trash around her.

"Chick, chick, come, come."

She knelt in the middle of the circle as dozens of chickens appeared and surrounded her, feeding. Her hand darted, grabbed a young rooster by its neck, and broke it. The birds momentarily scattered and returned to feed.

By 5:00 p.m., she served Tilly's dinner on a tray in her room. Songeeta hurried back to the kitchen, where the juicy remaining piece of bird in the pan seemed to call to her. Saliva dripped from her hungry, white lips. She sighed and served the leftovers to two demonic dogs while bath water boiled on the stove.

A stiff Tilly stood as if she was wearing a straitjacket as Songeeta peeled her dress off and led her to the steaming tub of hot water. Tilly stepped into the bathtub and sat, and Songeeta scrubbed her in water too hot for mortal hands. Silent tears flowed from Songeeta's eyes from the pain. She fanned and flapped her fingers as Tilly raised her right arm. Songeeta scrubbed and lifted the left arm, and Tilly gazed away beyond tomorrow or yesterday obliviously.

At dusk, a distressed Songeeta knocked on Tilly's door.

"Yes."

"Caan yu advance mi a penny, ma'am?"

"No, it's not your payday. Go."

She hurried away in tears.

Twilight dogged a distraught Songeeta as she hurried from the Great House, and her frantic hands shooed buzzing fireflies from her face. She hopped into the bushes, broke a piece of wild sugarcane and found a dozen eggs in a hen's nest. The scared girl's head turned 360 degrees as she searched the gathering darkness. Satisfied, she pocketed two eggs and sneaked away.

She tore into the sugarcane, but her jaws and legs suddenly froze, mid-bite. Her head whipped behind as a whip struck, and the tail wrapped around her neck.

"Puppa Jeezas, no."

She dug for the two eggs, and they fell from her hands. Tilly sat on her demonic horse wearing a malicious grin and tightened the whip around the girl's neck. Songeeta clawed at the whiptail as her tongue wagged.

"Wench, did you imagine you could steal my eggs behind my back?"

"No, no, ma'am. Please, ma'am. Mi mama and baby nuh hab nuttin fe eat."

Tilly spurred her horse and dragged Songeeta screaming over the rough stony track to her death. Her evil laughter and Songeeta's brief cry silenced the night insects.

CHAPTER 18

Birds sang, cackled and chattered across the green landscape to full man's remaining days much less a lazy midafternoon. The noisiest of them all was a flock of parakeets that soared and darted for a flowering red chin-chin tree in the green foliage. Large animals thrashed about in the brackish swamp water below the parakeets. The timid birds chattered about what made such awful noises and scattered across the woods.

On a small island, deep in the Negril swamp, stood a log cabin. Two crocodiles fed on the land crabs around the island and a woodpecker nailed a dead tree above the cabin. Feeding egrets flew away as a noisy giant crocodile crawled out of the black water into the sun in front of the hut.

Two sturdy, young, shirtless men strolled out onto the cabin's porch. The larger man picked the meat from a bone and tossed it. The crocodile caught the bone in midair and cracked it as loud as a fired gunshot. The men sat around a wooden table, and three other robust young men joined them from the cabin. One shuffled a deck of cards from one hand to the other.

The woodpecker found a spot and nailed the wooden cabin's roof oblivious to the men. Each man placed dice-sized gold nuggets on the table. The dealer flicked a card, and it froze in the air as it left his hand. Time stood still, the crocodile's mouth opened like an orifice in a hillside and a man's frozen hand held a card coming from a pants' leg. The woodpecker landed on the porch and transformed into Sanga. He observed the men for a long minute, standing still and hardly breathing. A breeze tore into the trees as he wearily limped into the cabin.

Massive raindrops the size of small pebbles fell without warning and washed away the lingering evening heat. The rain pelted the thatch on the cabin roof and sounded like small animals rummaging for something lost. Lightning reflected through slits in the rough boards and the two makeshift wooden windows. Land crabs crawled on the porch in numbers, and their legs made scratching noises on the wood as a bass-voiced toad cleaned its pipes. Answering croaks reverberated thick as the rain, back and forth across the swam.

Tilly stood in the buff on her second-floor verandah, watching the rain. Out at sea, frightened crimson clouds painted the horizon in doomsday's colors. Tilly held her hands out in the rain and her eyes mellowed like two sparkling emeralds. She recalled when a shower could make or break a planter. Now they fell on tropical vegetation, akin to vintage wine in street drunks' mouths. However, her plantation shall rise again into a slave's kingdom. She had used hunger to trap Sanga's daughter, killed her and now she waited for the game to unfold. A month ago, she had forbidden Songeeta to eat or take food home from her premises and last evening she finally succumbed.

Now Tilly waited for the coward, who had disguised himself to impregnate his daughter and disappeared.

She would hold for another week, and if he did not show his dastardly face, she would implement her plan. First, Westmoreland Parish would fall, then Hanover, St James and the whole damn island after.

She had hated Sanga from the moment they'd arrived on Earth, for no other reason than them having similar powers. A war of attrition between two equal powers spelled disaster for her aspirations and would tie her up for eons or longer. Not being the supreme evil power on Earth had eaten at her for two thousand years. As for the island, she would offer the coward forty percent. If he disagreed, she would up the ante to forty-five, and search Heaven, Hell or in the gutters of dimensions for ways to kill him.

"I kept my sons as lovers on pedestals and their faces or touches too many to recall."

Tilly spat in disgust. "How can a beast, who disguised himself to mount his daughter, ruin my plans? I detested consciences and the cowards who wielded them."

The light-skinned slaves on her plantation were her blood. She had many children and did not carry a pregnancy for nine months as women do. Days after conceiving, she grew the fetus and delivered it in two weeks. Last year, she entertained the idea of moving to New Orleans in America. She had spent time in the French Quarter and loved the natural way it unfolded. War rumors hung over America; nevertheless, conflicts always brought myriads of opportunities, but why should she leave, she asked, when she could be Island Queen?

Throughout Tilly's life on Earth, she enjoyed many wars, playing both sides and had even facilitated a few herself. As for skirmishes, they were too numerous to recall. Tilly's mind raced back to when court life in Europe became tedious to her. She had gotten bored, from Venice to St. Petersburg, it had become especially monotonous in the royal courts of soft, fat men. How many ways could one steal from, and kill, useless rich people?

After a five-hundred-year existence, Europe had become worn and repetitive. An encounter one summer's night in Spain in 1540 pushed her to the edge. She had moved to Palos, Spain, disguised as a Russian princess named Marina, whom she had devoured months earlier.

A Palos high official, one Juan de Croix, a short, fat, middle-aged man, called on Tilly the evening in question. After his second glass of wine, seated in Tilly's parlor, Juan de Croix delivered a monologue on a wide variety of topics. His witty, intelligent banter enthralled Tilly, sitting across from him. She laughed at his jokes and slapped his legs several times. Tilly kept refilling Juan's glass and dabbed at her teary eyes from his amusing stores. It was more than a pleasant surprise, how Juan de Croix's wits had compensated for his unattractive physical attributes. As the night wore on, Tilly drew closer to him, and Juan's rhythmic flow had lit a fire inside her.

She caressed his hand in the dimmed light and inspected his faint aura. Tilly's forwardness rendered Juan de Croix speechless. Her warmed probing hands had reduced his gaiety to dark anxiety. Juan tried to hide it, but Tilly sensed intimacy scared him to death. The more frightened Juan de Croix got, the more aggressive Tilly became. She ran a probing hand up his legs, squeezed and found out he was impotent. Tilly contemplated whether to magically enhance him, or feed on him. Juan de Croix broke and wept, and his painful crying doused the fire inside her, but she felt empathy for the first time and placed his head in her warm bosom. She rubbed his back and watched his body jerk until it settled at some level of comfort.

"Juan de Croix, I have something to cure you."

His puffy eyes pleaded, but he could not articulate the words.

"I will be right back," Tilly said.

Tilly poured wine in the kitchen, mixed plain pantry sauce in it, zapped it and her dress dropped around her ankles. She walked in on Juan de Croix, nude, held his head in her hands and fed him like a baby. After a few seconds, Juan de Croix felt movement in his loins. He grasped himself beaming and leaped on Tilly like a wild animal. She slithered away and took to her knees. He took her akin to a demon. Magic-enhanced lovemaking had a way to haul the most outlandish guttural sounds from deep inside a man.

"Marry me, princess. Please, marry me, princess," came from Juan de Croix between the demonic growls.

Tilly stood in the warm night air as Juan de Croix's carriage drove away. In retrospect, it hit her. She'd had enough of Europe, and something Juan de Croix said about the New World enthralled her. In the fall, she boarded a ship, and after a stop in Cuba, she landed in Kingston, Jamaica, in mid-1541. The breathtaking carriage ride to Villa de la Vega, now called Spanish Town, hooked her on the Island. She had planned to sail on to the South American mainland but decided to remain for a few years on the beautiful Isle instead. European women were scarce and eligible men in abundance. Many were sexual deviants and, she was an astute butcher, herself.

Tilly had settled in a red brick building, fifty yards from the Chapel of the Red Cross. One bright, sunny morning, she rode along the Rio Cobre enjoying the unspoiled beauty. The river ran on her left, and on the right grew tall flowering rainbow-colored blooms. Birds chirped from every tree; multicolored butterflies and bees drank nectar by the cupful from the wildflowers.

It was a dangerous place for a Spanish man traveling alone, and even more critical for a woman. Tilly approached a towering cotton tree and missed the enormous, shirtless African sitting on the spur until she rode abreast of him. The man's muscles competed and out did the tree spurs. She reined in her horse, impressed, yards from the man standing tall and coldhearted in front of her. Tilly's eyes fastened on the bulge in his tight pants, as he gaped unblinking at her. Tilly noticed he had two fingers missing from his right hand. A machete and a musket sat at arm's length, but she dismounted and approached him fearlessly.

The man was a Maroon turned bandit and went by the name Jack Tres Dedos. Centuries later, another bandit borrowed the name Three-Finger Jack under the English. He became a famous villain and freedom fighter, depending on which end his blade came at you.

Jack Tres Dedos could not understand the behavior of the beautiful, brave white woman who stood before him. He scratched his thick mop for answers. She should have galloped away screaming in terror. Instead, she had dismounted, held her ground and stared him down through fiery green eyes like the sea.

Tilly's tongue played on her parted lips. How could she not know his name and who he was? He had been the settlers' terror and nightmare since he'd escaped from Pedro Mazuelo's ship in 1534. He'd killed five the day he landed. No man he had met lived to tell tales, but a bold woman moseyed up and felt his arm muscles. She squeezed his upper arm, ran her hand across his bare chest and they had not spoken a word.

Tilly turned from Jack, lifted her dress over her shoulders, exposing her naked ass and bent between two tree spurs. Jack entered her forcefully and slammed her head into the tree trunk violently enough to break a mortal woman's neck or knock her unconscious.

On their many rendezvous, Jack told her the island's western end had free land in abundance. Tilly had not had an African before Jack. Two months after meeting him, she bought herself a few slaves, left the capital and they moved west, leading a wild stud stable. In the first year, Tilly bore

Jack and other slaves two dozen children and she devoured Jack somewhere in his late sixties.

When the British came, she wasted no time in telling them she was the boss around Western Westmoreland and Hanover parishes. Officers who did not heed her warning disappeared mysteriously.

Tilly sighed and removed her palms out of the rain, poured water between her tanned flawless breasts and it ran down the blemish-less body of a woman who had given birth to thousands. Her flowing black hair shone, and her green eyes were as bright as jade on fire. The merest of a glance at her body would inflame the coldest man. A cupped hand poured water on a firm, brown breast as she caressed a nipple, her eyes glowed. She whistled, her horse flew in the rain along the verandah, she leaped the rail onto its back and they darted away.

Chapter 19

Sanga had taken Kabba back to Africa by magical means, had him restored to his royal house and spent years teaching and roaming across Western Africa. He returned to Jamaica in 1840 and impregnated forty-seven-year-old Naana Meg. The village called it a miracle for he had married her at sixteen, and Songeeta was her first child. He spent ten years fathering Songeeta and went back to roam Africa.

Songeeta's nakedness was insignificant for he had decided to give her his gift before he left Africa. He sensed her deep love for the boy, and she would have rejected his magical offspring, an eternal sacred uncursed gift burning deep inside his core and a leftover from what Grace had given him. It fought stubbornly and refused to let go during the cleansing and it was burning like living flames inside him.

He could not have explained something beyond her understanding, and it was impossible to describe it to her, he had told himself a million times after the act. How did it remain untouched? Did they leave the dust of light kernel surrounded by darkness intentionally or was it by chance? How else could it have survived or kept uncorrupted? In the last few years, he felt time chipping at it. Its demise was imminent, and he had to pass it on to her.

Songeeta possessed the spirit and deserved his gift above his thousands of other children. Love remained beyond reproach, but she had to receive life and the future. He perceived the soothing raindrops in the darkness, but the peacefulness brought back longing to his troubled life, instigating sharp breath and loud, regretful sighs.

His shoulders sagged, a gush of air escaped through his clenched teeth as regret tore at him, for his actions had denied Songeeta her true love. In life, even the most straightforward deed led to a reaction; in retrospect, he should have possessed the boy, but lust, his weaknesses, and the instrument of his demise, overpowered him again.

Songeeta, his daughter, suffered and died at Tilly's hands for his infernal travelling and weakness. Two thousand years doing the same thing had worn on his psyche.

Sanga had taken Songeeta three times in the river, even though he had willed her to conceive the first time. He had not hurt her, but his action burdened and shamed him. After the deed, he wanted to run away from her, but she had expected him to walk her home, and carry the water gourd, as the boy usually did.

He followed her on the narrow foot track, carrying the water gourd and the mangoes. She glanced back at him every few yards, her eyes filled of love and the feeling inscribed on her smiling face.

Songeeta smiled to herself after eyeing the disguised Sanga. She had savored the sex and still tasted honey on her lips. They've never done it three times in one session and thinking about it had aroused her again. The spot behind her mother's shack sounded exciting when they got home. She could bite on her dress to keep quiet. She laughed, turned and caught his bowed.

"Wat wrong wid yu, boy? Yu so silent."

"Yu bruk mi dung."

"A yu, bruk mi dung, yu drown mi," Songeeta giggled.

Sanga raised his head. Songeeta pointed to a spot close to Naana Meg's house.

"Tomorrow mi ago help yu cut wood, fe wi build a little place right there," she said.

"Yes, wi can do dat in de mornin."

Sanga placed the water gourd at the front door. Songeeta held his hand, smiled and winked.

"Laata mi hafi go fe mi goat dem."

"Bring back milk, mi 'round back in the spot waiting fe yu," Songeeta smirked.

"Laata."

Sanga ran from Songeeta's house into the woods. At dusk, he had reverted to himself and sat on a rock weeping, surrounded by the wilderness. His evil aura had driven away the citizens of the woods and left him lost in regret. His weakness had denied Songeeta true, pure love and he wept for hours.

Fruit bats flew from a cave in a long stream, detoured around Sanga, their wings and sonar tweets were the only sound in the forest. He stood and howled in anguish at the gathering dusk. A passel of wild hogs scattered through the underbrush. Sanga transformed into a pig and ran in their midst as penance.

Sanga held the Padauk cross and gawked at it for a long minute in the marsh cabin. A year running as a pig had not absolved his sorrow and guilt. He inverted the cross in his hand, watched it glow red and clasped it against his chest. A burst of living flames emitted from the cross, seared his breast and burned into his body until the cross disappeared inside him. The room glowed crimson as his body transformed into transparency, showing the cross lodged between his ribs and burning like a living flame. He inserted an ethereal clawed hand into his stomach and retrieved the cross, leaving the crimson glow in his body. He tossed the cross above his head, and it hung upended from the ceiling.

Tilly had trapped five sex slaves in the swamp. She paid them gold trinkets for their amusement, and she devoured them after she had worn them out. Sanga had frozen the men in a corner and gazed at them pitifully.

"Humanity needed a break from myself and Tilly," he said, before he shimmered into invisibility.

The four lanterns hanging on pegs on the walls lit themselves and illuminated the spacious cabin. A large wooden bed sat in one corner, and three smaller beds scattered around a rough-hewn wooden table and stools. The men had their pots and pans hung left of an elevated cooking place. Sanga snapped a finger, and they woke from the induced trance and sat around the table not knowing they had lost many hours.

"Weh de cards dem deh?" one man asked.

Tilly's horse landed in the pouring rain as the five shirtless young men played cards inside. A gust of wet wind blew in as the door flew open, and Tilly stood naked in the doorway. The door slammed and shook the cabin; the sex slaves jumped to their feet, as each tried to outstrip the other.

"No," Tilly cried.

She stood under a white and black occult circle drawn on the ceiling above the Padauk cross hanging inverted in the center. A glowing mystical circle trapped her feet, and they felt like thorns were creeping through her veins. She tried to lift a hand, but only her thumb twitched. Her mouth froze open, but her green eyes moved and blinked, as Sanga dropped from the roof in front of her.

"Get out," Sanga bellowed in an unnatural voice.

The men bolted through the door as Sanga pulled an ugly occult white bone-engraved handle knife from his waist. He slit Tilly's skin from her neck to below her belly button and skinned her on her feet. Tilly's eyes followed Sanga's butchering hands closing and reopening wide every few seconds. Sanga watched her eyes and how they reminded him of Rosa, a woman who could not express herself sexually. The closing and opening of her eyes were how he measured her pleasure or her pain.

Rain fell on Tilly's demonic horse, and its color ran like black ink staining the ground. Bit by bit it melted away, like a saturated sand pile.

The storm had blown over, and the stars came out to witness as Sanga stood between two coffins and two dug graves. He glanced back at the Great House, a hundred yards back on the hill and regretted not setting fire to it before the ceremony. The remnants of the rain dripping from the trees tipped-tipped sounded loud as a waterfall in the woods. Sanga sniffed the wetness around him, filled his lungs and savored like a lovers' goodbye kiss. He had restored Songeeta's torn body, and he kissed her lips in her coffin on the right. Tilly's once-tanned olive skin was pallid from magical works and covered in ugly lattice stitches.

Sanga's magic lowered Tilly's coffin into the farther grave, and levitated Songeeta's coffin in the other. The knife and the cross stuck together as if they were magnets. He flung them into the night, and they sailed away like a comet's tail. Sanga bent over Songeeta's grave and vomited until his crimson life-force spilled from his body into the hole. The lava-like elements boiled and flowed over into Tilly's grave. Sanga withered and blackened until his crumbled shell fell into the grave. The wet soil refilled each grave, as a thick flourish of shrubbery sprung up, and hid their locations.

Inside Songeeta's grave, Sanga's life force suspended her body above the coffin's bottom and surrounded her. Tilly stretched out in her coffin, her mouth open and her eyes blinked rapidly in the fiery substance.

Songeeta's baby, Penny, cried, and Naana Meg picked her up, and found the cross and the ugly knife beside her on the bed. She did not miss the cross and her head whipped behind her. The empty string swung back and forth as if Sanga ripped the cross away seconds ago. Sanga's magical knife and the return of the cross meant one thing. She used a cloth to pick up the blade, wrapped it and placed it inside a bamboo joint and covered it.

"Yu mamma killa pay, Penny. She pay good too."

Penny grabbed the cross, and her body glowed a golden hue. The light spread to Naana Meg, covering her from head to feet. She fought to escape, but it dissipated before she did. Unknown to her for the moment, the years had peeled back and left her a forty-year-old, healthy woman.

Chapter 20

In 2009 Ranchie, a tall and elegant twenty-year-old unenthusiastic mother, walked four-year-old Hallie, dressed in her blue-and-white uniform, from school along the Prospect/Flower Hill main road. They skirted around yellow, red, speckled, and striped mangoes on the Hay Hill section. Large, black, shiny fruit flies and bees buzzed around the juicy fruit. The air smelled fruity sweet, and sour in the afternoon sun.

Hallie followed Ranchie, hefting a big red mango in her hands. The expression on Ranchie's face said 'I'm bored and Negril calleth my name'. Instead of frolicking on the beach, she had to walk an Obeah child from school. If they had told her not to seduce a man at sixteen for she could get pregnant the first time, laughter, laughter and more laughter would be her reply. At the time, Sasha and Cindy did it regularly and did not get pregnant. They worked Negril Beach, making money, and not having brats on their tails.

Ranchie's strides lengthened unconsciously and led Hallie by ten yards. She had planned to run away from her mom and daughter after Mother Penny relocated back to Moreland Hill in a month.

Hallie picked a wildflower and ran to catch her mother. Ranchie hated walking Hallie to or from school and considered it a waste of her time.

"Why should she have to babysit Hallie when she and her damn Obeah grandmother had powers? She had not experienced Hallie's magic, not even once but the smart little so and so possesses it."

"Mommy, I picked a flower for you."

"Don't call me Mommy. Call me Ranchie."

"But you are my mama. Grandmother Penny said you gave birth to me."

Ranchie glanced back.

"It fails me how an error made me your mother."

Hallie grinned at her. The memory of the rainy day flooded Ranchie's head like water from a wild river. Mother Penny had gone to Montego Bay, and weary Charles, her stepfather, evaded her throughout the house. Ranchie had intention written in her ultra-mini skirt from the moment her mother left home. She terrified Charles, and he kept out of her way. Thunder rumbled, and lightning cut the dark clouds touching tall trees. Ranchie ran out the front door to the house next door. Charles hurried out in the sprinkling rain to the clothesline and rushed back inside carrying the clothes. He dumped them on Mother Penny's bed as the bedroom door slammed, startling him. Ranchie had returned while he was outside and had hid behind the door. She grinned at him, exuding sexual intentions and her back against the door.

"You can run, but you can't hide," Ranchie said.

"This has gone far enough. And as soon as your mother gets home—"

"I'll tell the police you ripped off my clothes and tried to rape me first," Ranchie threatened.

"You dare not," Charles shot back.

A confused Charles glanced out the window as the rain slanted against the wind in sheets.

Ranchie ripped her flimsy blouse and tore her skirt open. Charles backed away from her into the corner. Ranchie pulled at her panties until the leg cut into her inner thigh, made bruises and ripped apart along pre-cut razor lines.

"You cut off my panties, Charles? Only God knows how you didn't slice me open."

"Please, Ranchie. Your mother will kill me."

"I don't care, and if you don't let me touch you now. I'm gonna run outside screaming rape."

"Ranchie, please, in God's name, I beg you not to."

"If I run out screaming, you're a dead man. Dem a go beat and chop you to death before the police arrive."

She stood an arm's length away from him, tall and filled out, like grown women at sixteen. Charles mumbled a prayer for his wife to walk in and save him from her evil daughter.

She could read lies, but if Ranchie ran outside screaming rape, he would die. To rape Mother Penny's daughter meant an instant jungle-justice death sentence, and he silently prayed again.

Ranchie laughed, grabbed his hand and he snatched it away from her.

"Don't do dat again," Ranchie said in deadly tones.

She placed his hand where she wanted it and moaned.

"Sit on the bed."

"Not on your mother's bed, please."

"Why not? You do her pon it."

Charles' backside hit a chair, and his head hung, a beaten man. Ranchie knelt before him.

"I'm not good at this yet. It's my first time, but we will do it every chance we get. They say it's gonna hurt, too, but make my pain your revenge. Only thing, though, I love pain."

Her sarcastic grin lit her fiery mocking eyes, and she buried her head again.

Hallie trailed behind Ranchie, and she turned and frowned. "How can an accident make me your mother, four-eyed Obeah pickney?"

Two malnourished kid ghosts, six and seven, cried in Ranchie's path, holding empty dinner plates. Ranchie tramped yards away from the specters. Loris, a gaunt angry spirit, appeared in front of the kids and swung a glowing machete in her hand. The blade did not seem to be from Earth. It shone an eerie silver blueish light as if it came from where people went when they died.

"Watch out, Mommy."

Hallie grabbed Ranchie's hand and tried to pull her away from the ghosts she could not see.

"What?"

"You're gonna collide into angry Loris Bissett and her two hungry pickney dem," Hallie said.

Ranchie snatched her hand away.

"I've got to get away from this. Go home to your grandmother. You deserve each other."

Ranchie turned and walked back the way she came.

"Mommy, come back."

Ranchie hurried around the curve, and Hallie turned her audacious attention to the ghosts. Loris raised her blade, but Hallie's right fist balled, and white energy spilled between her fingers.

"What do you plan on doing with the machete?" Hallie demanded.

Loris lowered her blade as she backed away.

"My mommy ran away."

"She ran from the day before you were born."

"I know but she would've stayed a month longer. What are you and your pickney dem still doing here?"

"They did not come for us." Loris said bitterly.

"Why?"

"I do not care."

"Are you going to Hell or Heaven?" Hallie asked.

"No one told me, and as I said—"

"Yu sound vex, ma'am."

Hallie gave Loris the flowers. White light emitted from her unclenched fist and enlarged into a portal.

"Go."

Loris dropped her machete, picked up her kids and ran into the portal. It flared, spun and took them away. The glowing blade vibrated on the ground like it was alive, and Hallie levitated it. The machete dipped, rose, darted and buried itself in the high embankment under a large mango tree deep beyond the handle.

"A ghost machete? I want it when I grow up," Hallie remarked.

<h1 style="text-align:center">Chapter 21</h1>

Present day Hallie raced excitedly through her front gate from school and ran through the church door into Mother Penny's office, bubbling on her feet.

"Grandmother, someone bought the diary."

Mother Penny continued to work her sewing machine and held an indifferent expression. Hallie eyed her, and Mother Penny's face said she was watching her demise play out somewhere.

"Grandmother, dem buy de diary, mind you explode from the bottled excitement. Let it out, Grandmother, mek it run," Hallie said.

"What excites me, may I ask?" Mother Penny replied.

"The diary, de gold, de everything," Hallie said.

"Gwan, go eat your dinner and come help me stitch these school uniforms. The old book sale was a formality."

Hallie shook her head from side to side as she headed for the side door.

"With the battle to come, not even a twenty-year-old stud could get me excited," Mother Penny grumbled.

"What did you say, Grandmother?"

"Never mind."

Chapter 22

Walden Bones stood lean and tall at his brownstone French window in his East Hampton, New York neighborhood.

The expectation on his clean-shaven, craggy face helped push the façade and made him appear well below his fifty-five years. The expensive suit marked him as a modern-day hedge fund warlock. A natural, black streak ran through his blond hair, from his forehead to the back.

A UPS truck soon pulled up. Walden Bones' face opened into a broad smile, and he dropped at least another ten years.

He signed for a package as he and the UPS man exchanged pleasantries.

"The midday heat reminds me of running into a hot wall," Walden Bones said.

"It's from one extreme to another, I tell you," UPS said.

"I'm not sure they designed this far north for human habitation."

"Blame it on the day men fell. Have a wonderful day, sir."

"You too, and be careful out there, man. Tempers rise in the heat," Walden said.

Walden Bones' study had old and contemporary occult paraphernalia, including a valknut, the alchemical symbol and a pentacle on the wall. The sigil shared space beside a thelema and three stock exchange monitors on the walls. He sank his lean body into a deep crimson leather chair at his desk, and his anxiety got in the way of his fingers; it took him clumsy minutes to get the box open— the expectations burned lines into his face. Kabba's old black-and-white goatskin-covered diary fell to the floor. Walden Bones gawked at it for a long minute and cuddled it to his breast.

"The folks at Amazon did not understand what they had. Thank you, Sanga, for having written this in pre-creation Twi."

He kissed the book, jumped to his feet and pumped a fist. He flipped a few pages carefully as he paced the study, his phone at his ear.

"Walden."

"Hey, Yancy my man, how's the bull market treating you?" he replied.

"Matadors are always comfortable around bulls."

"They shredded my cape," Walden Bones said.

"I told you to wait for a few days after the Orange Blabbermouth sank a stock before you take aim and rapid-fire," Yancy said.

"I got carried into preoccupied territory by a side project."

"Is it something I can cut into with my talons?" Yancy asked.

"No, it's in the dark mumbo-jumbo department aisle."

"I'll shop alongside the tech head merchants, thank you."

"I aim to blow off steam in Jamaica for a week or two. You practically live on the island. Do you know someone who could guide me around dark corners?" Walden Bones asked.

"Oh, yes, she's expensive and worth more than you'll pay," Yancy declared.

"Do you know someone handy outside the bedroom?"

"Walden, I said she's expensive, and I'd trust her with my life."

"I need her services," Walden announced.

"It's not a problem."

Walden Bones opened the book and gaped at a page. The neat handwriting was fresh as if Kabba had written it hours ago. He wished he could read the old language.

The summer fate introduced him to things occult in Louisiana had led him to a moment in time. Every road led to somewhere. He sank back into the comfortable leather, closed his eyes and recalled his hip, cool grandmother. She took him to fun places to meet people of the Earth. For the first time in his life, he had the pleasure of a Black kid's company. His parents had forbidden him, and none had attended his private school in NYC anyway. He called the long-ago summer his ten-year-old 'sunshine months'. Yancy taught him how to play ball and dance. Over the years, he had not had another friend as steady as Yancy. They were even roommates in college, but the turning point came one late, hot August night.

He and Yancy had lain on the grass under a magnolia tree in the front yard holding down an Outdoor Cooler, cookies and comic books. He had held a cold soda can against his neck, and it wasn't cool enough. He had to dip his hand in the water and dab his face to relieve the stifling heat. Yancy swatted at bugs beside him. He had forgotten what the hell they were talking about, and before he could ask, the first car pulled up in the driveway. One led to two, three, four until another until ten vehicles parked. Weird, sexy ladies alighted and Walden Bones lay both hands at his jaw, his eyes locked on the cars. Why had his grandma not told him about a party? He gawked in dismay and his ten years old eyes assaulted a woman wearing a red dress.

"No kids," Yancy said.

"What's going on?" he asked.

"They're wannabe witches."

"You're kidding. My grandma wouldn't—"

"Wouldn't do what? I'd say the same thing about my mother and put nothing beyond an adult."

"Your mother is a witch too?" Walden asked.

"Which part of a wannabe don't you understand?"

"Do they hurt people?"

"No, relax, man. They're stuffing their faces and boozing until midnight before hitting the basement."

"You snooped on them?"

"I beat them by half an hour every time."

Yancy grinned at Walden Bones.

"Cool."

"I'm getting too old to see my mother nude," Yancy said.

"Damn. What about the lady in the red dress?"

"My mother is built better than her."

"True."

"Your grandma also prances in her birthday suit, dude," Yancy said.

"Shit, again."

Night descended, and the muggy heat did not follow the setting sun. The boys mingled amongst the guests in a reception area, and Walden hung close to the woman in red, sniffing her perfume while he sipped from his soda to keep his mouth moist.

She had curves under her silky red dress. If they rated laughter, they would designate those obscene ones coming from the women as triple dirty X's. Walden and Yancy took goodies from the table before they marched upstairs.

The boys ate, played cards and listened to some tunes to pass the time. They alternated between Motown, Rock and the Blues. The boys realized that great music caressed a remarkable soul like grease lightning in any person who possessed one. Anxiety forced Walden to lose concentration several times and check his watch. Every time he did, Yancy's

North Pole-type cold eyes froze him. Even in the worst situation, the boy never sweated, and it followed him into adulthood.

At 11:30 p.m., the boys snuck into the basement. Yancy led Walden on tiptoes around the candle-adorned altar. He touched the skulls and bones, posed in front of the mirrors, commanded the crystal ball and picked up a dowsing rod.

Walden's eyes lit up as if a new, exciting world had opened for him and his maxed curiosity compelled him to circle the setup a second time. Yancy glanced at his watch and pulled Walden by his sleeve into an alcove.

Soon after, the women assembled in robes, sipping from bottles and glasses. Walden's grandma led them to the altar, dropped her robe and her disciples followed. They smoked weed, shouted, danced and sang mumbo-jumbo in multitudes. Walden angled his eyes and kept his grandma out of his vision line. Yancy did the same thing for his mother. *Boy, Yancy's mother had a butt and legs on her to fix war zones. God made brown soil from her instead of the other way around.*

Neither Walden's grandma nor any of the others exhibited any magical powers. Not even a damn spark flew. They played make-believe witches, dancing and prancing for hours until their hot, sweaty bodies glistened in the candlelight.

Something harmless for bored, overfed women to do, Walden guessed, but it lit his interest in dark matters, and the flames kept blazing.

Otherwise, he got enjoyment and a lesson in women's body sizes and shapes. The spectacle left a life-changing impression on him.

Walden sighed, gave his attention to NY Stock Exchange Monitor, and poured himself a drink, although his acquired magic did not make a powerful warlock out of him. His spells could wiggle him out of a jam here and there and stick the stock market in the right spot.

Over the years, he had gained knowledge of the art, much more than he could magically apply. He had traveled the world for over three decades seeking mystical experiences.

A trip to West Africa on a quest for magical tidbits a little under two years back had acquainted him with Tilly Whitelock and her buried gold. He had visited a few Nganga hounfors in dusty Nigerian villages, sifted through bits and pieces, but found nothing profound. He didn't know that he had picked up a tail from the day he landed in Africa. A powerful magician, one Prince Dinek, had a keen interest in him. Prince Dinek's ancestor was the slave, Kaaba, the diary writer.

On the fourth day of his trip, they had crossed into Ghana at the Aflao crossing, heading into the Volta region.

They traveled as far as they could from Wli Falls, fearful of crossing back over the border into Togo and have Border Patrol shaken them down. The African sunset glowed crimson, as it did in must-visit places in photographs. Walden watched birds fly across the orange beach ball sun in the distance and clicked a few photos. However, his body soon succumbed to the day's events, and he caught a quick nap. He woke at 9:00 p.m., stumbled and disoriented for a minute in his tent. After finding his bearings, he armed himself and strolled out into the warm night.

Nature's vibrant noises filled the humid air like an orchestra with too many pieces playing in a hot room. Walden wandered four hundred yards from camp through the light shrubbery.

Prince Dinek had mastered acquired magic and possessed excellent skills. He had followed Walden for four days; at some point, he lagged Walden ten miles and a hundred yards ahead as he pleased during his pursuit.

At one point, Walden stood under a small tree; one hand held a limb above his head as he played stargazer. *Which one of the distant planets does a man of his stature could migrate to, make crazy money, and practice potent magic? What else ignited and motivated men like himself but power and wealth?* A million idle things and ideas raced through his mind.

"Why does a poor man never want to destroy the world, but a rich one does?" He shook his head. "Whom could he ask?"

Walden had extensive military training and had dabbled deep in the mystical, yet Prince Dinek sneaked to a few yards of him. Walden did not sense him until he loomed two yards away, and the most profound voice he ever heard said:

"Hello, Walden Bones."

He didn't ask how the imposing warrior picked up his name, not wanting to disrespect the man. They sized each other up in the dim light. Prince Dinek sat on the ground before him, a sure sign he meant no harm. Walden sat across from him.

"I am Prince Dinek. Do you wish to get rich and powerful?"

"How much is it gonna cost me?"

"Not my prerogative. I am giving you the overall story. Whenever you find the book, you will call me to read it for you," Prince Dinek said.

"What's in it for you?"

"Twenty percent of Tilly Whitelock's gold."

"Who's Tilly Whitelock, my good prince?" Walden Bones asked.

"She lived in western Jamaica for over three hundred years, and she buried a Spanish galleon's cargo."

"Where did she do such a sweet thing?" Walden Bones asked.

"In Moreland Hill, outside Negril."

"I guess the wind has kept her secrets and her particular legend close to its chest?"

"Consider her and a hurricane in the same breath. Come follow me. The things you have never perceived are many, Walden Bones."

Two giant black fiery-eyed lions appeared from the shadows. Prince Dinek mounted one and eyed Walden, signaling him to mirror his action.

Chapter 23

The demonic lions raced away in the pitch-blackness. At least stars in the heavens witnessed his journey into the unknown. Walden Bones chuckled. His ride was much smoother than riding a horse and much swifter. He glimpsed trees flashing by under them in a continuous blur, and he understood the smooth ride.

He kept his eyes on Prince Dinek, yards ahead of him as they rode around thickets of tall trees and approached a lighted compound after twenty minutes. The prince dismounted between two massive gateless columns.

"Welcome to my village, Walden Bones."

Walden glanced at his watch and figured they were in western Kumasi, given the time and speed of the journey.

"My people have inhabited these lands for at least two thousand years."

The prince led briskly and made a left at the old quarters where the original beehive dwellings and replicas stood.

"My ancestors consolidated power from these primitive abodes to our sprawling complexes."

The compound gave Walden the impression of too much going on at once. They climbed a hill by a giant money-maker, the modern church. The prince, who did not care to become king, had a personal residence valued at millions, and it loomed on the hill. Prince Dinek's private study led to a mini museum. Artifacts from across the world and Africa dating back to humanity's cradled days filled the racks. Walden gave Prince Dinek his full eye in the light of the study and saw an impressive man of Idris Elba's status sporting a bald dome. Ebony and melanin teamed to produce the color of his skin. A shamelessly handsome man, the kind of person you gazed at twice, and his magnetism pulled you back to gawk. Walden possessed nothing the prince wanted, and he signed the partnership contract in his mind.

Prince Dinek lingered at Kabba's wooden sculpture.

"He was Sanga's writer and a prince sold into slavery for intruding into other men's harems," Prince Dinek said.

"When will us men learn? Has anyone ever eyed the book?" Walden Bones asked.

"Sanga brought Kabba and the diary back home. My people read the book and inserted its contents in our oral tribal folklores."

"Who were Sanga and Tilly?" Walden Bones asked.

"No one has the facts. Sanga had a wooden cross, and it held both their secrets."

"Is the cross in Jamaica too?"

"I think so, but it wields primordial magic or white magic. Acquired magic such as ours cannot open it."

"What was an evil entity doing with a symbol of primordial goodness?" Walden asked.

"The evidence points to theft." Prince Dinek replied.

Walden leaned back in his soft leather chair and closed his eyes in anticipation. One needed a vivid imagination to circumnavigate a ship full of gold. He placed the book on his desk while working on his laptop for a good five minutes and sent a simple email: *Prince Dinek, please check your ticket and hotel information. I've got the book in my possession. I'll see you in Negril on the 27th.*

Across the Atlantic Ocean, Prince Dinek and four topless female warriors worked out in his gym in loincloths. The women's abs and muscles competed and equaled the prince in the eye candy contest. Ebony wooden fighting sticks blurred and clashed, making hollowed sounds on contact. They attacked the prince relentlessly from all sides. After the women delivered their second kill strikes to his head, he conceded, bowed, and left the gym.

An expressionless Prince Dinek read Walden's email in his office, uncurled from the desk and paced. He sat on the polished hardwood desk, folded his arms and closed his eyes as if searching for a cozy spot to place the information he had received.

The gold meant nothing to him. He considered resurrecting Tilly, the crowning moment of his life. His research had told him Tilly and Sanga were not human, but evil creatures originated from somewhere in the universe, even aliens from the same planet came to mind? Both were sex maniacs, lacked sexual morals and had no qualms bedding their children.

Are they the angels the Bible claimed visited Earth to seduce and prey on humans? Kabba had not mentioned the cross in the diary. Oral stories claimed the cross terrified Sanga, and he kept his distance. It meant the cross could destroy him and Tilly. Aliens would not fear the cross, and there were no words in the diary to indicate Tilly had ever encountered the cross. If he managed to snatch the cross, Walden Bones could keep the gold. He had gold reserves on his tribal lands to rival what Tilly had stolen many times. He will not tell Walden Bones that someone placed the diary where he could find it, but why did they lure him there?

"He suspected it was to rob the treasure back when whosoever freed it, or it could be for something more diabolical," Prince Dinek mused.

Chapter 24

Ranchie had become a true legend on Negril Beach in the last 12 years, and one evening, she worked the treadmill in a five-star hotel gym flaunting her goddess-like physique. She stood a shade over six feet at thirty-two years of age, and every muscle reinforced her curvaceous body in the fitting locations. She had a tremendous aura, strength and uncanny beauty thing working for her. Her unabashed handle was a no-nonsense whore and a martial art expert from the dumps to the five stars hotels.

The yoga pants hugged her close like a second skin. Bodies like hers gave credence to the legend of angels flying from Heaven to work on Earth and mesmerize men's daughters and sons. Envious eyes followed her as she punched and kicked the heavy bag.

People typically locked their covetous and lustful eyes on Ranchie's erotic body. She enjoyed the attention and flaunted the extra yards. Gustav, a man of solid and fine substance, carried a touch of European aristocracy air about him and drew attention from both sexes on his exercise bike. He wore custom Adidas sweats, and his family's coat of arms was more extensive than the brand's logo. He leered at Ranchie without pretense, and she played him from her periphery vision, not lost to his royal type of aura. Gustav beckoned Ann, the attendant.

"Who is she?"

"She's available, sir."

"Do you mean?"

"Up in the high stratum, sir."

"Can you facilitate a meeting?"

Ranchie toweled off, and Ann whispered in her ear. Ranchie waved a hand Gustav's way, and her siren's smile beckoned him to her bosom. However, he had his eyes locked on her lower extremities and missed the wave. American mass media racist saints have used the discredit brushes on butts such as Ranchie's for years, but who can erase their DNA imprint? He savored and wetted his lips, for he decided to embrace all the goodies others had denied themselves, and he chuckled to himself. The future lies in the past, and women are paying good money to have poison pumped into them for a façade on Social Media. He lifted his eyes to Ranchie's face, and she wore nothing artificial. Even her yoga pants fit as if she had stepped from the womb wearing them. They both winked at the same time.

Ranchie and Gustav strolled the beach as darkness had set in, and fireflies played between the sea grape trees. The gentle waves licked their bare feet at the water's edge. A new moon hung on duty at the horizon's rim, and silver leaves rode the tranquil waters. Gustav gazed out to sea, an arm around Ranchie's waist.

Nude lovers frolicked in the quiet night ambiance and warm water as if they were water nymphs in their bedrooms.

"Gustav, I've got a prior appointment in a few days, and I don't overlap."

"I understand, Ranchie. Let us not waste a minute."

He pulled her against him, and his hungry fingers cupped her butt. Ranchie nibbled on his ear, and her hot breath excited Gustav as he squeezed her cheeks harder and dug deeper.

They waltzed under an overhanging sea grape tree, and two knifemen jumped from the shadows at them. Ranchie jumped in front of Gustav.

"Guys, it's a fantastic night, don't bleed on the moon," Ranchie said.

"Bitch, I even cheated at breathing oxygen. Fuck de moon."

"Well, he's with me, and I've nothing for you to rob."

The robbers laughed.

"We nuh seet dat way," the lead man said.

"If you insist, the end product is gonna be fatal," Ranchie said.

Ranchie stepped into the moonlight, shielding Gustav behind her. By the surprised look on Gustav's face, he wasn't used to a beautiful woman protecting him from ruffians. The first man bull rushed her. She danced away, kicked his knee and snapped it. She grabbed his knife hand in a jiu-jitsu hold, disarmed him and ripped the knife from his crotch up.

The man's howl turned into a gurgle and something unholy in his throat. Ranchie threw him in the water, and he yelled much louder. The second man ran for his life.

"Gustav, we better take the show indoors."

"Ranchie, you are an intriguing woman."

"You're rushing to judgment. You should wait until you experience what I do for real money and enjoyment."

Gustav's hand worked its way inside her pants and cupped a butt cheek.

Ranchie led him into a hotel compound.

"Sex is more profound to you than an act for monetary compensation, Ranchie?" Gustav asked.

"I enjoy every transaction as if it were my first. Money cannot change or influence it."

He grinned and dug deeper.

"If you see me crying, it will be from ecstatic joy," Ranchie said.

Chapter 25

Mother Penny's bedroom consisted of a queen-sized bed, a mahogany dresser, a night table and one hardwood bookcase of religious and occult books.

The padauk cross hung over the bed by a leather strap. An extended shoulder height vials-filled shelf lined one wall. Hallie opened the door, jumped on her back on the bed, giggled, bounced and settled. The engraving and grooves on the cross glowed red to welcome her.

"Rahtid, it's about time. Tell me your secrets. Lay it on me, woody," she said.

The red glow filled the room as a force from the cross lifted Hallie horizontally and leveled her face inches from it. She held form, suspended under the cross and her arms straight at her side. As it bathed her in the eerie red glow, her wide eyes shone white beams, piercing the red and striking the ceiling like two thin searchlight beams.

The cross carried Hallie's astral body back in time to the dusty road between Jerusalem and Gaza, two thousand years ago, where Queen Candace's caravan had camped for the evening. Hallie's astral patrolled the camp and headed to the royal tent and its broad-shouldered guards. She observed for a few long seconds and moved on into the compound. She heard coins jingling and voices up ahead.

The uproar was from the Ethiopian eunuch paying merchants and laborers from a wooden royal chest on his chariot.

The tall, balding straight-faced fifty-year-old eunuch wore a kind, wise and distinguished straight dirt brown face.

A belligerent laborer, about the same age as the eunuch, named Sanga, haggled over his pay, and his angry voice rose in the night. The Ethiopian ignored the man; he had paid him his fair wages and said enough. Two men led Sanga away, patting his shoulders, and the financial business continued without further incident.

Hallie watched the merchants disperse. She stood yards from the Ethiopian eunuch as he transferred the remaining few coins from the chest into a leather pouch around his waist. His duties behind him, he sat on the chest, ate bread and cheese, and drank red wine.

Tired animals in distress made a ruckus from farther back as handlers brought fresh horses for the Ethiopian's chariot and a runaway horse ran through Hallie's astral body. The Ethiopian eunuch rested his back against the chariot, reading a frazzled, old book by torchlight. A clump of trees zigzagged close by and running water from a stream trickled in the star-filled night.

Hallie floated to the creek's bank and listened to people speaking in four different languages as they bathed downstream.

She returned to the Ethiopian as he read and pondered as if he did not fully comprehend what he had studied. Footsteps approached, and a holy man, Philip, hurried past Hallie. He approached the Ethiopian eunuch, as bold as a lion, introduced himself and a lively discussion ensued with elaborate arm movements and nodding heads. Philip sat beside the Ethiopian eunuch on the chest, and they read the book together. The debate continued for twenty-five astral minutes and the eunuch nodded several times in agreement. Philip led him to the stream and baptized him in knee-deep water.

Dark clouds rolled across the night sky as a signal to the camp to settle for the evening. After Philip left, the Ethiopian eunuch broke an empty royal chest and carved the sturdy wood like a man possessed. After twenty minutes, he held the cross against the lamp, inspected it, held it on his leg, carved, filed and blew on it up against the light.

Sanga crept back, hid in the shadows and watched the Ethiopian eunuch work. Hallie recognized him as the man they'd escorted away earlier. The Ethiopian eunuch cut a mini cross where the two arms met, rubbed the cross on his garment, smiled at his artistry, went behind a bush, knelt, held the cross above his head and prayed.

A tennis ball size flame streaked from Heaven, struck the cross and sizzled like an electric current along the shaft. The dissipating light left engraved grooves on the shaft and arms. The frightened Ethiopian eunuch hurried back to his chariot, eyes looking over his shoulders and his smoking cross held against his chest.

Sanga pounced from the bush, stabbed the Eunuch several times, took his money pouch and wrenched the cross from his dying hand. The cross seared his fingers and fell. He cut the dead man's robe, held the cross and slithered away to a waiting horse tied to a tree. He quietly led it away, mounted the animal after a reasonable distance from the camp and galloped away into the night.

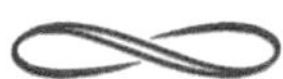

Mother Penny entered her bedroom. A startled Hallie fell on the bed, bounced and grinned up at her grandmother.

"What are you doing in—or hovering over—my bed?"

"The cross showed me secrets."

"Wooden crosses are generous these days," Mother Penny said.

"What do you mean, grandmother?"

"The wooden thing didn't show me jack until I was in my twenties."

"Moving with the times, I guess."

"Ask it to expedite your removal from my bedroom," Mother Penny instructed.

"Big words, grandma? It only showed me where the cross originated from and when."

Mother Penny sighed.

"I guess I have never sat in a classroom, and did not have formidable powers either? How much did it show you?"

"Sanga killed the Ethiopian and stole the cross," Hallie said.

"Go back and observe the light seconds before the thing hit the cross."

Hallie held onto the glowing cross and focused until her eyes turned white.

She revisited as the fire from the sky hit the cross.

Two bloody back fallen angels split from the light, their severed wing stumps red and raw. As the creatures hit the ground, they transformed into cloven hooves, hairy white hide beasts and scampered away in the desert miles apart.

Beast One raced on the road as Sanga galloped into view. The horse reared and threw Sanga in the dark. The creature pounced on him, placed a giant taloned paw on his head and absorbed his essence. It dropped the blackened carcass in the sand, transformed into Sanga's likeness, pocketed the cross and headed back to the camp.

"Sanga, old man, where are you? It's your shift," a man called.

"Can a man have his privacy?"

"Not while working, old man. The queen's chariot needs cleaning."

The cross took Hallie to a valley as the sun peeked over the mountain and raced across dew-wet meadows. She stood yards from the second beast as shepherds drove their flocks into the pasture.

The fallen angel observed the men from behind a rock. The sun glistened off its white hide as its large talons raked the rock. A small, dusty village perched on top of the hill and a persistent dog barked from a flat rock.

The beast followed the track to the hamlet and ran into a black-haired, piercing green-eyed woman, touching thirty, climbing the hill and carrying a water jug on her head. It leaped on the woman and dragged her into the thicket. A flame briefly flared, a scream snuffed in birth and the beast emerged from the bushes disguised as the woman. She frowned at her body and grew her breasts as her waist shrank; her butt got rounder, and her hips grew proportionately. Her overburdened legs straightened, alluring, long and flawless.

Her eyes got greener and penetrated as she transformed her face into the standard they judged beauty by, back in time and today—

The cross released Hallie. She opened her eyes, and Mother Penny brushed her locks, not the least concerned.

"They stole a ride on the light and made a detour on their way to Hell," Hallie said.

"Oh my, and you are getting F and G in school? I cannot figure it out."

"Do I ever get less than an A?"

Hallie took the brush and brushed Mother Penny's hair.

"But, grandmother, you're not normal. Your generations are demons, monsters and disfigured angels who fell."

"Back when I got my vision, they were more of a jumper. But what about you?" Mother Penny replied.

"I'm twice as far removed," Hallie retorted.

"Those two were sexual deviants who hankered for men's daughters and sons. They flew here to have their way and fell from grace in the eyes of higher-ups."

"It's a good thing we don't carry the trait," Hallie said.

"Are you being sarcastic, gal? Your mother and uncle are whores, and since you turned sixteen, you cannot walk the street without burning your panties to dust hankering after the footballer."

Hallie giggled and held two locks above Mother Penny's head.

"You could grow horns any day now, grandmother."

"Get your hands outta my damn hair. How is your football star doing, and how is peer pressure working out for you?"

Hallie sat on the bed, dejected. Her head dipped as if Mother Penny had uncovered a hidden wound.

"I will not interfere in your life and decisions, but you know what is at stake," Mother Penny interjected.

"I'm a sixteen-year-old girl torn between love, raging hormones and God-given abilities and responsibilities."

"At sixteen, you have more knowledge than most sixty-year-olds."

"I want to go about it naturally. I'll not even take a step ahead."

"When hearts and heads combine, they make wise decisions."

Hallie sighed.

"How did you manage the pressure, grandmother?"

"I limped from one day to the next until my early twenties."

"I don't want to limp through days or nights. I'm designed for speed."

Mother Penny glanced over at her, and her eyes conveyed what words could not say, but Hallie understood her.

CHAPTER 26

Sitira wriggled through the hallway flooring and flashed by Mother Penny's doorway. Hallie and Mother Penny glanced up.

"Coolie Duppy gal Sitira, a yu dat?" Hallie asked.

"I bet you she wants us to address her as a ghost and not a duppy," Mother Penny said.

"Yu and yu grandmother tek mi fe foreigner, bout ghost," Sitira said.

Hallie stepped out into the hall. Sitira posed near Hallie's room wearing her ghostly grin and her arms akimbo.

"Wat a gwan?" Hallie asked as she approached Sitira.

"Mi just scare a married 'oman out of a blue car backseat wid her drawers 'round one ankle, hee-hee."

"Wat, who dat?"

"Yu tek mi fi rumor monga nuh?"

"But Jeezas dough. And wat yu a do inna living people business?"

"Nuh mi cousin Butty…"

Sitira clasped a hand over her mouth. Hallie giggled.

"Gal, yu trick duppy?"

"How dat go?" Mother Penny asked from her bedroom door.

"Grandma, mi and mi friend a joke."

Hallie winked at Sitira.

"Come sit while I do my homework, Sitira."

"Yu a do de arithmetic dem again?" Sitira asked.

"What about algebra and calculus you can't recall?"

"Dem used digits, right?" Sitira asked.

"Lard Jeezas, Miss Selma a dweet inna car back. She's grandma's best friend. Lock my head away from her, please."

"You think only dat mi know?" Sitira asked.

"Wat else yu know?" Hallie asked.

"A mi yu waan dem bound inna mi grave forever?" Sitira asked.

"Who can bind yu…? Mi rahtid. Grandma, no sah," Hallie paused.

"Mi never tell yu dat, but today, it was one a dem young taxi man, and mi never see his face either," Sitira said.

"How come?"

"The boy had his head buried," Sitira said and made a face at Hallie.

"Wat dem call de new ting dat wi never do here inna my time?" Sitira asked.

"Wat yu talkin bout, Sitira? Damn, yu mean oral sex."

"Yeah, but dem young people call it a different name."

"You mean swipe?" Hallie asked.

Sitira grinned.

"Puppa Lord." Hallie tried to lock out the image.

"Miss Selma, getting a swipe from a young boy in a car back?"

"Ask the disfigured face Coolie Duppy gal if they don't have a plastic surgeon near Hell or something. Tell her to extract herself outta people business while you are at it." Mother Penny shouted.

Sitira bent over laughing, and Hallie joined her.

"If Mother Penny weren't a sweet Christian lady and your grandmother, I don't know, mon."

"Sitira, you can speak straight English?"

"Child, I'm a duppy. Je parle aussi Français. Yo Tambien soy fluido esspaol Tambien.

"Como Vivir y respirar. I can speak any language I over-hear from foreign ghosts," Sitira responded wholesomely.

"Where do you meet foreign ghosts?" Hallie asked.

"I guess you didn't know I went to the Olympics to watch Usain Bolt?"

"But see here…" Hallie remarked.

"Another thing you didn't know, back in the forties and fifties, a real Obeah man lived here. Not a Healer, a killer, and guess who was his hatchet?" Sitira noted.

"Lord, Miss Sitira, how many people did you kill?" Hallie pushed.

"Hundreds. I even did a man named Breadfruit Head and brought him back to life ten minutes later."

"Wait, how did you do it?"

"His girlfriend bought him a big, ugly, slate-colored gray Vauxhall car. The boy was more illiterate than a bat. A few months after, he walked out on the poor woman, and she came to the Obeah man seeking revenge."

"And what happened?" Hallie dug.

"I slapped him silly early one morning and disappeared. He ran and left his car as if his feet were faster. I watched him run for two minutes, then chased him down and strangled him in the Frome Factory parking lot. Unbeknownst, though, he had returned home to the woman the night before I killed him. Early, the morning in question, she had raced to my master to rescind the contract."

"Tell me the story, girl."

"The master summoned me, and ten minutes had elapsed by the time I got back to Frome. I hunted for his soul on the mystic road and found it at the astral crossroad. We fought, but I won and brought it back to him."

"What's your take on the crossroad?" Hallie questioned.

"It's a blinding, churning light in this vast plain of dark-ness at a fork, but guess what happened? The man came back as educated as a college professor, went into politics and served until the sixties as the Great Breadfruit Head." Sitira added.

"Grandma and her friends mention him every day."

"Guess where the term *'Mi nuh want dem set Coolie Duppy pon mi'* came from, my girl?"

"Did they coin it off you? Jeezas, Lord," Hallie blurted in disbelief.

"Do you think I was easy? I used to haunt dem before I killed them. I'd appeared over their beds, brandished my machete and disappeared. After they stewed for a day or two, I'd return, and bam."

"Yu wicked, dutty bitch," Mother Penny shouted.

Sitira laughed and wallowed on the floor.

"When you and your grandmother die, I'm finding an evil Obeah man or woman to work for," Sitira declared.

"So, you're not going home like other dead people?"

"I don't know which one of them owns the lightning bolt that burned me in my prime. So, I'm not taking any chances and end up in the guilty one abode," Sitira said.

Hallie shook her head in disbelief.

"I'm not condemning Miss Selma, though. I dated three men simultaneously, and none had small hands, Sitira said."

"What do you mean?"

"What kinda Healer gal are you again? Never mind, one night, the three of them visited me, hours apart."

Hallie held her head.

"The two married ones cut an hour apart and ran. When the third man knocked, I hid under the bed, but guess what? I remembered it was the stinker payday. The dog spent three days before he left."

Hallie dropped to her bed, laughing.

"You cannot still be mad at the lightning bolt that killed you?" Hallie said.

"Why do you have to bring up unpleasant things? If you were not my best friend, I'd race yu weh from over mi grave."

Hallie bumped Sitira's fists.

"If you all could give me someone to kill once a week..."

"We are fine, dear," Mother Penny shouted.

"We never used thin-ass drywall in houses back in the day, either" Sitira said.

"You lived in a damn bamboo shack, Sitira," Mother Penny said.

"Frock, slack, shack, do you know how many times we broke the bed?"

Hallie grinned and placed a hand over her mouth.

"Mek she sips on dat," Sitira said.

Chapter 27

On the day of Gem's healing, Dave had driven in silence on the way back from Mother Penny's, and Monica allowed him to sort out his inner conflicts. He had forgiven his wife for taking Gem to the healer and flashed her several brief smiles.

However, it had left him in a quandary. How can a devoted Christian explain an outside miracle to the church?

Not one as large as Gem's healed eyes. Expulsion stalked him like a dire beast for losing faith and taking his daughter to an ungodly healer. His 'siblings in Christ's' rebuking voices would cut like sharpened swords behind his back.

Satan did it to corrupt his soul. Brother Dave has blasphemed against the church and shall burn in Hell.

Dave's church denounced every other denomination as not worthy and unrighteous in the sight of God. He couldn't blame his wife, nor did he want to. Her actions and any transgression she committed, according to the church, lay on his head.

He had no intention of lying or warp into one of those husbands who took their so-called disobedient wives to church to confess. The church rebuked and sometimes flogged the wives. If he ever dreamt along those lines where Monica was concerned…; he shook his head as he killed the fleeting thought. He adored her independent spirit, although she had drawn him into various positions in bed, against the pastor preaching to do only the missionary position, but no one will hear him complain.

Brother Brown had his wife flogged for asking him to spend more time on his husbandly duties. He'd reported her, and the pastor accused her of being in collusion and keeping the devil company. Dave hoped he was enjoying his devil-free loneliness.

"The church prayed for Gem for two years without result but in less than five minutes, Mother Penny healed her.

"How does one explain it?" he mumbled.

He may have missed the positive side. A prayer was not something answered in glaring sunshine, dark clouds or falling rain.

Monica practiced her statue-imitating skills in the front passenger seat. She cringed at the dilemmatic haze surrounding Dave and gave him his space.

When he muttered, she glanced over, reached out a consoling hand for his shoulders, but changed her mind.

Dave had made an agonizingly difficult decision, which meant quarantining Gem indoors until they figured something out. Their hopes rested on time, for it had a way of dabbling in things and escalated or defused at its prerogative. He reached over, placed a hand on Monica's thigh and she dropped her hand on his.

Gem had sensed the tension in the car as she passed the time reading her dad's paperwork in the back seat.

"Boy, people pay big money to banks for things." Gem muttered.

She had not used her eyes to read for two years, and they devoured the words in a feeding frenzy.

Albeit an uncomfortable atmosphere, she still wanted to know how Mother Penny painlessly healed her eyes. From darkness to light in seconds. Her chest had beat, 'bu-dum-dum-dum' imitating a drumbeat as Mother Penny removed the blindfold. How can she recreate such a beautiful moment? Mother Penny stood over her, smiling and gave Hallie a sweet glance of accomplishment. The small moles around Mother Penny's eyes jumped at her, and she had about five more around the left eye. Gem's senses strained, her nine-year-old heart fluttered, but could not recapture the instant when her spirit and soul soared up to Heaven and gave thanks.

Gem gazed at the pages in her hands, but the words did not register. Her mind had raced ahead, and she showed off her eyes to Milda and Pauline, her two best friends, in her front yard. They laughed and hugged her, and she joined them in the games she had missed for the past two years.

As the car made the sharp left at Locust Tree she woke from the daydreaming and leaned. Even when she had no sight, she knew when the vehicle took the left turn coming from Burnt Savanna, because it slowed, and she had to hold on for dear life not to keel over on her side.

While attending the school for the blind, they had asked her to describe her village as she remembered it. Gem smiled to herself at how she had described Bath Mountain as a close-knit, small farming village. It had a Baptist church in the flat and a wild cherry tree in the front yard. The fruits left an acidic taste on the tongue when eaten. She almost spat in the car. The Church of God stood on the tall hill above the Baptist Church. Both churches were the community back-bones. Mass Reggie's two-floor concrete rum bar and grocery stood in the square. It competed against the church and had won over most of the older men and ninety percent of the young men. Either that, or it had not released them from their prior engagements, whichever, especially on Friday and Saturday nights after a hard week cutting sugarcane or work-ing their produce farms and at their trades.

A month before an election, they paved the street a hun-dred yards from the store in both directions. At that point, she could glimpse dark shapes, and the boiler thing they used for the tar made roaring noises. It appeared as a scary, dark, loud blob, dispending stinging heat waiting to burn her alive.

The churches had women's hearts and heads. The other members would drag a dropout's name to Hell's gate if one fell by the wayside. Miss Bess, my first cousin, ran the tiny post office beside the bar, next door to her boyfriend, Jewbert, who had a small shop and living quarters in the back. Across the street, tailor, as they affectionately called him, operated his shop. Sis, the dressmaker, was tall, skinny and white. Her daughter, Junie, had freckles and reddish hair. She laughed and screamed the loudest when they played. Sis plied her trade from her front room, next door to the tailor's shop. Mr. Lewis kept a small bar adjacent to a domino hall a few yards north. The wooden tables made for playing dominoes were sturdy. On any given day, lazy younger men loitered there playing dominoes. Monica took her into the domino hall once, and while she spoke to Mr. Lewis, Gem rubbed her hand over the chipped dominoes on a table. On their way home, she asked: "Mommy, how could the men play with those chipped dominoes?"

"Those are for idlers. The real players bring good dominoes to the game in the evening after work."

Uncle Tim's butcher shop sat under a large June plum tree next to Mr. Lewis's. Uncle Tim's wife and Miss Marry, Mass Reggie's wife the schoolteacher, were the only two fat women in the whole village. Why did they call a married woman Miss Marry? Gem could not figure out how adults did things. The same thing applied to Miss Maudy. Her little shop perched on a hillside across from the butchers and straight across the church. The other church on the hill sat right above her. Drummonds, bluey mangos trees and turmeric grew on the hillside behind the shop up to the church.

Gem would usually feel her way up the five wooden steps to enter the shop for her treats of sweet coconut drops, grated cakes, and coconut puffs. She slid on her butt to exit the shop and refused help when people offered it. Miss Maudy sold her candies during morning recess and lunch breaks at school, a mile north. They usually cut the distance in half by using the shortcut at Lulu Lewis's house.

Monica accompanied her family to church to avoid neighbors' razor-sharp wagging tongues than to worship, for her heart resided elsewhere in the Pocomania Church. Her soul longed for the traditional drums, songs and foot-stomping-style worship.

Monica sat in the passenger seat, chewing her sweet and bitter taste buds over time. She was so happy for Gem, but sad for her husband. She glanced at him, winced at the turmoil boiling inside his head and she touched his arm.

"Dave, let me drive for a spell."

Dave pulled over silently, and Monica slid behind the wheel.

"Mommy, me and my friends can play games now and walk to school."

"Gem, you will need to keep your eyes out of the sun for a few days," Dave said.

"Daddy, Mother Penny did not mention I had to shun the sun."

"I know, but it's best to take it easy for a few days," Monica said.

"Mi nuh believe sun caan hurt eyes after dem heal though."

"Speak proper English, Gem."

"Mom, I'm entitled to an exception, and I need friends at school."

"Are you saying that you will lose your friends if you speak proper English?"

"Somethings hafi seh in Patwa on de playing field."

Monica smiled. Gem slid from directly behind her, caught the smile and giggled.

Gem had a moment of clarity; her parents wore gloom-and-doom expressions because... Oh, boy, the church and Sister Gina, their neighbor, the holiest person in the world.

Troubles brewed on the mountain. Her parents could not explain the miracle. So, they planned to keep her healing a secret by quarantining her indoors. But for how long? Her mother cared not for anyone's opinions. She would figure out something.

CHAPTER 28

On her sixth day under quarantine Gem stood at Dave's side at the dining table as he ate his breakfast for work. After he finished eating, she kissed him goodbye, donned her radiation protective eyewear, and perched on a stool at the window to watch people. She observed the early bird kids who reached school an hour before the bell. Some of the late everyday kids hurried by after the first bell. Workers, on foot and bicycles, had passed an hour earlier. The women who worked in Frome and Savanna La Mar waited for taxis and buses in the square.

Gem slipped from the chair in fright. Mr. Dandy and Mr. Natty Runkus strolled by in a conversation. Mr. Dandy had his digging hoe on his shoulder and a machete in his hand. Mr. Natty Runkus had a fork on his shoulder. Both men had died two years back, the same year she lost her sight. Mr. Dandy was brown, short and sported a broad, balding forehead. Mr. Natty had a disfigured nose, and a jackfruit left foot and hobbled on the ball of his foot. She placed a hand over her mouth. She had seen two ghosts, and she planned to keep it a secret. Milda and Pauline waved on their way to school in their blue and white uniforms. Mixed-up concern and pity itched their faces out of love for her, and they earned the right, Gem figured. They had come over several times to play in the last couple of days and were none the wiser about her eyes.

Gem figured their sick neighbor to the left, Naana Bertha, had long touched two hundred years old. She lived closer to Pauline's house than theirs. She had noisy dogs, a gate and a fence. When someone walked by, the dogs barked the old yap-yap ugly-mutty bark. An annoyed Gem raised her eyes in the direction of the yapping dogs, and her eyes popped. She placed a hand over her mouth as a Black angel wearing shiny black wings and a purple toga touching golden sandals opened Naana Bertha's gate. His glowing skin was smooth as if someone photoshopped it on a smartphone. The dogs yelped and choked on their barks. Miss Shattie's Myrtle was the only person darker and was the blackest person on Earth, but gorgeous and sexy. Anytime the young men horse whistled and nickered, everyone knew Myrtle had walked by them.

A loud scream from inside Naana Bertha's bedroom announced her death. The angel led Naana Bertha's soul through the gate wearing a long nightdress. Sister Gina, Monica and two other neighbors dashed through the angel and Naana Bertha like they could raise the dead. Sister Gina would pray over the body while it was still warm. Gem chuckled at how Sister Gina carried her head high. Her hair must have tickled the bottom of God's feet when He walked barefoot upstairs. The angel and a young Naana Bertha smiled at Gem. She wanted to duck, but could not move. They waved to her as they climbed hand in hand up invisible stairs and disappeared. *A Black angel?* Gem asked herself. She had never come across one in a book at school or church nor in her father's religious books overflowing in the bookcase. She made a note to leaf through every single one later.

Monica's displeasure over Gem's house arrest rode her like a stinging red scorpion and had her dragging herself through the days. Sadly though, Naana Bertha had died. She had to prepare something for mourners to eat later, and she smiled as an idea sprang in her head.

Gem grated cassava for the duff and a proud Monica watched her immerse herself in the baking process, a well-pleased mother. Gem watched her from the corner of her eyes. *Why does mom never use the blender? Young women shouldn't do things their grandma's way.* Gem mixed the cornmeal pudding ingredients, bit her bottom lip and leaned her head to one side. As Monica glanced away, Gem picked out a raisin and ate it, but she turned and caught her. They shared a sweet mother and daughter laugh.

The wood coal stored in a burlap bag in the back shed blackened Gem's dress and hands as she loaded the coal pots and two zinc sheets. They used the sheets to cover the baking pans. Monica poured the kerosene and lit the coal. After they had a fire going, she grinned at Gem.

"Riddle mi dis, riddle mi dat, wat have fire below and fire on top and sugar in the middle?" Monica asked.

"Old riddle from slavery time. We've got a gas stove in the kitchen with an oven."

"Dem sweeta pon de coal fire. And dem bun nuff gas fe bake."

"And the coal is not even from pimento wood," Gem said.

"We're not jerking pork, Gem, but, if you go outside while I catch a nap and show your eyes, no one can blame me."

Gem stared at Monica, happy and surprised at once. Monica had something in her head from how she ogled the children on their way to school. *Gem going to school next week* shone like flames in her eyes.

As the afternoon dragged on a restless Gem paced around her dining table, picked up a book, replaced it and eyed the clock. She heard children's voices and she ran to the window, but it wasn't her friends. Half an hour later in Sister Gina's front yard Gem showed her eyes to Milda and Pauline holding her glasses in her hand.

"I do not believe you regained your sight, and a Mother Penny lady healed you," Milda said.

"I told you what color clothes you're wearing," Gem reassured.

"Wait."

Milda ran for her Bible, opened a random page and Gem read two verses. Milda squealed and ran back inside her house. Gem waited, and neither Milda nor Pauline came back outside to her. She stood in the yard fidgeting for half an hour and returned home. Gem caught Monica's smiling face through the curtains.

CHAPTER 29

Mother Penny and Hallie strolled through a five-star hotel lobby on Negril Beach. Mother Penny had always worn her whitest dress on Jamaica Tourist Board consulting gigs. She was out of place as a unicorn in a dogfight most of the time.

"Wait here for me, Hallie."

Hallie plopped on an expensive beige leather sofa, working her old, raggedy phone. Mother Penny continued to the front desk.

Hallie lifted her eyes from the phone.

"Grandmother."

Mother Penny stopped as Hallie hurried to her.

"By this weekend, you will get your intelligent phone and experience another life lesson," Mother Penny said.

"They're called smartphones," Hallie replied.

Mother Penny smiled.

"The same difference, child. I will be right back."

Hallie held Mother Penny's hand.

"A powerful magician and a dabbler await you," Hallie hinted.

"What hue?"

"The hazardous acquired sort, and he's not after gold. The prince seeks power," Hallie continued.

"The most dangerous kind, indeed."

"Maybe I should block your memory."

"No, not a roadblock. Do not raise anyone's curiosity."

Mother Penny glanced around and caught a woman pushing a trolley into an elevator.

"If he is not interested in gold, he came here for the cross. Replace the cross with that lady's memory."

Mother Penny pointed.

"Only the cross now."

"I could erect a firewall?" Hallie asked.

"Young people."

Mother Penny hurried off to the elevators.

"What the hell was a firewall anyway?"

Hallie hadn't told her Ranchie was in the room, and Mother Penny would not sense her until she was ten yards away from the suite. Hallie corroded the cross's memory in Ranchie's head. When Prince Whatshisname found the connection between Ranchie and Mother Penny, he would dig into her head.

Ranchie, Walden, Prince Dinek and two muscles, Terry and Norris, sat over drinks in Walden's suite. Walden glanced at his watch and shifted his eyes to the door.

"When she arrives, I will withdraw to the bedroom. I want to read her," Prince Dinek said.

"An excellent idea," Walden said.

"I should leave too, but she knows I'm here," Ranchie said.

"Why, Ranchie?"

"She's my mother, Terry, and we cannot agree on a simple truth in a civilized way."

Prince Dinek got to his feet, and Walden followed.

Mother Penny meandered the long hallway checking the numbers on the doors. She stopped at room #217 and knocked. Walden opened the door smiling.

"Mrs. Thompson, I appreciate your time, ma'am."

"It's a pleasure, Mr. Bones. Please call me Mother Penny."

Walden extended his hand.

"And you can call me Walden," he remarked.

Walden made the introductions: "My associates, Terry and Norris."

Mother Penny, Terry, Norris and Walden took seats. Ranchie sat aloof, slinging poison daggers from her mind. Mother Penny shot an icy glare to freeze fire.

"Okay, we're one big happy family here today," Walden said.

Ranchie frowned at the wall.

"The Tourist Board said you were the foremost expert on Tilly Whitelock and Moreland Hill. I'm researching for a book I'm writing on her," Walden said.

"A hundred and fifty years have left the Moreland Hill Great House in ruins," Mother Penny said.

"What happened to Tilly?" Walden began.

"Tilly Whitelock disappeared under mysterious circumstances in 1858. Local people have stayed away from her Great House over the years. I heard hippies braved the legends and visited the ruins in the eighties."

"Damn, why hippies?" Walden asked.

"They wanted to prove they were smarter than primitive natives."

"And escaped telling tales too. What a pity?" Terry said.

"Local legend says Tilly cannot die. Sanga's powerful magic imprisoned her in a deep hole on her property," Mother Penny said.

"How did he accomplish such a feat?" Terry asked.

"We're dealing up the supernatural echelon here," Mother Penny replied, wagging a finger.

"Sanga died a long time ago," Norris said.

Mother Penny shivered at Norris's ignorance.

"Obeah cannot die," she said.

"What is Obeah?" Norris asked.

"Acquired magic's big evil, ugly brother. Trust me. You don't wanna meet him," Walden said.

"No shit."

Inside the bedroom, Prince Dinek's eyes glowed, his forehead sweated and his face twisted in concentration. After a minute, he broke away, breathing hard closed his eyes and hid his emotions.

Mother Penny searched Walden's companions' minds back in the living room; the two men were heavy lifters and had no magical skills. The dangerous man hid in the bedroom, scanning her. She had felt his probe a minute ago. She only hoped the lovesick girl did not firewall the poor man to ashes. Where the hell did they get these names from anyway? It sounded as if it was something they used to inflict severe pain, Mother Penny chuckled to herself.

"Did Sanga use magic to hide Tilly's grave?" Walden asked.

"I believe Sanga buried her not more than two hundred yards from the Great House."

"Who had more power, Sanga, or Tilly?" Norris asked.

"Sanga followed an African princess sold into slavery from West Africa. When he got here, he found his love slaving on Tilly's property. Sanga and Tilly were angels who had fallen from grace in Heaven and were bound and tagged for Hell when they escaped."

"Humbug," Terry said.

"They cut a pact to avoid an eternal battle. Sanga married his princess, and Tilly got her slaves after she promised never to abuse a single Ashanti."

"What happened?" Walden Bones asked.

"Sanga went away for ten years. Tilly got overconfident and killed Sanga's daughter over two eggs."

"I guess as humbugs go, Sanga showed," Terry asked.

"One has to question how these things ran," Norris said.

"Sanga trapped Tilly, skinned her and stuffed her skin with magical stuff. Legend said he clothed her back in her skin and buried her alive."

"How do you destroy supernatural evil?" Terry asked.

"Holy fire can destroy any evil," Mother Penny said.

She helped herself to a handful of peanuts and a bottle of water.

"Who wields holy fire these days, Mother Penny?" Walden Bones asked.

"Maybe you're not aware of Creation's Pure Innocent Ones?"

"Who're the Pure Innocent Ones?" Walden inquired.

Mother Penny glanced at her watch.

"They are darkness and light and can destroy evil if a Neutralizer is not in the vicinity."

"Get outta here. What're Neutralizers?" Walden pressed further.

"Normal people carrying mystical powers that can neutralize good or evil magic. I mean, shut off and drain magical powers in their vicinity."

Mother Penny drank her water.

"This's a learning experience for me," Walden Bones said.

"Neutralizers' abilities may lay dormant for years and awakened on a Sunday by the wind."

"What's the trigger?" Norris asked.

"A walk in the sun, magic, trauma, emotional upheaval or a sundry of other things."

Ranchie watched her mother through unkind eyes. The years had dragged their relationship out into rough waters and sunk it. Ranchie hated her mother more so now than she ever did. Mother Penny had not wronged her in a specific way, but there was the unspeakable thing that Ranchie did, and her Mother had never said a word in anger. Instead, she showed her motherly love during her pregnancy. Mother Penny's silence did awful things to Ranchie's head.

Ranchie used her profession as an excuse to further hate her mom on the pretext that she disapproved. They'd not shared the same roof in twelve years or spoken to each other either. Her mother had not remarried and Ranchie presumed she must hate her. Ranchie's goal in life was to hate her more, but Mother Penny read her and wanted to tell her not to blame herself. The curse overpowered her and forced her to do what she did years ago. She did not hate nor was she capable of hating, and when her husband wanted a relationship again, he would return.

Walden accompanied Mother Penny to the elevators. They shook hands and conversed for a minute. Prince Dinek poured a drink at the bar when he returned to his suite.

"Prince Dinek?"

"She has limited powers remaining, but she knew much more than she had told us."

"She did great. We needed the confirmation," Norris said.

"I sure hope it's not a story," Terry said.

"What do you mean she has limited powers?" Walden asked.

"Magic like hers wanes after sexual activity."

Walden reflected and unwrapped Sanga's book from the black-and-white goatskin.

"It makes sense, a yin queued behind every yang, twenty-four-seven, and I love fucking Amazon."

Prince Dinek flipped the diary's pages and passed his hand over it. The Twi writing transformed into English. He handed the book back to Walden. They sat in silence while he read.

"Can you break the spell on the guard specters if we find the gold, Prince Dinek?"

"No, I cannot."

"Do you suppose Mother Penny can?"

"Not in her present state, before Ranchie, but primordial magic does not spill innocent blood to gain riches."

"It's always the hard road home," Norris said.

Walden caressed Ranchie's neck, and her smile said 'I love my job.' Ranchie may be crazy and hateful, but not enough to mention her daughter's abilities. She had seen the rolling calf's flames on several occasions. A shudder ran through Ranchie's body. *Can you imagine if the thing considered me a threat?*

"Did you ever locate the person who sold the diary, Prince Dinek?" Walden asked.

"No, I did not, but I can tell you, no one's read it in years."

"Something is bothering me. Why did Tilly kill Sanga's daughter?" Walden asked.

"Yeah, Billy the Kid did not ride over to Jesse James and cut his daughter down," Norris said.

"Sanga went missing for years. Tilly wanted him to return," Prince Dinek said.

"According to records, Tilly purchased four properties the day before she killed Sanga's daughter. don't think she wanted a war of attrition," Walden said.

"What about workers? The formerly enslaved people refused to work for their old masters," Ranchie said.

"Re-enslavement," Walden said.

"Songeeta became the pawn to induce Sanga's return, to cut a deal," Prince Dinek said.

"Shit, she needed Sanga's help to take the Island from the British."

"She may still want to," Prince Dinek said.

"I want her to show appreciation and be generous in her reward," Terry said.

"We've to break her spell to snatch the gold and run," Walden said.

"Will she return a dictator bearing a killer's mindset?" Norris asked.

"How can we know a thing fluid as a mind?" Walden asked.

"I saw a ghost and a thing once," Ranchie said.

"Is a ghost different from a thing?" Norris asked.

"Continue your story, Ranchie," Walden said.

"I was swimming nude in a stream fourteen years ago. At the time, we had an unusual number of spectral sightings. It was as if ghosts bloomed on trees."

Norris poured a drink.

"A tall man you could tell was a slave approached me from downstream, gawking and undoing his pants."

"Are you sure he was a ghost?" Norris asked.

Ranchie rolled her eyes, annoyed.

"Well, for one thing, only Jesus trod water."

Ranchie stared at Norris.

"Go on," Walden Bones said.

"As the ghost approached me, a raggedy red-eye, bloody mouth demon thing materialized behind it and slurped the ghost. It licked its black forked tongue and flew away as the ghost's clothes ejected from it."

"What?" Walden Bones exclaimed.

"They found me hours later, one hand covering my business and the other over my mouth."

Ranchie grinned at Walden Bones.

"I'd shaved a minute before, and my feathers hadn't grown back yet."

"Motherfuck. What was it?" Terry asked.

"They called it a Ghosteater. Legend said when there was an infestation of ghosts at one location, the creature rose from a dark corner of Hell and fed."

"A ghosteater would eat ghosts, made sense," Walden Bones grinned.

"We're back to yin and yang, huh?" Terry said.

Ranchie and Walden shared a private laugh.

"Ranchie, you shaved in an open river?" Terry asked.

"Yeah, back in the days. Boys wouldn't even hide and peek at me as they do the other girls. They feared my mother. I couldn't get any action, not even a fondle."

The men laughed.

"I sat on a boy's open palm at school once, and he ran in fear. His mother took him to my mom's church to apologize for accidentally touching me."

"It's called a rep. Your mom possesses an enormous one," Walden Bones said.

"Can we control her and get the gold?" Norris asked.

"I'm sure she will be grateful for her release," Prince Dinek said.

"We're on schedule. A fucking Spanish galleon full," Walden said.

Walden's eyes lit up, and he leered at Ranchie.

"Dreaming of heavy gold can indeed twist a man in knots and unravel him in a second."

Ranchie grinned at him.

"I wouldn't mind getting the dust beat the hell off me, either," Ranchie said.

"What's the story between you and your mother?"

"Do you want to lose your steel high right now?" Ranchie asked.

Walden stood and reached for Ranchie's hand.

CHAPTER 30

Meanwhile, four trucks pulled up in front of Mother Penny's house. Hard construction workers bailed, holding an assortment of beers, spliffs, cigarettes and tools in their hands.

Cars and pickup trucks parked along the roadside until about fifty men and women surrounded Mother Penny's house. Cooper, a brawny contractor, wearing a face hard as overnight work, stretched his muscles and donned his hard hat.

"Okay, fire up the cement mixer. Teppi, jump pon the Bobcat nuh mon," Cooper bellowed Cooper held back his head and stared at the house's unfinished second floor.

"Come on, mon, we a knocked it out dis evening. The materials are on the floor upstairs."

The work crew rolled as a well-oiled machine and attacked the unfinished second floor. Jerk chefs rolled out jerk grills. Two women, Miss Lyn and Cousin Darnet unfolded beach umbrellas.

"A so the one Cooper bark orders on the job?" Cousin Darnet asked.

"If I didn't lock shop on his rass and sleep in my jeans for the last two nights," Miss Lyn said.

Cousin Darnet laughed and dropped on her knees.

"Come on, Darnet, Sammy Fray brought the materials about a month ago. I had to let him know. Nobody was gonna mount me before they jumped on Mother Penny's unfinished house," Miss Lyn said.

"It's the same thing I did when I locked my shop. I'm not sleeping beside any strong man with my half-naked ass exposed after telling him no," Darnet replied.

"Temptation is too strong, misses."

"Yu ever gave in and changed your mind, and a ded fi him cut off your pants?" Darnet asked.

"And de two of you lay in bed under wicked agony, not speaking or making the first move."

The two women bent over, laughing until their eyes teared. Cousin Darnet wiped a tear.

"My dear, the house was so ugly, and tourists are regular visitors to Mother's." Darnet said.

"If it wasn't for Mother Penny, duppies, gunmen, scammers and drug dealers woulda eat us for food."

"Do you think I could operate my business anywhere else, and the extortionist dem nuh scrape the black off mi ass?" Miss Lyn asked.

The women bumped fists as Sexy Munchie waltzed up to them.

"Moreland Hill is the safest place in Jamaica night or day," Munchie said.

"Today, I fearlessly swam nude in the river. Thank God for Mother Penny," Miss Lyn said.

"Guess what happened last week. I forgot my place and stepped outta my drawers on the beach, thinking I was in the river," Cousin Darnet said.

The women laughed loudly and obscenely.

"I hope it was in the nude section," Munchie said.

"Mi fe go exposed mi grayness pon Facebook, at my age?"

"Bitch, shave," Miss Lyn said.

"What for? The last time Cousin Darnet got some, they hadn't even popularized sex yet," Munchie said.

Miss Lyn grinned at Cousin Darnet.

"I heard. She could only dweet in the dark too."

"Clap hand, Mary, mi ever dweet wid yu?" Cousin Darnet shot back.

"Lawd a massey, joke better than quarrel," Munchie said.

"Let's go set the refreshment bar."

"I carried red and white rum," Cousin Darnet said.

"Red Stripe and Guinness are on the truck," Miss Lyn said.

"Water, somebody please, have water," Munchie said.

A flatbed truck pulled up carrying giant speaker boxes and a dozen guys. It took an eternity to park. One man grabbed a roll of electrical cord, climbed a light pole and bridged the power lines. They strung their equipment in a moment and soon began pumping dancehall music.

Mother Penny and Hallie arrived in a taxi, as the carpenters placed their last touches on the upstairs front windows and the equipped painters stood by.

"We're Jammin, grandmother," Hallie said.

"Bob Marley sure sounds funny after his death," Mother Penny remarked.

"Grandmother, you have jokes. This is Jammin."

Hallie danced over to her friends as Mother Penny gazed at the men at work.

"Thank you, Jesus."

"Mother Penny, cum have a cold drink, nuh," Munchie called.

Faith and Irene, two of Hallie's friends and classmates, ran to her in distress before pulling her to the side.

"Hallie, you should've seen Steve and a girl kissing and how she nibbled on his ears," Faith said.

"My girl, the way they were carrying on, I know Steve hit it. She had him by you know what," Irene said.

"Yeah, you've got to do something, for real," Faith said.

"A true, mon," Irene agreed.

Hallie sobbed, and the girls consoled her.

"Call and confront him and tell him it was I Faith told you."

"Stinka," Irene snapped.

Hallie fumbled for her phone.

Chapter 31

Ranchie hurried along a dark alley, stopped under a pale streetlight and leaned against a lamppost. Loud voices came from a house behind her and a barking dog raised a neighborhood chorus. Blaacka, an evil disposition hoodlum, appeared from her right and leaned on the other side of the lamppost.

"So, can you do it?" Ranchie asked.

"Yu have de money?"

"Five Uncle Sam's on delivery."

"Later," Blakka growled.

"Later means ten p.m. on the dot, Blaacka, at the prearranged spot. Five thousand is big money."

Blaacka cupped his hands and lit his joint.

"Follow the instructions I gave you. It's Obeah business, and if you fuck up, your big guns won't help you," Ranchie said.

Blaacka disappeared back into the dark. The whole time they'd leaned on the post, inches apart, they hadn't glanced at each other.

"You hear me, Blaacka."

Blaacka did not acknowledge her from the darkness if he was still in her voice range.

Walden Bones and Norris drank beer in the suite. Ranchie joined them from the kitchen, holding sliced avocado and buttered warm hard dough bread on a tray.

"Hot buttered bread and pear gents. Oh, it's avocado to you," Ranchie said.

"Do you have a knife?"

"You break de bread, Norris mon. You break the bread."

Ranchie broke the bread and bit into the pear.

"Do you eat the avocado straight?" Walden asked.

"The connoisseurs of poisons got you sitting in a cozy corner. They have you adding shit to nature's bounty."

Norris bit the warm loaf and avocado, savored it and smiled up at Ranchie.

"Mmmmm, good, and for your information. I prefer my women as natural as spring water," Norris added.

"If your boss is not a hoarder, we could get at it. We've got work to do later."

The men grinned at her.

"Where's the prince?" Ranchie asked.

"He's out for a walk," Walden said.

"Good for him. I'm sure the high and mighty mother-fucker doesn't do whores," Ranchie said.

"His loss," Norris replied.

"Why do you hobnob with whores, huh, Walden?" Ranchie asked.

"Paying is cheaper and less messy for a man on the road."

"When one has something good, one should push it to the top."

"It sounds like you said you're a nympho," Norris said.

"Oh, my lord, everyone is a mind-reading magician these days."

The men laughed.

Night had descended on Tilly's gold depot and the Western world, but a star-filled sky could not penetrate the darkness in the forest.

Thick shrubberies shook, and the limbs ripped off trees as if a sizable invisible animal barged through them.

Loud trudging continued back and forth in circles until it came upon the strewn skeletal remains. The ghosts loomed from invisibility as elongated wraiths slashed their machetes left and right.

A force disturbed the trees. Prince Dinek materialized on his giant black lion, and the other stood in front of him, observing the riled ghosts in silence. Mother Penny's presence at the hotel had too many holes to fall in the coincidence realm. She was hiding something valuable, and ingenious camouflaging dabbled into her memories and woven it into a network of artificial web.

The Prince could only access two days old memories from Ranchie's memory bank. She wasn't blocking his probes or even aware he probed her. However, he got the impression mother and daughter's heads had moved off the planet and well out of his probe range. Yes, they're hiding the cross, but why were primordial magicians seeking damn buried gold? Prince Dinek tapped his lion shoulders and the beast's mane blew out like a fluffy afro. He could have ridden them on the mystical plain from Africa, but he let them travel alone and use Walden Bones' first-class airline seat.

Prince Dinek followed a hacked foot track to the Great House, and the other beast followed behind him. Frogs, toads and insects went silent for miles.

An hour later, Terry and Norris lit votive candles inside the Great House ruins, arranged in occult symbols as Walden riffled through the diary. Prince Dinek spray-painted a magic circle on the ground, stood in the center and chanted a few notes in a strange tongue facing a rising moon. He cleared his throat several times as he sang in a gruff, rhythmic tone.

Ranchie placed a five-gallon bucket of virgin human blood in the center. Blaacka came through as agreed.

"Are you ready, Walden Bones?" Prince Dinek asked.

Walden nodded as he joined Prince Dinek and mimicked his words. The diary floated between them, and the pages flipped as they recited from it.

Ranchie led Norris and Terry on drums around Walden Bones and Prince Dinek. She hadn't played the drums in years, but she was the best rattle drum player in her mother's den of water-washed saints. Walden Bones sprinkled black powder in the circle, and Prince Dinek poured blood on the powder. He stood back as thick red mist rose and the tempo of the drums grew as if unknown forces had hijacked them. Walden Bones and Prince Dinek chanted until it built to a crescendo in the fog. An ominous wind rustled the trees through the dark windows and lightning cut the partially clouded sky. The thunder cracked fearfully enough to drive dread in men's hearts and demons back to Hell.

Chapter 32

Hallie jumped from her bed, soaked in a cold sweat and whipped her head left. She scanned the room from top to bottom as if she had sensed danger. The bedroom door swung open quietly from a magical wave as she wiped her brow and dried it on her hip.

Mother Penny lay in her bed, in her street clothes, her arms folded across her breast. The glowing cross cast a crimson hue in the room. A perturbed Hallie rushed in and hopped up beside Mother Penny.

"My mother raised a demon from near Hell, and my boyfriend and a whore disrespected me in public."

"Whore is a strong word, dear and you are the only good thing associated with your mother. Are you ready?"

"Maybe we should stop them from resurrecting Tilly and destroy her ourselves in her grave," Hallie suggested.

"Sanga's magic is too evil and powerful for our magic to overcome. It requires spilling innocent blood. We cannot go there, ever," Mother Penny replied.

"Acquired magic people, used their powers in love and war. I can't even have sex. Lest I lose my abilities." Hallie added.

"You're too young for sex, and free will is sold as an expensive commodity."

Hallie stared at Mother Penny.

"After I kill her and break the magic spell she has on the gold, I'll be exploring an ordinary teenager thingy. Another thing, I'm not naming any of my daughters Penny," Hallie declared.

Mother Penny nodded.

"The first Penny back in the day was both Sanga's daughter and granddaughter."

"Nasty lot, is it too late for someone from Mars to adopt me?"

"Hallie, you are not a prisoner here."

"So, am I getting my second-floor white bedroom and bathroom?"

"Are you resorting to blackmail or yu chest damn high?" Mother Penny asked.

"Steve said they are high, and modern girls need space and personal facilities, including razor holders and stuff."

"You are saying I'm a Neanderthal?" Mother Penny pressed.

"You've got hairs on your legs."

Hallie ran from the room.

"You watched too many damn TV commercials," Mother Penny shouted after her.

Mother Penny's young son, Jeno, was a tall, striking man and his militant golden-end dreads gave him a unique rebel aura. He sat in the dark on his front porch smoking a chalice pipe. A track led to an open lot and a humongous guango tree in pitch darkness to the right.

Prince Dinek and one lion ambled under the guango tree. The lion's scent riled the dogs across the street and they barked frantically. Jeno unfurled his twenty-seven-year-old buffed body and peered under the tree. Prince Dinek hid against the tree trunk, went invisible and melted behind into the darkness.

Wes flicked on his porch lights across the street and came out onto his veranda.

"The dogs are going crazy. What a gwan, Jeno?" he shouted down.

"Do you have your piece on you?"

"Yeah," Wes affirmed.

"Come here. A man and a lion were under the tree."

Wes ran across the street and shone a powerful torch under the tree, but the dogs had settled, and the night returned to its country quietness.

"The dogs had sensed something, Jeno, but a fucking lion, Iyah?"

"Someone and something was under the tree."

"Come on, mon. You scared my dogs," Wes said.

Wes leaned against the porch and shone the light into the tree beneath it. Jeno handed him the pipe.

"Is she riding ital, Jeno?"

"Wes, you know I don't mix poison in my weed."

Wes pulled on the pipe and blew a cloud of smoke.

"You saw a rolling calf, dog," Wes said.

"Give me back mi rass pipe."

A light came on in Wes's second-floor window, and his wife called down to him.

"Weston, do not smoke Jeno's pipe and come back over here and bother my tail. I've to get up for work at four o'clock in the morning."

"Gwan, a yu bed nurse," Wes shouted.

"Please, do not go into Jeno's house, either. I want you to smoke outside and come back home."

"What's in my house?" Jeno questioned.

"Jeno, I was speaking to my husband."

Jeno and Wes grinned and bumped fists.

"She can stay deh. I'm gonna pick up a lady right now over at the Beach Club," Jeno said.

"Don't you take a rest?" Wes drilled.

"And get paid how?"
Wes gazed at him and shook his head.

Chapter 33

Steve's car pulled into lovers' lane, and Faith was in the front seat. They tore into each other, kissing and groping before the engine died.

Irene waited in the back anxiously, holding two phones in her hands. Faith undid Steve's buttons.

"Hurry, I'm on fire," Irene said.

"What Hallie did when you told her?" Steve asked.

"The innocent virgin cried as if she was in the movies," Faith said.

Faith fumbled with the recliner control for a minute, and her seat adjusted back, making popping sounds. Steve climbed over, and Irene kissed him from the back seat.

"Please pay me hard and long, Steve," Faith moaned.

Irene disengaged for air.

"Trust me. Hallie is gonna drop it by the weekend," Irene said.

Steve groped for Irene. She adjusted her lower body closer to his hand.

"Make sure my face is in the video, Irene. I wanna see my expression," Faith said.

Prince Dinek and his lion approached Steve's car from the soupy darkness. He went invisible as he passed a few feet from the vehicle. The mystery of Mother Penny's family deepened at every turn. He went invisible under the tree, but Jeno still glimpsed him.

Prince Dinek flew back on his lion to the Great House ruins and perched silently on a second-floor beam. The darkness behind him gave the impression of a vast void while the many lit candles below him glowed an ominous hue against the broken columns and walls. He gazed on Walden Bones, Norris, Ranchie, Terry, and a double of himself, worked their magic.

A sudden howling wind raged in the woods around Tilly's grave, and leaves and limbs flew off trees for five minutes. The lull came during the highest gust as if the wind-master commanded it. A strange stillness descended on the woods. It darkened as if the night had gone somewhere else and left nothing in its place.

The lion and Prince Dinek jumped to a lower beam, turned invisible and landed yards above Walden. His second lion doubling as him sensed and acknowledged his presence by glancing in his direction.

Walden chanted neck-deep in the mist. The frantic drummers beat their instruments as if possessed, but no sound came from the contact of hands and drums. Terry, Ranchie and Norris seemed lost in some magically enhanced zone, their eyes closed and laboring breaths whistling through their nostrils. However, the night around them remained silent. Prince Dinek's double poured the remaining blood into the misty apparitions around Walden and himself. They recited from the diary in old Twi, and their voices built to a crescendo. The apparitions' strands merged as one and spiraled away in a funnel cloud.

The air hummed in the thick bushes like a bass drum vibrating in a tunnel. The sound strummed low enough to rattle organs in people's solar plexuses, while trees quivered and sulfurous mist twisted away as yellow vapors. Night insects and birds fell to the ground, dead before a violent mini whirlwind flattened the trees, and blue fog rolled in and settled. Gusty wind dispersed the mist, exposing Tilly Whitelock on her knees, her forehead on the ground. Her scalp and white scarred skull were visible through thin, tangled gray hair.

Ugly stitches crisscrossed her wizened back in a cobweb patchwork. She shook her head as she rose to her feet on creaking joints, like an old bridge ready to give way. Her haggish face formed an awful, wizened scowl as the dead insects and birds awoke, shrieking and flew away. Tilly ran a hand through her hair, and the old stuff disappeared behind her hand as new, robust, milky-white hair appeared, accompanied by a black streak. She pivoted 360 degrees on one foot and a wind whooshed through the trees. She completed the pirouette, and a ravishing Tilly, age thirty, dressed in a red eighteenth-century gown, stood a yard off the ground. A mirror appeared in her hand. She inspected her face and nodded her approval as the howling night denizens quieted on cue.

The beating drums regained their robust sound. Ranchie's hands and sticks blurred on the rattle drum. It sounded as if a thousand souls pulsed to the same rhythm as one.

Tilly Whitelock floated between Walden and Prince Dinek's double, wearing a pleasant smile. Her crimson red dress gave her a royal celestial aura.

The wide-eyed drummers continued beating, possessed.

Walden's facial expression fought to show accomplishment as he backstepped, but dread and uncertainty surfaced instead. Sanga's diary dropped from Prince Dinek double's hand, wrapped in the goat's skin and slid under a fallen beam.

Tilly smiled warmly and extended a hand to Walden Bones. He shook her hand, forcing a sheepish grin.

"I presume you oversaw my resurrection, sir."

"Yes, I did."

Tilly shrieked like a banshee in Walden's face, and his flesh blew off his bones as black dust in the wind. The skeleton rocked, and the bones fell into a pile.

"It glitters, far from my gold."

It took an eternity for Norris and company to comprehend what had happened. The drums had not fallen silent, as if they were unaware, or the drummers could not control their beating arms.

Walden's death must have traveled worldwide by slow mail and back before it hit, but everyone bolted in unison a minute after, and their yells came from deep inside their dreadful souls. Ranchie fell and shuffled on her butt to escape.

Tilly flung Walden's thigh bone through Norris and killed him.

"Ranchie, come back here, wench. The rest, here are your rewards."

Tilly lashed crimson fire and burned Terry and Prince Dinek's double to dust. Ranchie hyperventilated on the ground, and she could not find her legs to stand, much less run.

"I was never a gracious paymaster."

A deep scream of terror echoed from Ranchie as she shuffled on the ground.

"Oh god, nononono."

"Wench, come here. I can smell my blood, in a tangled mix running with the dotard Sanga's through your veins," Tilly announced.

The terrified Ranchie struggled to her feet and ran. Tilly reached out a hand and floated Ranchie back to face her.

Ranchie's horrified eyes bulged, and her body shook from within, hard enough to break her apart.

"You have nothing to fear. I said my blood is in you."

Ranchie crossed her legs and locked them.

"Pee and come right back. Do not try to upset my good mood."

Ranchie hopped behind a broken wall.

Prince Dinek and his invisible lion flew away silently as if they were butterflies. Tilly jerked her head skyward, fired flames from her eyes and in her weakened state stumbled against the wall. Ranchie caught her arm and helped her to a beam to sit.

Ranchie perched on a broken wall stiffer than a column. The dark clouds revealed the moon above their heads, a spectator to an awful, painful night. The slowly dissipating magic and moonlight gave a dreadful silver ambiance to the country night. The shrubberies shifted in the wind, simulating silhouetted monsters on the prowl.

Fear had taken hold of Ranchie's bones and had her shivering, ready to break apart.

"Please breathe, Ranchie, breathe. I need you to live."

Tilly tapped Ranchie's leg and transferred a relaxing spell. Ranchie forced a smile.

"Your great-great-great-grandfather was Redebo, one of my sons. Are you ready to raise Hell and have fun with me, girl?"

Tilly slapped Ranchie on her shoulder, and she managed another weak smile.

"Who named you Ranchie?"

"I guess you figured right away why I hated my mother."

Tilly laughed. Ranchie stared at her.

"What?" Tilly exclaimed.

"You speak modern English. But how could you? Who are you? What do you do?"

"I do the opposite of angels."

"Where do you come from, Tilly?"

"They had me wrapped, tagged and ready to ship off to Hell, and I bummed a ride instead."

"Fuck, you're a fallen angel," Ranchie said.

"I jumped, Ranchie. I did not fall. So, do you ever have a man?"

"Do I ever have a man?" Ranchie repeated, searching for clarity.

"Ha-ha-ha-ha, take me to where I can find wild, strong, hard men, not scented soft pricks."

Tilly got to her feet, stumbled and grabbed the wall to steady herself.

"I need their wild, fiery primal essence to reenergize me and reach my peak. Someone wielding puny magic escaped me."

Ranchie grabbed Tilly's arm, picked up a flashlight and supported her outside into the night.

Chapter 34

The night had settled back around the graves, and the firm ground appeared undisturbed. The serenity could lull an insomniac to sleep. Songeeta's head rose above the ground, and she slowly ascended vertically to her knees. She used her hands to pull out her left foot, before she glanced behind and pulled out the other in no hurry, as if she did not care to walk the Earth a second time. Her flawless beauty remained intact as if Sanga had buried her an hour ago. Flames danced in her eyes as she gazed up the hill at the ruins.

Hallie stood under a tree, gazing at the broken Great House's walls and cast a white shadow against it from the moon. Paranormal chicaneries were not the only thing troubling Hallie; the greater portion of her pain came from something more primal. She had left her heart elsewhere, and she made an anxious telephone call.

"Hey, babes, what's up?" Steve answered.

"Where're you, Steve?"

"I'm home in bed watching tapes for my next game."

Songeeta flashed by the ruins through Hallie's shadow and disappeared as fast as she'd appeared. Hallie's head whipped in the direction Songeeta had vacated as she put away her phone. Her eyes lit as she peered into the dark like two headlamps.

Mother Penny, a gentle woman, had two children, taking the same path. Jeno was a Rent a Dread by profession (Gigolo).

He rode into his driveway on a motorbike carrying Ruth, a sixty-year-old tourist, as his pillion rider. A light ball floated low over the back wall, wobbled, lost cohesiveness, and crashed into Mother Penny's backyard. Hallie transformed to herself rolled on the grass and stumbled to a stop.

"Ouch, ouch, damn. I can bet Uncle Jeno is close by."

Hallie brushed off her clothes and hurried around the house, bumping into Jeno and Ruth in his front yard.

"Hallie, where are you coming from this late?" he asked.

"Your bike woke me, Uncle Jeno."

"Oh yeah, and I'll not smoke weed again. You take me for an idiot?"

"No, Uncle Jeno."

"What were you doing around the back? Were you messing with a boy?"

"Grandmother would kill me. You and my mother are the perfect role models, too," Hallie grumbled.

"You're far stronger than Mother. You could hide things from her," Jeno whispered.

Hallie giggled and ran through the front door.

"Is she your niece?" Ruth asked.

"Yeah, she's my older sister's daughter."

Jeno waited until Hallie closed the door behind her.

Songeeta walked through the broken equipment and the burned bodies in the ruins. She levitated the remains and sailed them away toward the burial spots in the dark. The diary floated into her hand as angry flames flickered in her eyes, her head whipped to the side and she went invisible.

Prince Dinek rode in on his last lion. Tilly had destroyed the second one impersonating him. The lion's eyes illuminated the grounds bright as daylight; the prince dismounted and searched for the diary. He levitated the trash and crashed it all back in his frustration.

Tilly was a killing machine before and after her resurrection, as he rightfully suspected.

The moment she had sensed the men's intentions concerning her gold, she destroyed them.

Evil, selfish creatures had no conscience or grasp of gratefulness. The prince wept for his beloved lion.

He only hoped acquiring the cross would compensate him.

CHAPTER 35

Ranchie and Tilly reached the vehicles parked under a tree. The wind was still and the night strangely quiet. Five male ghosts rose from under a clump of bushes behind Ranchie. Tilly pointed a stern finger, and they plunged back underground.

"These are our horses and buggies," Ranchie said.

"They are not demonic horses, but I guess they will do for now," Tilly replied.

"Okay, let's roll," Ranchie continued.

"Wait, show me the latest dance moves. My magic will mimic them," Tilly added.

"Okay."

Ranchie cranked her car stereo and danced freely like the wind. Tilly observed, leaning against the car, joined her, and they danced around the vehicle under a half-moon.

Half an hour later, Ranchie led Tilly through the trendy Addiss nightclub's front door. Wolfish iron-hard tattooed men loitered at the entrance, scrutinizing the new arrivals. Tilly and Ranchie made their way through the hunters' gauntlet.

Inebriated revelers crowded the dance floor, jamming to the song "Burn Me with Love."

Tilly stopped, inspected, surveyed, exhibiting a wild abandoned air and sauntered head high onto the dance floor.

The ranks and regulars closed in on Ranchie. Zappa, a big, strong, tough man, blocked her path.

"A who de white gal, Ranchie?"

"She's Miss Tilly Whitelock."

"Tell her fe cast a rassclaat spell on me tonight."

Zappa wheeled away to Tilly on the dance floor.

"You're welcome, Zappa," Ranchie said.

Zappa grabbed Tilly's hand, brash, overconfident and aggressive in behavior. She waltzed into his arms, wearing a sultry smile on her lips and danced dirty on him. He led her to the bar after the song.

"I'm bad boy Zappa."

"I am Tilly Whitelock. I am hotter than your worst bad."

"Two double white rum, bartender," Zappa ordered.

Zappa felt Tilly's hair and curled strains around his finger. Tilly knocked off her drink in one gulp and pulled Zappa to her.

"It has been too long for everything," Tilly said.

"Have another rum," Zappa replied.

"Yes, but you need not douse me with rum. I am wet already, boy."

"I've got a roomy ride outside waiting."

Tilly kissed him in reply, and Zappa strolled by his envious friends, escorting Tilly on his arm.

The song "Dry Night" boomed from the boxes, and the bassline and drums intoxicated the house into a dancing frenzy.

"Fuck, Zappa, dat was fast, mon," said a guy.

"Zappy a punnany terrorist, mon," another man said.

"So, wat a gwan, Ranchie? Yu ago run dry all night?"

"I'm on work to rule, but she wants to run a train. No one boy can dagger her."

They stared at her astounded.

"Weh she from, Ranchie?"

"I'm not going down fe rape, yu nuh Ranchie. I leveled my machine at rapists, yu nuh."

"Gwan, go ask her. She's from the Big-Wallman's family up north. She has a bigly appetite. Gwan, go beat white meat, boys."

"Why yu never seh she was related to Bigly Wall in de first place? Revenge."

The men hurried after Zappa and Tilly.

Ranchie waited a few minutes and searched for Zappa's SUV in the rear parking lot, and she found it under an almond tree in the back. Zappa's men waited in line before the opened door.

A security guard on a golf cart rode between the rows of vehicles toward the men's location. The man in the rear stepped out in front of the cart.

"Guardie, wi have it covered, check the front, where de nice people dem parked. Yu wouldn't want things fe happen to dem," an impatient man said.

The guard made a U-turn and rode by Ranchie between two cars.

Zappa backed out of the SUV covered in flames and collapsed at his captivated friend's feet. The first man in line hopped over his body and entered the vehicle, and the queue moved forward. One man stood ankle-deep in Zappa's burned-out shell. Tilly serviced another man, and his blackened carcass crumbled to dust.

The next spell tied man stepped forward, and Ranchie grinned from her vantage point.

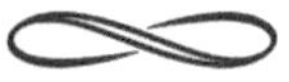

Ranchie zipped along Norman Manley Boulevard through light traffic. Tilly kicked back in the passenger's seat, wearing a full tan. Ranchie suspected her supernatural familiarity had helped her and Tilly to bond.

"I felt like sixteen and free, but I was never a sixteen-year-old," Tilly announced.

She slapped Ranchie's arm.

"I guess it's time to stop being nice."

She lit a joint from the ashtray.

"Did you cast a spell on the men?" Ranchie asked.

"Yes, I hate doing it, though. I eat fear, but I was too ravenous tonight to chase anyone."

"What do you want to do next?" Ranchie asked.

Tilly blew smoke through her window. Ranchie overtook a truck, her horns blaring.

"Tell me the major happenings of the last hundred and fifty years. I also need somewhere decent to live until I rebuild my house."

"The Moreland Hill Towers is the best hotel in Negril. It has residential suites and penthouses."

"To the Moreland Hill Towers. What do you do around here?" Tilly asked.

"I provide exotic services for high-end clients, and you damn well knew," Ranchie offered.

Tilly sucked on the joint and blew the smoke on Ranchie.

"Yeah, a dribble-down effect from you and Sanga's genes, I guess. I can't keep my legs closed for more than a few minutes," Ranchie said.

"I would put my talent to use too, dear. Whew, I feel damn good."

"It's a double whammy, pure joy and the money too is good."

They shared a hearty laugh and carried it for a long minute. Ranchie dabbed at her eyes.

"They were playing a song a while back called 'Ghetto Slam.'" Tilly Said.

"Oh, my God, you could hear things in your grave?"

"Sanga restrained me underground, but I was not deaf. Now, what is a Ghetto Slam?" Tilly asked.

"It's licentious sex, given and taken without restraints."

"Ha-ha-ha-ha, the wheel reinvented."

Tilly puffed away and coughed on the joint.

"Have you ever boiled a man in oil?" Tilly asked.

Ranchie's eyes popped, and she hit the brake for a second.

"I love boiling a man minutes after he worked me for two hours."

Ranchie stared at her, and they grinned silly. Tilly wiped tears from her eyes.

"But why?" Ranchie asked.

"What does the word *evil* mean to you, Ranchie?"

Tilly puffed and choked on the joint, coughed and smiled at the lit end.

"Ranchie, I had the first Ganja farm on my property in 38."

"Which 38?" Ranchie asked.

"Don't be funny, child. Indian indentured servants brought the seeds over from India."

Tilly filled her lungs and blew smoke rings at Ranchie.

"What do you think about the modern world?" Ranchie inquired.

Ranchie handed her tablet to Tilly.

"The internet will fill you in on what you've missed in the last hundred and fifty years."

Tilly stared at the tablet in her hand.

"Say your name to it," Ranchie said.

"Does it recognize me?"

"Show me, Tilly Whitelock," Ranchie said.

Tilly's face popped on the screen in her favorite red dress.

"Damn, my son painted this portrait, but I had to kill him a few nights later." Tilly announced.

"What for, Tilly?" Ranchie asked.

"I caught him behind a house wench in the kitchen. I do not share my men." Tilly replied.

"I wouldn't even say another fucking word," Ranchie said.

Tilly passed the butt of the joint to Ranchie.

CHAPTER 36

Hallie sat on her bed, dejected and Mother Penny hovered at the door, wearing her 'mad-as-hell' iron-hard face.

"We had planned to attack her in her weakened state," Mother Penny said.

"Another entity I couldn't read came out. I couldn't take the chance."

"Are you sure now? When the demon fed and strengthened, she will be a bitch to kill," Mother Penny warned.

Hallie wilted under Mother Penny's steady gaze. Her grandmother figured out why she had not attacked Tilly. Broken hearts fought no battles and saved no worlds.

Mother Penny wheeled away, and Hallie's shoulders sagged in despair. The news of Steve and the girl together had cut Hallie to the bones. The temptation to use her powers to spy on him was compelling and twisted. For the first time, she fought a personal battle inside her soul that could affect those she loved adversely. Hallie curled on her bed, her back to the door. Should she have unpredictable Sitira check on Steve? Hell had rejected Sitira, and she tossed the idea for she may take it as leave to do something rash. She would have to depend on her friends, Faith and Irene, to keep her informed.

She lay across the bed and folded her arms across her stomach. She suspected that sleep had lined up in the Australian Outback or farther away from her bed.

<h1 style="text-align:center">CHAPTER 37</h1>

Jeno drank a beer at Wigan's Place in the Beach View Plaza, and his keen predator's eye hunted for prey through the storefront window. Wigan's functioned as a takeout liquor store and a small bar. It had six stools around a small counter and emphasized the takeout part of its business more. Jeno, the lone patron, swiveled west and east, sipping a beer. He caught sight of Tilly as she sauntered from the more expensive boutiques, half-covered in a red miniskirt and accessories to match. Tilly adulated her reflections in the glass windows as she strutted. Jeno hurried to intercept her.

Mr. Wigan, a short, mustached man, returned through a side door as Jeno beelined for Tilly, and shook his head.

Jeno shook his dreads, imitating a lion. Tilly posed, and a relaxed, inviting vibe radiated from her body language.

"Yow, my empress, do you ride your lions in hotel rooms, or do you prefer the great wide open?"

"I am still searching for a hotel," Tilly replied.

"Where's the empress rest?" Jeno pressed.

"Does it matter where you want to take me?"

Jeno grinned and pointed to his Ninja bike.

"Let's go for a ride."

Two mangoes dropped, 'brapp', as Jeno rode Tilly through his gate. She hopped off the bike, picked up a mango and inhaled its aroma. Hallie ran from next door and met them on the lawn.

"Uncle Jeno, Uncle Jeno."

"Hey, Hallie."

"Hallie, meet my friend, Tilly."

Hallie stuck out her hand to Tilly.

"It's a pleasure," Tilly said.

"Is your surname Whitelock? Hallie asked.

"Oh, yes."

"No, you're pulling my leg," Hallie said, in denial.

Hallie grinned silly and ran back inside her house. Tilly gazed after her for a minute.

Jeno sat on his back porch, loading his pipe. Tilly stood at the rail gazing at the azure and green Caribbean Sea as she did the Spanish Galleon centuries ago. She turned away from the sea and squatted in front of Jeno. He flicked his lighter, puffed, and blew smoke clouds between her legs. He handed off the bong, and Tilly sucked until the pipe gurgled like a sinkhole swallowing a river.

Moments later, Tilly straddled Jeno on his bed and rode him home, wearing a misanthropic grin on her face. She pinned his shoulders, brought her mouth inches from his, sucked at his life force and nothing happened. She tried several times, met the same result, jumped to the floor and lashed her arms to zap Jeno, but they fired blanks.

"What're you doing?" Jeno asked.

"Don't you love my dance?" Tilly whispered.

"Come dance on this."

"I need a breather," Tilly replied.

Tilly slipped on her clothes.

"Rasta is too hot for you, eh?" Jeno let out.

She bolted from the room and slung a mean finger spell without result from the door.

"A fucking Neutralizer," Tilly whispered.

She hurried out into the yard.

Hallie watched Tilly run through the gate from the living room window.

"I guess you met Uncle Jeno, the Neutralizer, Tilly Whitelock?" Hallie muttered.

Mother Penny joined Hallie at the window.

"The hair on the back of my neck stood and tingled," Mother Penny said.

"Tilly Whitelock ran from over Uncle Jeno's a minute ago."

"He will be the death of us," Mother Penny added.

"Tilly may have eaten your son, grandmother."

"Your uncle," Mother Penny said.

"He was your son, first, and the way Tilly motored she found out."

"You meant she ran?"

Hallie rolled her eyes.

"It's too dangerous for us having him next door. I am sending him to Miami for a few days," Mother Penny said.

"Wait, it's not a game day. Steve lied to me," Hallie picked up.

Hallie ran for her phone. Mother Penny shook her head in resignation.

"I have two whores for children and a lovesick granddaughter. Healing people sure got a negative bounce to it. Take my case, Jesus, and soon," Mother Penny said.

The setting sun hung crimson over the sea, bearing witness as Jeno ate a mango under the tree. His eyes latched onto the sun as he used the garden hose to wash his hands and face. He fanned his hands dry and walked across the lawn to Mother Penny's porch. Mother Penny came out to meet him.

"Good evening, Mother Penny."

Jeno sat on the steps. Mother Penny sat beside him.

"What mi a go do wid you, Jeno?" Mother Penny asked him.

"I'm not sure you need to interfere or dabble into my things, but I recommend you stay here on Earth for as long as possible, because I'm not coming to Heaven to visit, period," Jeno replied.

"Boy, you smell like a Ganja warehouse. Have you any idea who you brought home today?"

"A Tourist lady, mother."

"No, you brought home Tilly Whitelock."

"Mother, you're tripping. Tilly is a legend, a duppy story for children."

"Your Neutralizer's ability saved you today."

"My what?"

"You are off to Miami until Hallie kills Tilly. We cannot take the chance of an attack while you are here."

Jeno stood and gawked at Mother Penny. Her eyes became dark, grave slits and he shivered.

"Did you say Hallie was gonna kill Tilly?" Jeno asked.

"What's wrong? She owes you money?"

"Mother, Hallie is a schoolgirl."

"Who possesses the power to destroy evil... I want you to move away from next door," Mother Penny ordered.

"Why mother, and where shall I go?"

"If we come under attack while you are here Jeno, it could go bad for us. Why don't you check out the Orange Bay Housing Scheme?"

"The two bedrooms cost half a million US," Jeno belted out.

"We will get you one," Mother Penny said in a beat.

"Where're you going to get the money?"

Hallie joined them, rubbing her eyes, and Mother Penny shook her head at her.

"Hallie, tell Mother that Tilly—?"

"When she lashed her arms at you and tried to zap you, did anything happen?" Hallie asked.

"How do you know? She said it was a dance."

Jeno stood and plopped adjacent to Mother Penny, his head tangled and he furrowed his brow.

"How can I help?"

"By leaving for Miami tomorrow," Mother Penny said.

"Bring back a pair of men's brown size ten and a half Clarks for school and plain brown socks," Hallie said.

"What happened to the pair you got the other day?" Jeno asked.

"They don't make them like they used to back in the day."

"You sound edgy. What days are you referring to, my girl? You're sixteen," Jeno remarked.

Hallie grinned.

"I'm gonna need you to collect a WU for me," Jeno said.

"I'm underage, and I'm not dropping like a scammer, either."

"It's not scamming money," Jeno said.

"Jeno…" Mother Penny warned.

Hallie winked at him and whispered, "Whoring money."

A taxi pulled up in front of the church, and Prince Dinek alighted.

He gazed high on the flagpoles at the black cross and smiled slyly.

"The plot gets thicker than sweet yam soup," Hallie said.

Mother Penny glanced back at Hallie.

"Here comes the prince who dug into your head," Hallie said.

"What am I missing?" Jeno asked.

"A lot," Hallie said.

"He is a guest. Wait here, Jeno, and don't move until he leaves," Mother Penny said.

CHAPTER 38

Prince Dinek sat in the pew and crossed himself. Mother Penny entered from the side door displaying her Holy Mother Superior persona.

"Good day to you, sir, how can I help you today?"

"Your reputation precedes you to Africa. I am pleased to meet you, ma'am," Prince Dinek said.

"I am honored, sir. I am Mother Penny."

Prince Dinek stood and extended an arm.

"My pleasure, madam. I am Prince Dinek from Ghana's Ashanti Kingdom."

Mother Penny shook his hand.

"You are from so far away, and yet so familiar. Have we met?" Mother Penny asked.

"We shared an old primal connection, and possibly blood, also."

"Ashanti blood courses through my veins." Mother Penny said.

"I suspect we shared common ancestors," Prince Dinek added.

"Sanga was my great-great-grandfather. How is he regarded in your kingdom?"

"With reverence, Madam. Your presence humbles me."

Prince Dinek reckoned Mother Penny had the cross in her possession. Although security measures were nonexistent on the compound, his experience told him not to take it as an invitation and pay the ultimate price for his mistake. The promise did not include time, as Tilly was behaving like a hurricane at a kite exhibition. He had to make haste and leave Negril carrying the cross by any means possible lest he tripped himself across Tilly's path.

"Mother Penny, why is the black cross inverted, ma'am?"

"I never asked my mother, but it has something to do with tradition, my son. It has no significance."

"Very curious," Prince Dinek added.

Hallie walked through the side door.

"Grandmother, you have an emergency call. Hello, sir, I seem to have forgotten my manners."

Prince Dinek got to his feet.

"Good evening, young lady. I will take my leave. I hope to meet you again, Mother Penny."

"You are welcome here anytime, my good sir."

Hallie watched Prince Dinek drive away in the taxi.

"I had no idea I owned a phone," Mother Penny uttered to Hallie.

"When are you getting one, Grandma?"

"Why do I need one, though?"

"To break the questions for answers saga, and why did the sweet prince come to Negril to die?"

"You should consider a career in comedy later," Mother Penny added.

Hallie's phone rang the Whitney Houston's "Your Love Is My Love" ringtone.

"Exactly what I was saying," Mother Penny said.

"Hello, Steve."

Miss Jerald, a woman in great distress, barged into the church, crying. Her breast heaved from some deep agonizing mental pain. She had left her home without doing her hair, and her eyes were red from crying.

A concerned Mother Penny ran to meet her, and she collapsed into Mother Penny's arms. Hallie paused her conversation and held the phone against her leg to muffle the receiver.

"Mother Penny, I need your help, ma'am."

Mother Penny sat Miss Jerald on a bench. Hallie rushed her a bottle of water, and she gulped as if a furnace burned inside her. Mother Penny tapped a comforting hand on her back as Miss Jerald caught her breath.

"They murdered my only child in broad daylight in Norwood, and none of the twenty eyewitnesses will help the police, Mother Penny."

Miss Jerald exhaled like a dragon and emptied the water bottle into her parched mouth. Hallie stood over her.

"What do you want me to do, dear? We do not hurt people," Mother Penny asked.

"I want justice. I want the witnesses to my son's murder in a line at the police station singing like nightingales."

Mother Penny glanced at Hallie.

"Tell us what happened," Hallie said.

"He stopped his taxi in the vicinity of a bar, and as the passenger exited, a man shot my son in the head. He robbed his body and used the money to buy liquor while he bled out."

"My God," Hallie said.

Hallie placed a hand over her mouth, in shock.

"Can you help me, Mother Penny?"

"Your son will get justice. I can assure you."

Miss Jerald held Mother Penny's hands and squeezed.

"Thank you, Ma'am. I thank you from the bottom of my heart."

She gathered herself and even managed a smile. She had never met Mother Penny, but she had total confidence in her ability to help her. She stood fulfilled as if her son's killer had already paid. Mother Penny accompanied Miss Jerald to the car. Hallie observed through the window.

Sitira zipped beside Hallie, and her wake blew up Hallie's dress tail around her; Hallie shivered for a second. Sitira grinned as if she got her 'resurrection from the dead' ticket and was about to execute it.

"Give mi dat job deh nuh mon. You have a witch to kill already," Sitira said.

Hallie turned.

"It's not a killing job."

"Wat? Dat boy fe dead. The grief in de lady's voice had me trembling in my grave."

"It's a job for the law, but you can add a little bonus pain."

Sitira laughed and rubbed her palms together.

"I'm dragging my coffin along."

"Are you Bob Marley's Mr. Brown?" Hallie asked.

"A weh yu tink mi get de idea from?"

"Don't tell me you're a Marley fan. What were you doing in your grave this time of day?"

"But si yah, where do I reside? I lay there speculating. Did your grandmother update you about the birds and bee's situation? Christian people hide things from their children."

Hallie grinned at her in awe.

"Do you want de talk? You don't even know what a large hand means," Sitira added.

"An internet page tells more than you learned in your thirty years on Earth," Hallie replied.

"Okay, no magic, what's spermatozoa lifespan?"

Mother Penny came back and eyed Hallie and Sitira.

"What sweet you so, dead woman?" Mother Penny asked.

"Mi gi her de haunting gig, Grandmother."

"When did you and the killer become musicians?" Mother Penny inquired.

"No, Ma'am, Hallie warned mi bout dat."

"If you kill anybody, you cannot come back here," Mother Penny instructed.

Mother Penny headed for her office.

"The next time you sneak in your boyfriend, I will expose myself to him and watch him run and break his neck and leave you dry," Sitira grumbled to Mother Penny.

"Peeping damn Duppy-Mary-Tom, if you tell Hallie my business yu si," Mother Penny grumbled back in her office.

CHAPTER 39

Hardworking, blue-collar, gritty people built their dreams one block at a time when they carved the Norwood, AKA Gulf subdivision, from limestone wilderness in the mid-eighties. The estate was situated on a hill above Montego Bay and the blue Caribbean Sea. By the late nineties, resentful eyes envied Gulf's prime real estate under the wrong feet. The original builder's offspring took different routes in life's pursuit and discarded their hardworking elder's lifestyles.

The killing had taken place at Fire Red's Spot, a small board-and-zinc-roofed building, painted red under a guango tree. It operated as an informal bar and drug spot in Gulf's grittier section. While Gulf's denizens were not an eternal incorrigible lot, they lived under the unwritten cultural mantra: *Informa fi dead.*

The criminal culture and its sheer brutality has sickened most folks to their souls. Moreover, the adverse effect it had on their children had many parents asking God if the trend could reverse. As they slept, criminal elements hijacked their lifestyle and cornered them into gutters of despair.

The nation's politicians squabbled as the people's lifeblood depreciated and drained away into abysses as if it were the clean energy the Earth needed to reverse the greenhouse spiral.

Over decades, crime-infested neighborhoods such as Gulf suffered while inept governments, churches and service clubs held many prayer breakfast spectacles. After every hearty meal, they hurried home to sit on their asses, waiting for miracles.

Sitira had a not so endearing name for people who prayed to their capturers' gods and expected favorable results.

Meanwhile, no one stood or came out from behind their burglar bars and high walls to fight the corrupt culture or step into the light from the backwardness.

Frazer's killer was a twenty-five-year-old man nicknamed Gulf Marshal and answered to either Gulf or Marshal.

A lively group of young people loitered, danced and drank at Fire Red. Sitira stood invisible in Frazer's blood-stained mark and identified five women and six men amongst the crowd who had witnessed the killing.

Although they didn't have a speck of the dead man's blood on their person, it stunk on their souls. The absent killer's scent reeked in Sitira's nostrils as she watched the people in awe, enjoying the dead man's spoils.

Where were the love and respect the rulers of her days and time had? Hardly anyone had locks on their doors in the country. People closed their doors using a string tied to a nail from the elements when they were going somewhere. Sitira used to sleep nude by an open window where anyone could climb through, day or night, and had no problem. The degradation proliferated during the devil's philosophies upheaval in the ugly seventies. Marley sang about it, and they heard, but never listened.

"Someone shook dirty water in a glass, and the dregs never settled again."

She sighed and yearned for bygone days.

"I wish I didn't die before Marley's time. He woulda love mi cute coolie backside yu si," Sitira said.

She smiled and turned up the hill, hauling her invisible coffin in the dark.

Marshal killed Frazer on a dare to impress Diana, a dancer, and his action paid a dividend for him. Sitira sneaked in on Marshal, taking Diana from behind and locked her eyes on the sweat traversing the gutter in Marshal's back in the hot room. She picked up a machete from her coffin and slapped Marshal using the side of the blade across his broad back. The blow flattened them on the bed. Marshall bellowed and scrambled to his feet and gawked in Sitira's boney ghost face.

"Hello, duppy maker, put your clothes on. We're going for a coffin ride," Sitira announced.

Diana screamed as she crawled away on her hands. Sitira slapped her on the ass, and she crashed into the wall head-first. Marshal dove for his guns, and Sitira severed the fingers on his right hand. He howled and jumped about, holding his hand. A blow across his face slammed him against the wall.

Diana crawled into a corner, hyperventilating and her legs spread.

"Gal, yu lucky mi a nuh man duppy. Put on some clothes before mi cut yu front."

Diana searched blindly on the floor for her clothes, her eyes locked on Sitira.

"You have a clap-hand model front instigating murder, my girl," Sitira said.

Sitira levitated Diana in her panties and slapped her several times across her backside and back. Diana kicked and shrieked until her cries gurgled in her throat like a horse toad.

Marshal held his hand, favoring the bloodless stubs as the coffin lid opened and banged at his feet.

"Nuh worry bwoy, you won't bleed out you're off to jail fe murderer riding inna coffin."

By the time Sitira's coffin reached Albion Road, people had gathered on both sides to observe the supernatural phenomenon. The witnesses to Frazer's murder marched in a line, and the coffin made noises on the tarmac behind them, like a car driving on four punctured tires. The twelve witnesses to the murder whimpered like hundreds of dogs in pain. Sitira had squeezed Marshal into the coffin and placed his guns in his lap. His limbs hung out over the side, and the coffin front lifted as invisible hands pulled it along.

Cell phones snapped, and flashes lit the night. They got the people, but none captured the coffin. Diana, dressed only in her G-string panties, took most of the shots. A brave woman ran and gave her a jacket to cover herself, but the coffin remained invisible above the noises it made on the road.

"They said a coffin was making the noise. Did you get the coffin?" a man asked.

The guy next to him inspected his phone.

"Hell no, I took several shots, and none had a shot of the coffin, but I got the Gulf Marshal."

"I didn't get it either… but how could Marshal's body move at such an angle, and his feet are off the ground?"

They glanced around and backed away.

Traffic crawled at the rear of the proceeding, and not one enraged motorist honked a horn. A woman dropped back, and a machete slap echoed on her backside. She pitched forward, uttered sharp guttural sounds from her nostrils and stampeded the crowd.

Chapter 40

Ranchie had slept through the day, partially to avoid Tilly, but at 6:00 p.m., Tilly barged into her bedroom and demanded they go disturb the night. She didn't give Tilly her address or let her in, but she was standing over her bed wearing an end-of-times smile.

After running through Negril, they stood on the beach drinking rum from the bottles and puffing joints. The waves broke in white foam around their ankles, and the moon hung so low over the water one could spot silver pebbles on the surface.

Ranchie gazed at the play between the sea and the moon through mellow eyes and hummed a tune.

Rhythms of the Earth are sounds one never heard, but felt. They slowly moved Ranchie's waist and hips at first, but soon warped into a seductive dance called bubbling. Her right hand shot over her head, holding the rum bottle and her free hand grabbed a handful below the belt.

"Let's go tear a dance to pieces, Tilly," Ranchie said.

"What time is it?"

"Close to midnight."

"It's a howling moon and snack time."

Ranchie executed a fist pump.

Dancehall promoters had moved out of the city and into the sticks, surrounded by farms or wildernesses, to beat the 2:00 a.m. night ordinance law. Ranchie parked in a grassy field, doubling as a parking lot.

Bare light bulbs, strung on bamboo poles, provided lighting, and Partygoers streamed uphill to the dancehall nicknamed Blue Walker Hill.

The camera operators followed the women in revealing costumes and gave scant attention to the more elegant, but modestly dressed Rastafarian women. A roots-and-culture dance would reflect on the food served, and the music played. Ranchie expected heavy Marley's clan and other revolutionary minstrels' music in constant rotation.

"Tilly, they'll be playing music for the soul."

"Yes, I love my souls vibrant and running scared at dinner time."

Tilly took in the wild men's aromas and nodded at Ranchie, excited as a schoolgirl at her sweet-sixteen birthday party.

"Ranchie, my property used to extend beyond here."

"How many acres did you own?" Ranchie asked.

"My property stretched to Little London and Orange Bay in the north."

"I bet you stole lots of property."

"Ranchie, you are a funny girl. I had bought property hours before Sanga ambushed me."

"I guess the government repossessed your holdings a long time ago."

"I want it back, Ranchie, and I've figured out how to get it."

"How're you going to do it?"

"Run for office."

Ranchie stopped in her tracks.

"Do jumping angels qualify under the Constitution?"

"What is a Constitution?"

They busted out laughing.

Ranchie paid and led Tilly through the loud-mouthed human bottleneck at the entrance. An awe-struck Tilly observed the hot, skimpy-dressed women until her gaze became uncomfortable for some people. She shifted her eyes to the vertical bamboo cast into concrete for the walls and how they used the split bamboo for roofing over the bar, kitchen and an elevated DJ stage. The builders left the grassy dance floor opened to the elements, and the porta toilets placed against the back wall. A pungent mouth-watering aroma came from Jankrow Batty rum, curried goat, scotch bonnet peppers, steaming jerk chicken, roasted fish and Ganja.

Tilly danced across the floor, and after two songs, her alluring moves and aura captured everyone's attention. To impress the world's most curvaceous dancers in a Jamaican dancehall was not an easy task, but Tilly's dancing wheels, beauty, curves in the right places and chrome bumper to match any ebony ones pulled it off. Dancehall queens and princesses joined Tilly, barely covered in revealing outfits and surrounded by rowdy men. Traditionally Rastas jumped on one side, smoking large joints and drinking expensive liquor.

The high-testosterone males danced in packs. Tilly pirouetted into their midst and sandwiched herself between two men.

One man danced on her butt, while the other man danced in a bump and grind motion before her. A forward man dug his hand into Tilly's bosom, and she played him and his gang. Hard men, carnal intentions, men gathered around Tilly and her partners, ready to pounce. A third man tried to get between Tilly and the man dancing on her rear.

The two men got in each other's faces. Tilly stepped in the middle of them, placed her arms on their shoulders, and whispered in their ears. They led her out a rear exit, and another four men followed. Delroy turned back at the door.

"What's up, Delroy?" Que asked.

"My mom told me to avoid easy women."

"Maybe you and your mother should change the subject to the weather."

Delroy fanned Que off and headed back to the dance floor.

Ranchie danced in a zone at the edge of the floor like a lost star dancing its way home, and her arms opened wide like wings opened wide. She absorbed the primal drums and bass and regurgitated them in stunning movements. Ranchie had long taken freedom and her relinquished spirit as her mantra. She had always chosen what she wanted, chewed on it and spat out the trash. However, her flying lanes narrowed in Tilly's town. *Run the country?*

Ranchie's mind could not conjure Tilly running the country. What would happen to the seabirds, such as herself, whose cage extended from the water's surface to outer space and beyond? Would she dig up Negril's beaches and turn them into sand quarries or back to crab swamps? *I hate stinking crabs.*

It was time to cut Tilly, and she would after a visit to the bank the next day. Gustav had said he had a welcoming Manor far away, and she would see the inside of those walls much sooner than later.

CHAPTER 41

Tilly led the men down a grassy slope into a flat, wooded basin, giggling like a child. The five enthusiastic men jostled for position and kept their eyes on her butt.

"This is far enough," a man said.

Tilly ducked into a bush.

"Whosoever catches me can have their way with me, two at a time."

Que rubbed his hands together in anticipation and ran after her. Tilly jumped from behind a tree, grabbed Que, and ducked back into the dark.

"Jesus Christ, ugh—" Que cried.

Flames flared. Que's yell cut off in his throat, and the men bolted in fear.

"Ha-ha-ha-ha. You can run, but can you hide?" Tilly asked.

Tilly chased the second man, dived on him and dragged him away by a leg. The man's yell stuck in his throat as a short, sharp flame illuminated his terrified face. Another man collided into a banana tree trunk at full gallop and bounced back into Tilly's arms.

"I believe your affections are waning for me. You could hurt yourself running in the dark."

The fourth man charged through the underbrush and climbed up a tall tree. He perched on a limb, searching for movement below. Tilly silently appeared on a branch above him and hung her leg inches from his head. The man twisted his body, and his free hand grabbed for a better hold. He missed Tilly's leg by an inch. He hung his head and searched the darkness below while sliding his hand along the branch.

Tilly transformed her leg into a cloven hoof beast's leg, covered in long coarse white hairs. The foot followed the man's searching hand until he grabbed hold. She jerked her leg, and he stared back into the ugly face of a seven-foot beast from Hell.

"Laaaad gad noooooo."

The beast jumped on his back and rode him into a thicket in a flaming sphere.

Jamaica had folklores piling on each other, searching for space to breathe. A major one in the country said, 'If you ran into a croton patch where the trees grew tall as bamboo, you might be in an old burial slaves' people burial ground.' If you found yourself in such a place, run, for they are merciless; but who checked bush species when chased by a demon? The last man barreled through the bushes and jumped an old stone wall. He crept on his stomach and hid behind two old gravestones in a tall croton thicket. The tree-like croton bushes' leaves had lost their array of colors and were solid green. The music sounded close and comforting to the man. He felt the vibrations from the bass and drums in his solar plexus. Foundation's "Fire Burning," one of his favorite tunes, thumped from the boxes. Only true reggae purists played Foundation's music. The closeness of the music gave him some respite, and for a whole minute, his fear dissipated. His head told him that supernatural danger from Hell dare not invade the space of good music and happy people. Another beat echoed from somewhere nearby as he listened, he realized it was his heart thumping.

Tilly's presence evoked ghosts and other night pestilences in her vicinity like gas on a burning fire. Gatta, a bony-faced slave-era ghost, crawled from her grave behind the man, grinned and pulled him by his ankles. The yelling man grabbed shrubberies as Gatta dragged him and the roots into her grave. Her head popped back above ground, smiling ghastly seconds later and another ghost emerged from her tomb, hideously stupefied.

"Who stuck a pig, Gatta?"

"He is no pig. Mi calter, a lively young fellow."

Gatta sniffed, and fear inundated her face.

"Puppa Jeezas, mi smell de mistress."

"Weh she did deh fi three' undred years."

"Yu tink she cum fe relieve wi?"

"She nuh 'member seh she lef wi a guard her Spanish jars."

They submerged back into the ground in fear of Tilly. Deep underground, the man had fallen flat on his back on old Spanish jars and shattered them. Gold and silver coins glowed in the ethereal light. Gatta floated, landed on the man and he opened his mouth wide as a whale. If he screamed, it could only reach dogs' ears.

Back in the dance, Ranchie danced dirty on a girl named Peggy. A pissed-off Rastaman approached them, shook his locks and cut his mean disapproving eyes.

"Fire fe de wicked."

Ranchie disengaged, kissed the man, and pushed him away.

"Bruk Pocket, motherfucker. You can't afford a good front," Ranchie said.

She danced away, guzzling champagne.

An awkward Songeeta staggered across the dance floor, as out of place as a green lawn on the moon. The night hunters smelled easy food, and two men descended on her. One man shoved a bottle in her hand as the other blew smoke and forced a joint in her mouth. Songeeta puffed on the joint and giggled aloud. One man whispered in her ear, and he led her by the hand to an exit.

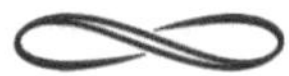

Tilly rejoined Ranchie on the dance floor, glowing in her cheeks like a midnight sun on a distant planet.

"Damn, Tilly, I'm tired," Ranchie said.

"The night is but young, child," Tilly replied.

Ranchie rolled her eyes.

"I can zap energy into you," Tilly offered.

"No zapping for me. I worked a client into intensive care a couple of months back. By the time they placed a drip in his arms, my business had graced Social Media."

"Okay, your loss. I think I will fly over to the beach and grab whatever the sea washed ashore."

"Do you have wings, Tilly?"

"Do birds fly without wings?"

"Okay, catch you in the morning."

The two men groped a docile Songeeta against a tree in the dark. Roy kissed her and her eyes gleamed fire. He tried to break, and flames blasted from between their mouths.

"Bloodclaat, a duppy gal," the other man cried.

He bolted into the dark. Songeeta reached out a hand, and the man ran in place, squealing like a weird pig.

Songeeta sucked Roy's life force until his black carcass crumbled. She hauled in the second man to face her, and a prolonged kiss withered his body into a dried prune. Her actions left a sour after-the-fact expression on her face. She slung an apologetic eye at the burned remains and ran.

Chapter 42

The alarm clock rang three times and stopped at 5:00 a.m. on Moo Wang's night table. He sat up in bed, yawned and stretched his sinewy sixty-year-old muscles. He sprang to the floor from a sitting position, and steel-like potencies held firm. He walked lazily over to his penthouse bedroom's blinds in the Moreland Hill Towers and gazed below at the dark water.

Moo Wang's skin color shone like the Island sun on oriental brown. He picked up the sand grit in his skin tone from outside Negril's white sands. Moo Wang's generation had worked on Tilly's farm as indentured servants a hundred and seventy years ago. Nevertheless, after the dust blew away, established banks took a sweet liking to specific colors and the rest they said became history.

Tilly strolled the early morning beach, searching for the Moreland Hill Towers Ranchie showed her from the street side earlier. The towers stood gray against the dawn light, two hundred yards from her like two giant columns waiting for bridge pylons to set across them.

Negril lay on Jamaica's western end, famous for beaches and sunsets, not for the sunrises. Blue and emerald dominated the water during sunlight, but it wore a dark, rejuvenated hue from the beating it took during the days early in the morning. Tilly walked by a tired couple entwined in knee-deep water.

Moo Wang power walked on the beach, as he had done every morning for the past decade. He had run into half-drunk tourists on the sands of all-inclusive hotels, as well as whores and hustlers, but never a woman of Tilly Whitelock's caliber. Tilly's unusual gorgeousness gripped him and induced him onto a collision course from ten paces away. He ran his eyes from her bare feet to her face and smiled.

"Good morning," Moo Wang said.

Tilly had not met a victim she did not gyrate to, and her parted lips said bunches to Moo Wang in silent language.

"Hi, I am Tilly. One of the last lonely people left in the world."

"Who said you're alone, though?" Moo Wang asked.

"People enjoy jumping to conclusions."

They conversed for ten minutes, held hands and Moo Wang led her back the way he came. He tried to step into his old footprints missed by the waves, and Tilly giggled in step. After the brief meeting and small talk, they figured out each other's wants and wasted no further time. One couldn't tell it wasn't two old lovers strolling hand in hand on the beach.

"Imagine meeting you on your second night back in Negril," Moo said.

"Destiny sometimes wrote events in invisible ink years ago, Moo Wang."

Ten yards behind Moo Wang and Tilly, an invisible person made footprints in the sand. The hair on Tilly's neck stood on end. She whipped her head back as waves reclaimed her and Moo Wang's impressions. Moo Wang stopped in the Tower's shadow.

Thirty-five yards away, phase two towers were under construction, and work crews labored twenty-four hours a day, banging and drilling. Tilly bumped into Moo Wang, recovered and caressed the hairs on his neck. Moo Wang pointed high.

"I'm in the penthouse."

"Your bed is probably much softer than this cold, hard sand."

"Now I wish I had wings."

"Do you want to fly?"

Moo Wang placed his arm around her shoulders.

"Maybe next time, the elevator will do this morning."

"You are missing a great ride."

Moo Wang smiled at her and led her through a gate. Tilly flashed another puzzled eye over her shoulder and disappeared inside the building.

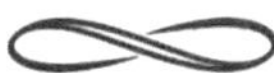

Moo Wang lay on his back, closed his eyes and his body was sweaty from lovemaking. He interlocked his fingers across his chest, and Tilly ran her finger through his hairy chest.

"I believe I may have excelled beyond sex. I've never experienced this kind of ecstasy," Moo Wang said.

Tilly released her claws on Moo Wang's stomach, retrieved them and caressed his chest.

"I tossed in a cup of hellish magic," Tilly said.

"It could become addictive," Moo Wang said.

"Yeah, maybe I overdid it."

Tilly got on her knees and elbows. Moo Wang scrambled to get behind her.

Songeeta rushed along the beach, her eyes on the Moreland Hill Towers. Sand clung to her ankles and bare feet, but she left no footprints. She stopped under the Moreland Hill Towers, tilted her head and exhibited a profound sadness on her face as she gazed at the upper floors. She whirled away and swam out to sea, and her powerful strokes propelled her through the water like a fish.

Hallie tossed and turned from one end of her bed to the other. A force lifted her upright and transported her to the floor to a light landing on her feet. Her body transmuted into pure white light. The surprised expression on her face said it was not her doing, as she shot out the window into the early morning light.

Tilly leaned on the rails of Moo Wang's penthouse balcony in the nude, and the waves danced in the dawn light below her. A crimson glow on the horizon signaled the imminent shift change. She inhaled lungs full of morning air and savored a breeze as it blew her hair. Moo Wang strolled out and stood beside her.

"I love your place, Moo Wang, and that will not work out for you."

"What do you mean?"

"Do you still want to try your hand at flying?"

"I've soared and landed, babes. Didn't you feel me?"

"I meant to fly this way, Moo Wang."

Tilly grabbed his lapels and tossed him out to sea.

"Nooooo."

"I have chosen your penthouse as my party place, and you are not welcome here anymore."

Tilly ambled back inside the bedroom.

Moo Wang fell from the sky, bellowing loud enough to wake the dead half a mile out at sea. Songeeta stood on the waves, generating a broad water sprout. It met Moo Wang and washed him to shore uninjured.

"Help, help," Moo shouted.

Hallie ran into knee-deep water and helped Moo Wang onto the beach. He gasped on his knees in the sand.

"What happened? Who was she?"

"Who are you talking about?"

"The woman, Tilly… she's a demon."

"Where is she, and where do you live, sir?"

"She's in my penthouse, and I'm not going back there."

"So, where do you want to go?" Hallie asked.

"Somewhere far from here. Wait, how come you're not scared?" Moo asked.

"Scared of what, babbling? Come with me. My grandma, Mother Penny, may have something to say to you about your bad dream," Hallie assured him.

"Mother Penny is your grandmother?" Moo asked.

"Are you waiting here for this Tilly monster, or are you coming?"

"Are you still in school?"

Hallie wagged a stern finger.

"Do not venture on hallowed ground."

The sunlight hit the buildings, and long shadows raced across the beach.

Hallie led Moo Wang to the taxi stand on Norman Manley Boulevard. Who had the hell compel her to fly from her bed to the beach? Evil pulsated through the man's body, yet she had to save him. Even her formidable powers cannot unlock all the secrets of the mystical world or her gifts.

"Something transformed me and had me flying as if I were a damn toy. Oh well, the truth will slam me soon enough," Hallie grumbled under her breath.

She gazed back at Moo Wang as they hurried along.

"Damn, Tilly made the day Satan told Southern Evangelists to support Trump look like a glorious day," Hallie mumbled.

Chapter 43

Mother Penny sat on the edge of her bed, brushing her hair. Hallie pocketed her phone, climbed up, knelt behind her and took the brush from her. Hallie's face played anxiety, guilt and a broken-hearted thing sucking her emotions. Mother Penny's somber mood didn't assist the morning sun rays fighting the blinds either. Hallie held a salt-and-pepper lock by the end to break the ice, and the salt disappeared.

"Don't you dare."

"Grandmother, the gray had an ancient touch to it."

"Do you want your grandmother to become a laughing-stock in the Obeah fraternity?"

Hallie forced a smile as the hair reverted to normal.

"Tilly is raising hell," Mother Penny said.

The guilt on Hallie's face overpowered the other senti-ments.

"When is Uncle Jeno leaving?" Hallie asked.

"Later today, you will be free tonight," Mother Penny replied.

"I'm meeting my friends at the mall when school is out, and I'm wearing my school uniform to the thing."

"You were not in school. What are you going to tell them?"

"Nothing. I want my friends to pree me as a bad gal."

Mother Penny turned her head, and her eyes slew Hallie.

"Are you building a rep? And what monster accompa-nied Tilly Whitelock out of the hole?"

"I'm sensing a lost spirit. Moo Wang is untrustworthy, period, Hallie said.

"How he did not kill his mother for a late breast as a baby remains a miracle."

"Time will not give him refuge," Hallie said.

"We'll see."

Mother Penny's steady gaze peeled back an energy field around the bedroom door.

Moo Wang tiptoed away from the door, opened it and slammed his room door. He tramped back and knocked on Mother Penny's bedroom door. Mother Penny glanced back at Hallie.

"What time are you going to the mall?"

"After the thing," Hallie said.

"The thing, as you call it, is on you."

Hallie glanced away from Mother Penny's intense stare.

Moo Wang stood by Mother Penny's fence, juggling a ripe mango in his hand on a gorgeous, cloudless morning. Birds' and children's calls reverberated and added to the beauty of life. A curious young mother, Cherry, approached Moo Wang, lugging her baby at her side.

"Mr. Moo Wang, what are you doing in Moreland Hill, sir?"

"Why, Cherry?"

"Mother Penny is a healer. Are you sick, sir?" she pressed.

Moo Wang met Cherry in the street.

"I'm going to make a documentary on Mother Penny, and I'm writing the script, but I want you to keep it low, Cherry."

"Nice of you, sir."

"What's Hallie's story?"

"She's Mother Penny's granddaughter. Her mother's Ranchie."

"Do you mean Negril Ranchie?" Woo asked.

"Yeah, said one, sir. Ranchie the rich man's mattress."

"What about Hallie's power?"

"Mother Penny, a de woman, Hallie has no powers."

"Thanks, Cherry."

He glanced back at Mother Penny's house and wrinkled his brow.

Moo Wang traversed the street, questioned an older woman at her gate and made notes in his book. He took notes from the ever-alert Brushie Brissett on his front lawn. Mother Penny and Hallie soon waved at Moo Wang from a departing taxi.

He hurried back to the church and found Prince Dinek at the gate holding a steady eye on the flags waving in the breeze.

Moo Wang stopped beside Prince Dinek. He figured him as Mother Penny's husband.

"Good morning, sir," Moo Wang said.

"Good morning."

Prince Dinek's accent surprised Moo Wang.

"West Africa, I presume?"

"I am Prince Dinek from Ghana."

"You missed Mother Penny by a few minutes," Moo Wang said.

"I came to sit in the church last night and had a great night's sleep for the first time in years," Prince said.

Moo Wang glanced at the open church door and back at Prince Dinek *and wanted to say it aloud: Strangers could not enter and sit in Mother Penny's absence.* Prince Dinek read him.

"She assured me it was okay to visit any time last evening," Prince Dinek said.

Moo Wang did not show his surprise. Each man stood gazing at the church, focused on their agenda.

"I will sit and meditate," Prince Dinek said.

"I'm a guest, not a family member," Moo Wang said.

Moo Wang headed for Mother Penny's office, closed the door, searched her desk drawers, knelt, peeked under the bed, peered at the vials, cut a skeptical eye, opened a peculiar blue twisted bottle, sniffed and recoiled.

"Damn."

He went under and behind everything.

Songeeta stumbled through the church door, disoriented, like someone nursing a bad hangover.

She sat on the opposite aisle from Prince Dinek, and they did not acknowledge each other's presence.

Songeeta gazed through the wall ahead as Prince Dinek's eyes were dead set on the curtained door.

Moo Wang tiptoed from Mother Penny's office, headed in the other direction and out the front door.

A minibus dropped six people in front of the church. They waved at Moo Wang as they marched into the church and sat in front of Prince Dinek. The eldest woman glanced back at the prince and across at Songeeta and raised a hymn in a sweet husky voice. Her companions beat tambourines, their faces aglow and joyful tears rolled down their cheeks.

Prince Dinek walked out perturbed. Songeeta remained seated, her eyes locked on a spot above the pulpit.

Chapter 44

Greg and Lonesome were two large junior college football players from the American Midwest. Lonesome's folks were wealthy farmers for over two hundred years. The elder Lonesome was a generous man who had lavished on his only son.

Lonesome moved from one major college to another and got the same news from each football program. Talents were the only currency needed on their football field. He and his best friend, Greg, marched back to junior college and played ball well into their mid-twenties.

The boys had not left their custom pickup trucks or the rural Midwest before landing in Negril two days prior. They had found the all-inclusive five-star hotel accommodation, as advertised, but had run into social roadblocks.

Both Lonesome and Greg were clumsy around the sophisticated women in the resort. Lonesome's entitlement attitude did not help their cause either.

A night ago, Lonesome had approached two Ivy League coeds at the Tiki Bar, and before he said a word, the girls hurried away, leaving their drinks.

"I could buy you and this hotel," Lonesome shouted.

"Don't forget to spend something on palm Vaseline," a coed retorted.

"What will you have?" the bartender asked.

"Rum, strong rum," Lonesome said.

Greg joined him, glaring his displeasure at the girls. "Bitches."

"You should have walked the seven-mile beach," the bartender said.

"Man, what is it with these stuffed-bosomed girls?" Lonesome asked.

"The redhead who cold-shouldered you earlier today…"

Lonesome and Greg nodded. Remembering the day's terrible memories of the gorgeous redhead and the dirty eye that murdered his intentions fresh like an open wound.

"She's a Ph.D. chick, and she hired the local guy who won the coconut tree climbing contest as a carpenter," the bartender continued.

"What's she doing with a carpenter?" Lonesome asked.

"He nails her, hammers her and drills her."

"We got you," Greg said.

The bartender served drinks to two other patrons and returned.

"Braggadocious eat sand around here. People come to Negril to get what they never had."

"What do you mean?" Greg asked.

"We don't carry hamburgers or hot dogs on the menu. That should've told you something. Take a walk, check out the strip."

"We'll miss meals and shit," Greg said.

"Your problems ride in your heads and guts, dudes."

"I don't get you," Greg said.

"You should've found two locals, bent them over under a sea grape tree, and got your whistles wet already," the bartender told them.

The bartender addressed other customers' needs. Greg and Lonesome sank tall glasses of colorful liquid.

"Tomorrow, we'll check it out. If the beach turns up cool, we change hotels," Greg said.

The two last rum punches had hit the boys like heavy sledgehammers.

Lonesome nodded his head and staggered off his stool. He barely made it to his room, asked himself a couple of questions and passed out. How could someone so wealthy end up so lonely in a crowd? Why're the girls treating him like how honest and wise world leaders treated the president in a conference room?

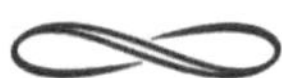

Lonesome and Greg crawled from the hotel and hit the hot and humid streets around noon.

Meanwhile, Tilly led traffic in a slow line behind Moo Wang's azure Bentley convertible wheel and maxed the stereo. She wore a mischievous grin plastered on her lips and swore to drive the thing without utilizing her powers. *I love this impressive car-carriage thing the British made. It must have gotten sunny on their Isle. They could not accomplish such an engineering feat and manufacture a magnificent machine in fog and gloom.*

She rocked to the music, driving at fifteen miles per hour, holding the wheel awkwardly. An irritated motorcyclist pulled alongside the car, shouting and cursing until his words came out distorted. Tilly's pointed finger zapped him, and he skidded in front of a bus going in the opposite direction. Tilly cringed at the sound of metal tearing into metal.

Greg and Lonesome waited for the light, and Tilly had stopped a few yards from them. Lonesome turned and locked Tilly's eyes. She gawked at the boy.

"Damn, boy, you so resemble the giant, loud-mouthed Texas farmer I met in Louisiana in 1846. What was his name? Dev or Zeb something, oh yes, Zeb Lonesome," She said to herself.

Tilly savored a memory. She grinned, remembering the horror on Zeb's face when he walked around a bush and caught her devouring two of his slaves.

"When did he stop running to settle and have off-spring?"

Skipper Drake's actions had taken him above a mere criminal. Although not defined by law, he lived in the terrorist's stratum. The clean-shaven, fresh-faced young man terrorized Westmoreland worse than a hated nightmare.

Only a few people could identify him, and those who did were too scared to do anything about it. He had several murders, rapes and robberies under his belt, and he operated freely like any average person, fearlessly.

Skipper Drake pulled alongside Tilly on a crimson Harley dressed in a starched white shirt and expensive jeans. Satan spoke directly to the boy's heart whenever he wanted to relay his daily message to avoid his twenty-four-year-old angelic face.

He gawked at Tilly's exposed legs and felt a stir. She instantly disliked his angel-type mug, pointed a finger and zapped him twice. Skipper Drake grinned at her for her effort, winked and ran the light.

"Another Neutralizer from Sanga's bloodline. I'm gonna kill you one by one in the most terrible way," Tilly said.

A young woman strutted by Greg and Lonesome in a sheer, white strappy dress. The grinning boys whistled at the woman; she flashed a contemptuous finger, turned and spat. Tilly zapped Miss Contemptuous, and her dress fell around her ankles. A heel broke, and she spread-eagled on the sidewalk.

Greg and Lonesome bumped fists and leaned their heads for a better view.

"Spit now, baby, spit," Greg said.

"Come hit something on me instead of hitting each other, boys," Tilly called.

The boys gawked at each other.

"Are you coming, or what?"

The boys squeezed in the front beside Tilly, Greg at the door.

Tilly guzzled from a rum bottle, her hands off the wheel as the car rode the sidewalk and dropped back onto the road as she passed the bottle. Lonesome took a huge swig and gave the bottle to Greg.

Tilly's dress rode high. She placed Lonesome's hand on her naked thigh.

"I am Tilly. Grab my leg."

Lonesome pinched himself. He could not believe a woman of Tilly's class had spoken to him and tried to seduce him. Fuck, his luck had changed. He never made a note to book another all-inclusive cage anywhere in the world.

The car weaved dangerously through traffic, and he braced on the dashboard.

A police cruiser wailed behind Tilly's car. Greg and Lonesome gawped at the police.

"The cops are trying to bust our threesome before we've left the ground," Tilly said as she reached for the bottle. "Should we let them interfere?"

"Hell no," Lonesome said.

The car leaped forward as the accelerator hit the floor. Greg and Lonesome raised their hands.

"Yippee, yee-haw."

"Floor it, baby, eat fumes, Five-O," Greg yelled.

Chapter 45

Moo Wang had finished his patties and a cold beer at the Sandy Beach Cafe. Police sirens wailed up the road, and all eyes turned as his Bentley flew past, followed by two police cruisers.

"Fuck."

He raced on the sidewalk, following his car until it disappeared around the bend, and he turned his eyes back to the Moreland Hill Towers a mile away in the opposite direction. He had planned to stalk Hallie at the mall, but he could grab his essential things from his penthouse first, and he rushed away.

Tilly wove through traffic and clipped a red compact car into an oncoming pickup truck. The fun dripped from Greg's face leaving a disapproval mask. His eyes roved the mayhem as Tilly eyed him from her peripheral vision.

"If you guys were packing, we could make this worth their while," Tilly said.

"Yeah, baby," Lonesome said.

Lonesome pointed his fingers at the lead cruiser and mocked fire like he had a gun.

"Bam, bam, bam."

He blew imaginary smoke from his finger. The lead cruiser opened fire and shattered Tilly's windscreen.

"Hell no, they did not shoot at me," Tilly said.

"Motherfucking cops are the same worldwide," Lonesome said.

He flung the rum bottle at the police officers, and bullets buzzed them. Greg and Lonesome ducked as Tilly slapped her pocketbook.

"Hey, do something."

"With what?" Lonesome asked.

"Check my bag. I want to party, not this shit."

Lonesome fished two revolvers from Tilly's pocketbook, smiled at the guns gleefully, and dropped one into Greg's lap. Greg gawked dubiously at the weapon.

"It's not cool anymore, dude."

"Drop the yapping, dude. I wanna do..." Lonesome fired at the lead cruiser and shattered its windscreen.

"Wanna do what, man? We don't know these people," Greg said.

"A cop is a cop. If you're chicken, give it back," Lonesome said.

Greg handed back the gun. His door flew open, as unseen forces ejected him on the pavement, and the lead cruiser ran over him on purpose.

"Ouch, I should not speak poorly of the departed, but Greg seemed like he had lacked team spirit," Tilly said.

"It appeared he did, huh?"

Lonesome dug for his maniacal grin, firing both guns at the lead cruiser as he did; he ducked from the returned fire. A dauntless Tilly kept driving.

"Watch those bullets," Lonesome said.

"Brace yourself."

Tilly turned into a side street and smashed through a road-closed barrier at high speed.

"Drive, baby, drive."

Lonesome shot out another cruiser's windscreen.

Moo Wang had changed his clothes like a thief in his penthouse. His trembling fingers fumbled as he retrieved cash, documents and a gun from his bedroom safe. His eyes darted as he snatched a beer from the refrigerator and wet his mouth, parched as a dry leaf. He flew through the front entrance, ran toward the elevators, changed direction and charged through the fire escape door. Ten minutes had elapsed since he'd seen the police chasing his Bentley.

The local elementary school had decorated banners and flags that lined both sides of the street. Tilly's car sped by and rattled the shouting spectators standing on the sidewalk.

Along the street, a children's marching band dressed in colorful costumes danced curb to curb.

Families and spectators cheered from the sidewalks. Hallie and Mother Penny enjoyed the spectacle under a Poinciana tree, their faces stiff as the tree trunk.

The fallen flowers randomly decorated Hallie's hair and Mother Penny's wrap in nature's flair. Hallie jumped, trying to catch the flowers as they dropped.

Tilly sped down the narrow street, and the children marched on a collision course. Lonesome fired, hit a driver, and the cruiser hydroplaned through a fence.

"Fly, baby, fly," Tilly hissed as she turned and kissed Lonesome, long, and hard. The car swerved from side to side, rode the sidewalk, and dropped back onto the street under a hail of bullets.

"Wild boy, we are going to the top. Do you know I'm somewhat of a witchy?"

"Get outta here, Tilly."

"Ha-ha-ha, how many bullets hit us?"

The car screamed around the bend in the road, swerving side to side.

People shouted, screamed, yelled and bolted.

The children, marching in formation, panicked into a petrified, screaming horde as they scattered before the approaching car and imminent death.

Hallie swung a hand and froze the children in the street, but their screams continued. Ten yards from impact Hallie punched a fist left behind Mother Penny, her eyes shining like searchlights on her grandmother's back. Tilly's car careered left through a fence and crashed into the ground floor of a house.

Screaming mothers raced for their children as the patrol cars skidded to a halt and armed officers advanced on the house.

Mother Penny gazed at Hallie sternly.

"Do you want another example why people eat cakes and beat iron while they are hot? Tilly should've died before she regained her strength mowed down those kids" Mother Penny said.

"I guess your analogy doesn't go for hot boys, and stop exaggerating grandmother," Hallie said.

Mother Penny smiled from the corner of her mouth.

"What you call the thing is twenty-five bloody dead children on the street. What do you and your friends usually do at the mall?"

"Pree, gossip and pose."

"Oh, I can relate. There is no better way to pass exams, too."

"Grandmother, you missed your call. Your fifth or sixth HBO special slipped away from you. We should get cable, too," Hallie said.

"No one is getting tied up into any cables until after Tilly dies tonight."

Hallie rolled her eyes.

"If the people of Moreland Hill want us to have cable, they will install it, don't you think?" Mother Penny asked. "I had to leave my sewing machine to come out here and save these children, and it's not a thing, as you called it. It's your damn fault," Mother Penny said.

Hallie bowed her head from her grandmother's icy gaze.

Chapter 46

The police officers found Tilly's empty car buried under broken concrete and wood. Sergeant Smith led the cautious officers, their weapons drawn through the unoccupied ground floor rooms. Sergeant Smith pointed up the stairs, and they rushed to the closed primary bedroom door.

"Come out with your hands above your heads," Sergeant Smith shouted.

Nothing stirred behind the locked door.

"Kick in the door," Sergeant Smith commanded.

An officer kicked the door from its hinges. Tilly and Lonesome sat on the bed, and fifteen guns covered them.

"Put your hands in the air."

"Your new friend has crashed the ride, dude," Tilly said.

Tilly leaped at the nearest man.

"Get down on the floor."

Two officers tackled her. She swatted them away and transformed into a snarling old witch.

They opened fire, and bullets knocked dry dust from Tilly's body. As the men backed against the wall in fear, she transformed into a crying bloody six-year-old girl.

"Mommieee, where's my mommy? Mommieee, big wicked-ass men are shooting me."

The shocked officers backed away. Tilly took the stairs two at a time.

"She's a witch."

"A rassclaat Annie Palmer," An officer said.

"Annie lived in Rose Hall, idiot. A Tilly fucking White-lock dat," another announced.

"How many white witches did we have?"

"Each rassclaat great house had at least one."

Lonesome tried tiptoeing by the distracted officers and Sergeant Smith slammed a gun butt into his head at the door.

"Quiet down. I need to think," Sergeant Smith shouted.

"What now, Sarge? Bullets can't hurt her."

"Clark practices Obeah, sah."

They turned to Clark.

"Buying Obeah for protection and promotion is not practicing Obeah," Clark said.

"You've been a constable for over twenty-five years, Clark."

"Did you get the message, sir? I'm not good at it."

Tilly, as the bloody child, ran outside screaming. A crowd waited across the street.

"The police shot my mummy and my two sisters. They killed them."

Tilly stomped her feet and tore at her hair.

"Mommieee. I want my mummy and my sisters," she wailed.

The crowd gawked at the house. Old confrontational resentments against the police resurfaced.

"Bomboclaat Babylon dem shoot, and dem shoot and shoot," a woman said.

She lifted Tilly in the little girl form and consoled her against her bosom. Tilly pointed her index finger and zapped the crowd over the woman's shoulder. The possessed men and women broke fence posts and picked up rocks. Some snapped tree limbs as they converged on the house.

The police raced from the house into the angry mob.

"Stop where you are," an officer shouted.

Sergeant Smith took in the situation.

"Withdraw, run," Smith bellowed.

A trigger-finger officer fired in the air. The frenzied mob screamed in fiendish voices never heard coming from humans and attacked. Tilly jumped from the woman's arms.

Lonesome stumbled behind a tree, punched, bloody and cuffed. His cuffs dropped and clanged against something metallic on the ground.

"Are you waiting for another pair of handcuffs?" an adult Tilly asked.

Lonesome rubbed his wrists as he followed Tilly away from the maddened mob.

The mob chased the officers over and through fences, past pool parties, nude sunbathers and backyard killer dogs.

Tilly's spell soon dissipated. The chasing mob slowed and stopped, disoriented and the dogs chased them back the way they had come. The barks, yells, shouts and screams blended into one awful voice.

Chapter 47

Teenagers descended on the mall in multitudes, and their many color uniforms rivaled the rainbow on its brightest day. The reason for the invasion was, the schools were out for the day.

Moo Wang leaned on a column and eyed the children. Irrespective of what they had told him, he had his suspicions of Hallie, and he was sticking to them. No ordinary fearless sixteen-year-old schoolgirl waited on a beach to save a man thrown from his penthouse by a demon. It also was too damn early in the morning. A friggin' waterspout, large as a city block, cushioned his fall and washed him ashore. The whole affair was too coincidental for comfort, and he could not get her off his damn mind. Ranchie's daughter? They had a few bouts back in the day, and he preferred not to be in the same building with Ranchie again. He felt his wrist; the excruciating pain he felt the day she had twisted it over a payment issue, came back for a second.

Skipper Drake, the murderer responsible for many of the missing schoolchildren in Westmoreland, shopped and prowled near the girls like a hunter. He took an interest in Hallie's posse and followed them from across the aisle.

Hallie and her alpha posse crowded an electronic store showcase. A girl pointed at an expensive phone.

"Hallie said she's getting an iPhone this weekend."

The girls laughed and pushed Hallie.

"She must have a sugar daddy. Mother Penny is not buying her an expensive phone," another girl said.

Hallie grinned as her eyes roved the lanes.

"I adore trolls. Let's walk this way," Hallie said.

Tilly and Lonesome approached from the direction Hallie pointed. She took an intercept route.

"Miss Tilly," Hallie said, pretending shocked to run into her.

"Yes?"

"Oh, you rode my uncle's bike yesterday."

"Where is he now?" Tilly asked.

"He's probably out somewhere doing what he does."

"What does he do?" Tilly pressed.

"He has never discussed his business with me. Who's your friend?" Hallie dodged.

"Oh, meet Lonesome."

Hallie stuck out a hand, and Lonesome shook it.

"It's so sweet to meet you, Mr. Lonesome. I'm Hallie."

"It's a pleasure."

"Bye, Miss Tilly. I hope to catch you later. Bye, Lonesome," Hallie said.

Tilly and Lonesome strolled away and Tilly glanced back on cue into Hallie's eyes. Tilly's brow wrinkled as if something she couldn't explain lodged in her brain.

"She has zapped the poor boy into wonderland, back bush. He hasn't even registered the death of his best friend yet," Hallie said.

"Who's the weird woman, Hallie?"

"You've met Tilly Whitelock. She scares even ghosts."

"Do you mean the Old Witch?"

"Yes, the same one."

"Girl, you got to stop drinking your grandmother's Obeah liniments."

"Hey, why don't you steal Mother Penny's oil to help me pass my exams and gimme a rub?" Rose asked.

"You need a full bottle of gimme back my virginity, please," Hallie said.

"If it tightens back, I will give my new gift to experience, and not to a fumbling, ramming, impatient young fool, when I'm ready," Rose said.

"Which would be minutes after you get it back," a friend said.

"They only teach life lessons once," Hallie said.

They laughed raucous and vulgarly.

Faith and Irene hurried to Hallie, swinging their troubled, sympathetic faces.

"Did you run into them, Hallie?" Faith asked.

"Run into whom?" Hallie asked.

"Steve and the girl were shopping, and the way she flashed money, she's a working girl," Irene said.

"Oh, my God. Hallie, he didn't," Madge said.

"Oh, he's a stinker."

"Call the dog," Irene said.

Steve's phone rang several times, and no one answered it.

"He's not answering."

"Call him again," Faith said.

Hallie cried out in mental agony and ran away. The girls gathered in a whisper.

An astonished Moo Wang ranted behind a column when Hallie spoke to. As far as he was concerned, the mystery fell into place as the girl and Tilly apparently working together. He needed answers, and when Hallie stormed away, he followed.

Skipper Drake had marked Hallie from the other girls as his victim.

Hallie stumbled to the taxi stand like a horse wearing blinkers, drunk in her soul. Skipper Drake had measured her at an angle and made ground on her as Moo Wang followed from her right and had Skipper Drake in view. He considered Skipper Drake a shopper on the move, flirting, and he could relate. He had seduced many schoolers himself.

"Hey, my girl, do you want a ride?" Skipper Drake asked.

Hallie ignored him and continued ahead, her wild eyes searching for a cab. Skipper Drake mounted his bike and rode alongside Hallie, his feet dragging on the pavement.

"My girl, tek a ride with me, nuh."

He grabbed at Hallie's hand. She swung her arm away as she backed away from him. Moo Wang drew abreast of them and crossed the street.

Skipper Drake's evil eyes locked on Hallie as he dismounted. She clenched her fist but did not feel her powers, and she backed away, intending to run from the evil Neutralizer.

Moo Wang crossed the street at the rear of Skipper Drake. She glanced left, away from Moo Wang, and Skipper Drake followed her eyes and showed her a gun in his waistband. Moo Wang sensed Hallie was in trouble six yards out and pulled his firearm. Hallie realized why unknown powers had her save him at the beach that morning.

Hallie played the damsel in distress perfectly and backed up against the wall in livid fear as her assailant yards advanced. He reached for her, and she dove to her right.

"He has a gun, Moo Wang," Hallie shouted.

Skipper Drake turned, drawing his gun, and Moo Wang placed two bullets into his chest. He backed away and collapsed. Blood spread on his starched white shirt in seconds. Hallie jumped to her feet, and pure white holy fire spilled from her fists against the wall.

"Sanga's offspring, a distant cousin," Hallie muttered.

Moo Wang figured he had made a mistake. If she had powers, why didn't she save herself? Hallie smiled at him.

"You played it well," Moo Wang said.

A crowd gathered, and phones clicked away.

"Dem kill Skipper Drake," a woman cried.

"Thank you, Sir. My grandmother said a fiery cloud hung over your head, and you should visit relatives overseas today," Hallie told Moo Wang.

Hallie melted into the crowd and disappeared.

Chapter 48

Tilly and Lonesome waited under a gray evening sky at the far end of the mall's parking lot. The police had caution-taped off the streets to their right. Emergency vehicles raced back and forth as Ranchie's car pulled up at Tilly and Lonesome's feet.

"I slept through the day," Ranchie said. "What about you guys?"

"We raised sweet hell," Tilly replied.

"So, how're you enjoying evil, dude?" Ranchie asked.

"It worked as advertised."

"Cool. Tilly, can I walk into a bank and make an invisible withdrawal?"

Tilly zapped Ranchie, and her body glowed for a minute.

"You have got an hour, and after tomorrow I'll reclaim all the money in the banks over the Island."

"A woman can wreck a kingdom in five minutes," Ranchie said.

Ranchie's car pulled up before a bank, and she ran to a Rastaman ground produce stall under an orchid flower tree close by.

The falling purple flowers decorated the merchandise like wedding tables. Breadfruits and yams in hundred-pound bags leaned against the tree trunk.

"Ras, let me hold a bag of breadfruits."

"De daughta means the crocus bag?"

"Yeah, Ras, and can you sell it to me today?"

Ranchie dug into her purse and gave the man a US $100 bill.

"I hope a bill covered it."

Before the Ras reacted, Ranchie cut the bag open, pushed it over and breadfruits rolled along the sidewalk.

She folded the bag under her arm and hurried across to the bank. Ras watched her enter the bank and shook his head.

Ranchie passed security, pushed a swing gate, rushed by the busy tellers, cut around a desk and bolted into the vault.

Minutes later, Ranchie hurried out of the vault carrying the heavy invisible bag on her shoulder. She eyed the clock, danced around bank employees to avoid collisions, and darted through the door.

She squeezed the bag down and slammed her car trunk, wearing a well-pleased smile in the parking lot.

Jeno pulled into the spot next to her on his bike.

"Hi, sis."

"Where did you drop from?" Ranchie asked.

"I am hitting the bank for shopping money. Mother wants me to grab a few things in Miami for her today."

"Good for her. I hit them myself. Hey, rumor has it you and an old princess from Europe rode a month ago."

"Are we in competition?"

Ranchie laughed and held the bike handle as Jeno dismounted. "Running princesses, and you're broke like a bitch. What about a decent job, boy?"

Ranchie bent over and guffawed.

"The pot turned on the kettle, only in Negril," Jeno said.

Ranchie dabbed laughing tears from her eyes.

"By the way, when was the last time you ran into Hallie?" Jeno asked.

"Jeno, nuh bother with no bomboclaat… Mi nuh have no time fe dat."

"You nuh have no time fe your mother and daughter?"

"Fuck yu and de two a dem too."

Jeno slapped Ranchie and backed her up; her eyes widened as if the blow had awakened her from a slumber. She shuddered, her teeth and fists clenched in a rage. Something primal took over, an uncontrollable force shook her core and her teeth chattered for a few seconds.

"Watch how you refer to our mother," Jeno yelled.

"I can't believe you hit me. You know I could kill you with my bare hands," Ranchie said.

"I'm willing to die for our mother's honor," Jeno shot back.

Ranchie's body shivered furiously, and it ran to her clenched fist. Her breast heaved, and her body quaked involuntarily. She took deep breaths until a calmness overtook her, but it seemed something unknown had awakened inside her.

"Kill me with one punch like you did, Kebo Brown," Jeno said.

Ranchie's raised fists unclenched and dropped back by her side. Her teary eyes blinked rapidly for a moment.

"Why do you hate her so much?" Jeno asked.

"The only man I've ever loved refused me in school because of my mother's rep. He's our next prime minister. I would've been his wife."

"What? Foster Johnson? You were about fourteen when he left school," Jeno said.

"Neither he nor any other boys wanted to touch me because of her, and the urges drove me crazy."

"What are you talking about?" Jeno asked.

"Mi and yu, wi have no magic. We're extreme nymphomaniacs instead, fool," Ranchie replied.

"You're wrong again. I'm a satyromaniac, not a nympho," Jeno said.

Jeno turned and hurried away.

Concerned women had gathered and closed in on Ranchie when Jeno left. Songeeta stood amid the women and stared at Ranchie.

"Mi call de police fi yu, my girl," a woman said.

"You and the police get the fuck outta my business," Ranchie barked.

"Excuse me. I see why you're a fucking beating stick," the woman said.

Ranchie's eyes threw daggers, and she slammed her car door.

Songeeta gazed at Ranchie's car until it disappeared and cried bloody tears as if she mourned for her. Ranchie bore an uncanny resemblance to her mother, Naana Meg. She even had a mole between her right ear and eye. The women dispersed, leaving Songeeta alone, dabbing at her eyes like a lost child.

Chapter 49

Hallie bailed from a taxi, raced toward the church, changed her mind and dashed through her front door. The news of Steve and the girl had twisted her insides into a corkscrew. She repeated over and over as she staggered to her room. "How could Steve hurt me so terribly?" Her trembling hand missed the doorknob three times before she darted into her room and slammed the door. She jumped onto the bed, piled the pillows on her head, balled her body and sobbed in mental pain.

A million icy threads crisscrossed her mind, tied her in a lover's quandary and she could not use her powers for selfish reasons. The red-hot electric shocks searing through her head were unbearable. She held her head and slithered across the bed in agony.

"Why do I need powers if I cannot use them to please myself or even check what my boyfriend is doing?"

"Hallie, Hallie, open the door."

"Go away, Grandmother. I don't want to talk to you."

"Tell me what is wrong, child," Mother Penny pressed.

"I'm not saying and stay away from my head."

Hallie reburied her head under the pillows.

"Yu and dat footballer. You have Tilly to kill."

"I don't care if she destroys the world anymore," Hallie replied.

"If you want to see the world destroyed, go borrow ten nuclear bombs from America and cold-ass Russia."

"Grandma, call HBO, your special awaits and leave my heart alone to bleed out in agony."

Hallie curled in the fetal position and fixed a pillow over her head.

CHAPTER 50

Sunset watchers had descended on Rick's Cafe in numbers. They began amassing from 4:00 p.m., two hours ahead of the sunset. A generous Mother Nature worked to please her audiences and painted a beautiful crimson and orange canvas in the western sky.

Liquor, laughter and the fantastic sunset caught on a string at the world's end fired the moment and mesmerized like liquid happiness to grasp before it drained away. Moo Wang sipped a tall drink at a corner table, his eyes locked on the Moreland Hill Towers' top floors in the distance. Weighty things rested on his mind, but none was about how the sun rays played the upper levels of the building and left the lower section in the shadows. He had no idea that the drama playing across his stage began yards from where he sat, almost three hundred years ago. If he were prudent, he would heed Mother Penny's warning, but who had walked away from their earthly possessions without a fight?

His research had convinced him that he and Tilly could work something out, but Prince Dinek, who had spliced Mother Penny and Hallie's shenanigans concerning Tilly's gold in his head, sat a few tables away eying him. The spell compelled him to seek out Tilly and hold a reasoning. He had no idea the prince had sacrificed him by placing pieces of information in his head. Prince Dinek paid his bill, made his exit from the crowded building and when the smoke cleared, he would pick up the cross. In his mind, it wouldn't be long before Tilly destroyed Mother Penny, and he decided to wait close by, but out of sight.

The local evening news carried the Skipper Drake killing, and Moo Wang stood in front of the TV monitor to catch it. He had sneaked away but had nothing to fear. If the police wasted time investigating who killed the most wanted man in Jamaica, they would hand him a medal. He swallowed the last bit of his drink and stood resolute, his eyes still on the Tower.

The builders had lavished the Moreland Hill Towers' mezzanine beyond what five-star flair required. Comfortable leather, marble, waterfalls, hedonistic glitters and the affluent shared space engrossed in the luxurious living experience on any given evening.

House security skirted the festive atmosphere as they escorted two uniformed police officers and two plain-clothes detectives to the elevators.

The officers searched Moo Wang's penthouse, room by room, returned to the living room and shielded their firearms.

"We'll wait for her here," the sergeant said.

"They say she's a witch. We should shoot her on sight," detective one said.

"A witch, my ass," the second detective said.

He sank into the deep leather armchair.

"If she smiles crooked, I am shooting."

"You're running true to form, Officer Random Lead," the sergeant said.

"Let's check out the bar."

"Not on my shift."

"Sarge, are you with us?"

"I'm an officer on duty. Who're you?"

Uniform One plopped on the couch, dejected, eyed the bar and licked his dried lips. If the witch killed him in his parched state, he would come back from the grave and fuck up the Sarge's family.

A speeding car braked hard in the Moreland Hill Towers' parking lot, and Tilly hopped from the driver's seat in her zestfully. A tired Lonesome crawled from the front seat.

"Welcome home, boy," Tilly said.

"What about the police?"

"They do not worry me, and you should not worry about them either, love."

"We humans are allergic to bullets," Lonesome uttered.

"What you need is a makeover, Lover boy."

Tilly's snapping fingers clothed Lonesome in an expensive suit and accessories.

"Let's go home."

"I love this. I love this, baby," Lonesome said.

The four officers in Moo Wang's penthouse jumped to their feet on cue and squeezed into a bathroom. Each man aimed his gun at the other man's face and fired.

The front door swung open as they dropped into a pile. Tilly and Lonesome stood in the front doorway, locked in a kiss.

"I smell gunpowder," Lonesome said.

"I bet you've never seen cops dispose of themselves."

Chapter 51

Songeeta wandered the streets, lost, out of her time and place before stopping under a poinciana tree brooding. The sun was deep in the western sky and was as beautiful as she remembered it. Two young women in tight jeans giggled at her. She snapped her fingers, copied their attire and overcooked the jeans' tightness. An older woman going in the opposite direction gawked at her disdainfully and grumbled under her breath. Two motor vehicles blasted their horns, and the drivers leered.

The ungodly hunger gnawed at her gut, and reluctance could not stave off the inevitable for long. She watched the fading sunset as she doubled as a sunset watcher and a honeyed bait. How the land had changed, but the beauty of the evening remained the same.

Two young men, Randall and Paul, spotted Songeeta from the opposite side of the street and cut across, lugging tons of carnal intentions on their faces and everywhere else. She sighed under her breath, as regret and a profound sadness raced through her.

"Black Beauty, a who trouble you?" Randall asked.

Songeeta eyed them for an eternity before she smiled, showing the whitest teeth.

"Have you seen my boyfriend? Someone said he's followed a girl home. Do you have somewhere private? Two can play the game."

Randall's grin would have brightened a cloudy day.

"I live over there. Paul, I'll see you later."

"Bring him too. I am hot, mad and hungry, bad."

Randall threw his hand around Songeeta's waist as he guided her up the street. Paul's eyes danced along the lines and motions of Songeeta's butt as he followed behind.

Minutes later, a reluctant Songeeta stood in Randall's living room against the wall. Paul and Randall appraised her from across the room as the precious prize they were too shy to collect. Her expression had not changed from somber, and they had difficulty reading her.

"Songeeta, please have a seat. I'm gonna get you a glass of juice," Randall said.

Paul followed Randall into the kitchen. Songeeta lifted a finger and zapped sexual energy into the men's back; the invisible energy wave ruffled their shirttails as if a soft wind had hit them. Her jeans did the impossible and fell around her ankles. She wished they did not have to die, and meant it but she had to fed.

Randall poured fruit juice into a glass on the kitchen counter; an apprehensive Paul hovered over his shoulder.

"You think she's having a second take, mon? I'm not feeling a vibe from her," Paul said.

"You think so?"

"After you give her the drink, call her in the bedroom, and if she obeys, we're good."

"I'm trying everything I ever saw in a blue movie on her. I tell you, dog, it's gonna be all night until daylight," Randall said.

"Suppose she's not freaky?" Paul asked.

"If she wasn't a freak, she wouldn't have invited the two of us."

Paul grinned, "She's pretty, mi boy."

Paul and Randall's eyes surveyed the empty living room.

"I'm in here, fellows."

Songeeta knelt on the bed, her back arched and her rear end elevated. The men rushed into the bedroom. The glass fell from Randall's hand, and he flicked on his hidden PC camera.

"Go to the front, Paul. I'm mounting right here," Randall said.

Hours later, Songeeta stood nude over the two blackened carcasses on the queen-size bed, wearing a dry and lifeless mien. Her eyes roved the room, and seating was missing of any kind. "Why did he not have a chair or a bench?" She asked the empty room.

She touched the bed and continued speaking to herself. "Oh, visitors had to sit on the bed, for it was a hassle moving them from chairs to beds sometimes. Even getting hands to relinquish phones in a delicate moment had become a chore."

"I saw a thing been pried from a woman's hands, but what was a phone?"

Songeeta didn't know, but anyone who owned the astute players' manual read the seatless bedroom scene in the first chapter.

She stood on the scattered clothes on the white tiles, drawn to the red LED light on the PC monitor on the night table. She held back as they enjoyed themselves for hours, but human endurance has a limit, and she fed. The poor souls had obliviously taken one for humanity.

She sat on the bed straight back like a statue until darkness consumed the room. The men's carcasses became dark shapes from a few yards away. Hours later, she stood in the dark, and her statuesque body shuddered in revulsion twice.

CHAPTER 52

Dave's car took the sharp right at Locust Tree; the headlight hit the old Sinko's building, traveled by the breadfruit tree branches, leveled off and hit the Burnt Savanna Main Road. Gem sat behind her dad as he drove, as her seatbelt prevented her from sliding across the back seat. They had another forty miles to Mother Penny's church for night service. Monica wore a long white dress and her face was alighted under a white head wrap. How her mother held her soul from bursting forth in all its celestial glory in the car, Gem will never know. Monica cuddled a goatskin rattle drum in her lap.

"Why don't you put the drum in the trunk?" Dave asked.

"You asked me five times already. Are you nervous, Dave?"

He glanced across at her, and a thoughtful expression marred his rugged face. Dave's family had not missed a single church day until he missed last Sunday in over a hundred years.

Monica leaned as far over as she could, placed probing fingers on Dave's shoulder, and whispered, "It's the same God, but he doesn't frown on a non-missionary style from this church."

"You're my Hell and my Heaven," Dave replied.

"We Eves have paved the famous road."

Dave tried but could not hide his smile.

Gem learned as she go that sometimes, the verdicts and the executioners struck simultaneously.

The evening Gem exposed her eyes to her friends, Sister Gina sat Pauline and Milda in a corner and peeked through the curtain at Gem standing in the yard, waiting. Gem got tired of waiting and walked away, and Sister Gina pointed a mean finger at the girls.

"You are not to speak to Gem or her parents ever again. The devil has possessed them."

The teary eyes girls cringed and bowed their heads, anticipating a beating, but Sister Gina's breasts heaved as she dialed her phone.

"Brother Brown, a grave and vexing situation..."

She listened for a beat.

"My brother, two of our members have fallen into Satan's net," Gina charged.

She changed the phone from her left to her right hand and listened, eager to speak.

"I recommend an emergency meeting for 7:00 p.m. tonight," she said.

At 10:00 p.m., four grim-faced church elders knocked on Dave's front door. Dave opened the door, and Elder Jarrett handed him an envelope and backed away. Monica took the note and read it.

"Brother Simms, we must inform you with great regrets in our hearts. You and your family are no longer welcome at our church for your remaining days. We have found you guilty of devil worshiping. May God have mercy on your soul."

Dave crashed into a chair, a broken man, and his face dropped on his knees. Monica threw a comforting hand around his shoulders.

Despite their mother's warning, Milda and Pauline had played and studied alongside Gem at school but did not acknowledge her at home. Hopping back to the trip with her parents, Angels and ghosts flashed across Gem's mind on the ride. Many kids her age claimed they had seen ghosts, and no one believed them. How can you, though, when someone points and says, it's under the banana tree, and you strain your eyes, but see nothing? Gem had made up her mind to keep her ability a secret. She would wait and see how long it lasted or what else it brought. *Wait, how come I'm not scared? Ghost stories used to make me tremble.* She sighed, sank back in her seat and gazed at the light as darkened shapes rushed by her window.

Chapter 53

Night had descended on Negril Beach, but nights around there were a clarion call to rise from your rest. Torches flickered from the various beach parties, and sunbaked tourists rubbed on aloe vera gels and ventured outside, smelling like fresh cut plants. The locals came out too, ready to sing and dance. At birth, destiny stamped many souls and allocated them destinations; they often stood the course throughout their lives. The Negril recipients took the stage, playing their role as either hunter or prey. As preordained, the night ran true to form and did not deviate until demons hijacked reality.

While the players strutted the evening stage, Tilly and Lonesome locked each other in their arms in Moo Wang's bed and intertwined their legs. Lonesome extracted an arm and propped up on his elbow.

"They said witches use and devour their lovers," Lonesome let out.

"Who is the expert on things witchy?" Tilly replied.

"Certainly not me," Lonesome confessed.

"Witches are bitches, huh? What do they say about witches' words?" Tilly asked.

"Witches never give their word, they say," Lonesome offered.

"Ha-ha-ha-ha, well, although tempted, I am holding you as a keeper," Tilly said.

She turned to face Lonesome.

"I am not a witch," Tilly said, looking at him.

"Cool, so can you make me into a warlock or something?"

He ogled Tilly's face.

"You're gonna need help with those cops when they show up here," Lonesome said.

"The evacuation is underway, but we have our police squad," Tilly said.

She kissed Lonesome.

"The cops should have gone into missionary work," Tilly said.

She snapped a finger in the dead officers' general direction.

The dead men came to life and jumped to their feet. Lead Detective had his right eye shot into his brain. He inspected it in the mirror, frowning at the neat entry hole the bullet had made, stuck a finger in, and pulled out the tissues until they hung on his cheek.

"How is it?"

The uniform Cop inspected the eye.

"Great, squaddie, great."

Moo Wang tiptoed toward his bedroom door as the ghosts shuffled out into the hall. Many people have mastered the art of acquiring, but none have studied the art of relinquishing when the odds are insurmountable.

The ghost-squad cuffed and pushed Moo Wang in on Lonesome and Tilly, propped in bed.

"We found him sneaking into the apartment."

"Moo Wang, what a surprise."

"Listen for a minute, Tilly—"

"I do not think you can tell me a lot," Tilly said.

"I can tell you who saved me and is after your gold."

"Can we raise hell now?" the dead detective asked.

"Oh yes, I am gonna make out there, dead people friendly in a minute," Tilly said.

The four dead officers shuffled away and Lonesome shuddered.

"I hate to kill a man twice, Moo Wang."

"You didn't even sense her. Doesn't it tell you someone powerful is after you?"

Tilly reached him in two strides against the wall.

"It's a powerful young Obeah woman," Moo Wang blurted out.

She clasped a hand on Moo Wang's forehead. Her hand glowed until it seared into his forehead. Moo Wang yelled, his eyes rolled white and black like marble in their sockets. Tilly fired a crimson blast and incinerated him.

"I have played nice since I returned, Lonesome, but now I must prepare a welcome party for Miss Hallie and her grandmother's plans for my gold."

"She's the girl we met in the mall, huh? You have gold?"

Tilly eyed Lonesome.

"Never mind. I'm not into shiny things," Lonesome replied.

"They are planning to use my gold to build a fucking church, the gall of Sanga's bitches."

Tilly rushed out to the balcony, jumped over the rail and flew out to sea. Her dress flowed behind her like a red nocturnal bird of prey.

The moon hung low like a molten glow, and the calm water reflected it like a mirror. Tilly tread the water in a rage and spread her arms wide.

"Come forth, ye angry, restless souls. Come drink revenge and vengeance from my cup."

A fierce, hellish wind howled around Tilly, and the water put on an angry, choppy edge as locals, pirates, Haitians, Cubans, Joes and Marys' ghosts rose from their watery graves from across the centuries. The ghouls formed a mighty circle around Tilly, howling like hungry banshees into megaphones.

The demonic wind blew Tilly's hair, as the water wrapped around her body like a living thing, and she pointed ashore.

"Hurry ashore and unleash your vengeance on the living until the night is no more."

The angry ghosts tramped water to the shore on a high swell.

Chapter 54

Ranchie staggered along her apartment hallway, the burlap bag riding over her shoulder and shopping bags in her other hand. Chemmie, a tattooed, gold-tooth hoodlum, loitered on the rails smoking a joint.

"Ranchie, where did you steal the bag of weed?"

"You wish, Chemmie."

"When are we gonna have the drink, Ranchie?"

Ranchie dropped the bag.

"I'm a high-end-tourist whore, Chemmie… and based on how great I am in bed, going local gets personal and complicated quickly." She grinned at Chemmie. "No offense. We can burn a joint anytime, but…"

"You can't kill a guy for trying," Chemmie chimed in.

"Your eyes are also tearing me behind to bits. They twisted my thong in a nasty way the other day," Ranchie added.

"It must be the same time I felt a monster rise," Chemmie said.

Ranchie smiled at him.

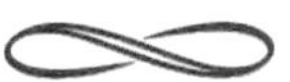

Mother Penny opened the last of the four church windows and placed the stick braces to keep them open. She lit one candle on the wall, and the others sprang to life around the church. She flicked on the overhead fans and a couple of the enhanced candles flickered, but none went out. She rolled out two new MaxxAir thirty-inch fans on the pulpit. Sylvia, a young woman Mother Penny had nurtured, had given them to her last week. She wanted to buy an air-conditioning unit, but Mother Penny would not let her. Her plans for the combined mega-church and healing center were shaping nicely. Although Sylvia made good money overseas as a chemical engineer she didn't want her squandering money and bought sand for the beach. Someone banged the church door urgently and broke her musing.

"Mother Penny, Mother Penny."

"Come on in. The door is always open."

Freddy and Addi, a country couple in their fifties, wheeled in their young son, Omar, in a wheelchair. The evolution concept had a perfect run-on, Omar. A casual observer could tell he had jumped two generations above his parents' status in looks.

The young man was suave, and alpha; even the agonizing pain that twisted his face could not hide the fact. He contorted in pain, held his right leg under the blanket, leaped out of the chair, and dropped back in agony, holding his leg.

"Oh, God, Mother Penny, please make it stop. Mek it stop, ma'am."

"Uncover his legs," Mother Penny instructed.

Addi pulled the cover. Omar's right leg and foot were swollen as large as a five-gallon bucket.

"Dem a move. Oh, God. Dem a move."

"He woke this morning wid him foot like dis," Addi said.

"You're a woman beater. Did you warn your son not to lay his hand on a woman?"

"Puppa Jeezas, Omar. You beat a woman and get a jackfruit foot?" Addi asked.

Omar shook his foot, yelling, "Dem moving up and down, oh God no."

Mother Penny poured oil from a vial in her palm and rubbed the leg. Two-inch worms wiggled out onto the floor.

"Lawd God, mi son ded now."

"Oh, my. Get out, get out. I must call for spiritual help," Mother Penny said. Addi and Freddy hurried through the door.

Mother Penny blindfolded Omar and wailed in a chant.

"Oh, ye ailing spirit, wracked by lover's pain to your soul. I calleth upon your eternal goodness. The sick needeth healing, and the unvanquished devil walked the Earth."

A disheveled Hallie raised her head from under her pillow. Her dreads knotted, like Medusa's hair the day a hurricane trapped her in a corner of the world. Her arm labored to six inches off the bed and expelled a pinpoint light beam from a finger as she shuffled back under her pillow.

Hallie's energy beam illuminated Omar's leg and moved from his ankle to his knee like an electric current. A dozen dead worms fell from the leg and withered to dust. Mother Penny removed the blindfold, and the boy watched the swelling dissipate an inch per second.

"Thank you, Mother Penny."

Mother Penny pointed at Omar's manhood.

"Your healing came with a price. The next time you hit a woman, your manhood will rot."

"I'll never hit another woman, ma'am."

"Don't convince me. It's your private parts."

He embraced Mother Penny.

"I'm sorry, Mother Penny, it will never happen again."

"I love how you learned proper English fast. Please open the church door for me. We have an early service."

"Him staying for the service too Mother Penny," Addi said at the door.

Chapter 55

The police and wealthy, obstinately angry residents glared at each other on the Moreland Hill Towers' fourth floor. A routine evacuation exercise had turned into a huge hostile no-win standoff.

"Where're my children?" an agitated woman asked.

"We've evacuated the children to safety, ma'am," the sergeant said.

"Well, you can go to Hell. I'm not leaving my home."

She wheeled away and slammed her door behind her.

Twenty-five ghosts bolted from the water into building two under construction and began the wanton killing Tilly ordered. Carpenters, electricians and plumbers worked throughout the building. The mezzanine had taken shape, but was a jumbled mess of building materials, scaffolding and piles of trash scattered everywhere.

Eko Singh, an easygoing local man from Delveland, pushed a cart of Scrubbers and Heaters at a snail's pace across the mezzanine floor as if his thirty-five-year-old body were a burdensome ninety-five.

Jae was a business-and-bustle American from the northwest, brought in by the builders to do remediation work on the penthouses. A freak storm two weeks ago had blown water into the apartments, saturated the walls and pooled on the floors. He pushed his cart past Eko Singh and held the elevator as shadows flashed in the corner. Eko Singh whipped his head around.

"Dude, we don't have all night on this sh-t," Jae prompted.

"Why not? I'm paid by the hour… I guess they paid you for speed," Eko Singh replied.

Jae released the elevator door. The ten days he'd spent on the Island had taught him so much. He especially loved the laid-back lifestyle, and Eko Singh had invited him to his lovely home several times. He had built his house one brick at a time without a penny coming from a bank loan. It had taken him years, but in America, a home-like his sold for three quarters to a million and a half dollars, depending on the neighborhood. Echo said he spent about fifty thousand dollars over three years.

Even though Jae loved the laid-back lifestyle, he could not put his wife's panties in the washer, much less touch her, if he should lose his job. Some of these lucky motherfuckers wanted to exchange their island life for Trump's third-classism regime. *Damn, Eko Singh's wife better cook hot curry chicken and coconut rice for their dinner*, he salivated, gazing into space.

Eko Singh watched the elevator climb to penthouse four. He waited a minute and jabbed the button.

Falling metal crashed into a dark corner, and he whipped his around but saw nothing. It wasn't unusual for stuff to fall in a building under construction, but he hurried aboard the elevator anyway.

The severely hit Penthouse four had water settled in patches on the floor. Tilers were going to have problems laying tiles on the unplumbed levels. Heaters and scrubbers worked against the walls, containing mold. Eko Singh hauled his load into the room as Jae placed his last scrubber against a back wall.

"The mildew is more excessive up here," Jae said.

"Thus, our continuing employment and paychecks," Eko Singh replied.

Jae glanced at Eko Singh.

"Did you smell the elevator?" Eko Singh asked.

"It smelled okay," Jae offered.

"You know what? Cigarettes shot your nostrils, mon. The elevator smelled putrid," Eko Singh said.

Crashes and bangs echoed from the master bedroom. Jae pressed a finger to his lips.

"Shhhhh, someone is probably banging an electrician girl in the bathroom."

Jae tiptoed away to investigate. He peeked into the bathroom as eerie, macabre shadows danced on the walls behind him. Reddish, dirty water filled the Jacuzzi, and a rotten-fleshed female ghost emerged from underwater. It rotated its head 360 degrees and submerged, leaving the water ripple less.

Jae tiptoed through the door as the ghost resurfaced, and he ran, but opened-arms specters blocked him at the door.

"Help, Eko Singh. Oh, my God."

Another female ghost pushed him in his chest, back into the bathroom. The Jacuzzi ghost held him by his collar and pulled him into the water.

"Aaaugh. OOH. Help." He struggled to yell.

The grinning ghost straddled and submerged him; the water bubbled and settled.

Eko Singh raced into the bathroom, a monkey wrench held high into his hand, but when he got there, the Jacuzzi was dry, dusty, dirty and wrapped in factory wrapping.

"Jae, Jae, Jae. Where're you, mon?"

"I'm trapped in the closet. Help me."

Eko Singh ran into the large walk-in closet. Eight ghosts surrounded him from out of the walls.

"Bomboclaat, duppy. The Lord is my shepherd—"

A female ghost slapped and backhanded him into a corner.

"Shut the fuck up, boy."

"Laaad gad. Help me." He yelled.

A ghastly rotten-faced female ghost pulled him to her by his shirt front, and Eko wet his pants as she smelled him.

"Dis piss pants fucker is my relative. Yeah, he's my Grand-aunt Bella's boy."

The ghosts lavished kisses on Eko's arms.

"Boy, yu a do good, yu a wuk pon billionaires' penthouses, gi mi a money nuh mon?"

A petrified Eko remembered his mother's old saying: *Beggars in life, beggars in fucking death.*

His relative touched his wet pants, and they dried instantly. Eko Singh wetted them again as he crumbled to the floor. The ghosts laughed as the echoes bounced off the walls around Eko's head. His eyes rolled back, white and he collapsed on his back, foaming from his mouth.

The spell broken as the ghosts disappeared and Jae hyperventilated in the dusty Jacuzzi's bottom, stroking his arms as he tried to resurface from under nonexistent water.

One floor below, male and female electricians ran numbers ten and twelve AWG wires. They had jumbled live cables hanging from control boxes, and a playful twelve-year-old Boy Ghost climbed along the wall close to the ceiling like a toad. A woman held her nostrils and made an ugly face.

"Someone needs a doctor. Who the fuck farted?" She asked.

They gave Nick their disgusted attention.

"Fuck you. It wasn't me this time."

"It was never you, huh, Nick?" the fat electrician said.

The young spook hopped to a junction box, and his nimble fingers sparked as he twisted the live number wires. A cable snaked around the fat electrician and tightened around his neck. He jerked; his hair stood on end, his facial skin drew taut, his lips melted away and his cheekbones protruded. The flaming cable burned his head off and attacked the fleeing, panicked electricians.

"OOHH, mi bloodclaat, aaaugh, Jeezas Christ. Motherfuck, ugh," they wailed.

The wires hoisted two tardy folks and the room turned into a fiery smoking barbeque pit. The last electrician ran for the door and a cable cut him off, imitating a king cobra in the doorway. He moved to his right, and the wire followed, darting at him. He howled as he jumped backward. The cable moved from side to side, covering the doorway and a second wire crawled toward him out of the smoke like a sidewinder snake.

He glanced behind in terror and rushed to the open door. The cobra wire launched into his stomach and ignited. He bellowed in agony, grabbed the cable and his hands stuck to the flaming wire. The wanton killings Mother Penny dreaded about Tilly began and the night was still young.

Chapter 56

Tower One's long fifth floor hallways exhibited a peaceful ambiance, and the deep crimson carpet gave it a virgin appearance.

A seven-year-old male ghost, clad only in new Batman and Robin underwear, staggered from an apartment like a drunk, and its mouth foamed as if it had drowned minutes before. It stumbled, lost across the corridor and disappeared into the left wall, but seconds later reappeared from the right. Something heavy crashed on the floor above, vibrating the building, and Boy Ghost bolted through the nearest closed door.

Boy Ghost wandered into the dimmed apartment living room, drawn to the red electric LED lights on the appliances. A human-like finger poked finger the couch, sat tentatively, sank through the cushions, ascended and tried again and again until it could sit.

An intoxicated couple slept off too many tall drinks in the bedroom, and a light snore emanated from the man down the hall. Boy Ghost entered the bedroom, rubbing its eyes, yawned, climbed between the pair and spooned against the woman. The man's snoring seized. The woman sighed in her sleep and threw a hand over him.

Ten adult ghosts in various degrees of decomposition barged in through the apartment door and scattered like marauding insects. An envious female spirit admired the expensive kitchen fixtures and appliances, while Filthy Specter, another ghost, drank and ate from the containers in the refrigerator, spat in them and replaced them. Another male ghost urinated seaweed, sand and a dead fish on the bathroom floor.

Filthy led the others into the master bedroom. Boy Ghost gazed up at them like a lost kid, far from home. Its eyes said, *where am I, and what are those ugly, awful things?*

"Poor soul, I don't believe it knows it has died," a female ghost said.

The massive marble bureau rose above the bed until it touched the ceiling. Boy Ghost flew from the bed. The dresser dropped on the couple, ascended, dropped, rose, fell and bloodied the bed.

The scope of Tilly's spiteful evilness flipped like a horror movie scene through the building, and hapless police officers moved in fours, covering each other on the fourth-floor corridor blocked by angry residents. It was only the first hour of the mayhem Tilly had planned for the Island playing like a dress rehearsal in the two buildings. Mother Penny reminded Hallie that she should've beaten the iron while it was hot. However, Hallie had dropped the ball when she didn't attack Tilly as planned in her weakened state.

"This is an unlawful government intrusion and invasion of privacy," the lead man shouted at the police.

"Two dangerous killers have taken refuge in the building, sir," the patient officer said.

"I don't have to listen to you… my monthly light bills are higher than your damn salary," Niranda said.

"I don't give a fuck," the man said.

A young officer lost his patience and advanced on the man. An infernal screech reverberated throughout the building and stopped him. A loud creak followed until the building shook and vibrated as if the entire foundation shifted. Cops and residents stumbled across the uneven, shifting floor. Niranda slammed her apartment door as two blood-curdling screams echoed through the building.

The officers stared at each other. Niranda flung her door open.

"Investigate the fuck outta what made those screams."

She slammed her door and shrieked for her life behind it. An officer kicked down the door, led six others inside, and they found themselves in a hellish dark, steamy swamp. A large dark creature splashed brackish water, and snakes slithered from twisted ball moss trees.

A demonic crocodile, the tail to its midsection natural and its upper half-skeletal bones, held Niranda in its powerful jaws. An officer pulled his gun.

"Run."

They bolted through the door into another surprise.

The corridor had transformed into an unkempt graveyard, with bottomless opened graves and scattered gravestones like there was an eruption. Macabre trees and living killer vines curled like they searched for food. The officers dispersed, each man for himself and Corporal Bell fell away in an abyss, bellowing.

A curling vine pulled an officer by his leg into a tree. As he spun, yelling and reaching, trying to find something to steady himself, a female specter climbed from a hole, held his leg and steadied him.

"Aaaugh, help," He hollered.

"Hush, dear. Who did this to you, boo?" she asked in soothing tones.

She gazed into his terrified face.

"I bet I can make you smile."

She tickled him, and he screamed in terror.

"Must be the damn vest you're wearing."

She stripped his vest, caressed his chest and he howled louder. She tickled his side, he hollered, and it cracked into gurgles.

She grabbed his head, twisted and ripped it from his neck, before frowning and tucking it under her arm.

"We could've had fun together, but I couldn't get a shitty smile outta you."

She jumped back into the pit, carrying the head under her arm.

Millionaire tenants and the cops bumped heads on the mezzanine floor. The shouting match played back and forth as a kind of 'my shout over your shout.' Mrs. Brandon's facial chinks cut deep as a well-used battleax and she was the most belligerent of the lot.

"I'm not leaving my penthouse unprotected. In fact, I don't trust the police one bit."

"Cuff her ass and drag her out," Sergeant Brown ordered.

"I'll have your badge for speaking to my wife like that," Mr. Brandon said.

"If I've got a dull battleax for a wife, I'd not admit it. What type of billionaire are you?" Sergeant Brown remarked.

"She's the fucking billionaire, officer."

"Oh, sorry, sir, keep up the excellent job," Sergeant Brown said.

Brown turned to his officers.

"Play time over. We're dragging these rich bomboclaats out. Mi sick a dem."

Senator Thomas bustled his way up front, oozing power and authority as if he had invented arrogance.

"I'm Senator Thomas officers."

"Is that so?" snapped Bobby, a tall officer.

Senator Thomas flashed a contemptuous eye at Bobby.

"And who're you?" Senator Thomas asked.

"I'm a dead political victim. My name is Bobby Knocks, and I love fucking politicians."

Bobby Knocks metamorphosed into a putrid ghost. Senator Thomas ran for his life.

"Sergeant, do something. Protect me."

Bobby Knocks grabbed Senator Thomas by his coat's collar. The police opened fire, and bullets flew through Bobby Knocks' body, killing Senator Thomas. Sergeant Brown shouted on the run.

"Cease fire and run."

The resident and the police bolted for the exits. The waterfall spluttered to foam, the lights dimmed and a deep rumble rocked the building. The runners stumbled as if an earthquake had erupted under them. People slipped, fell and slid on the unstable ground. The lights brightened, the flooring stabilized, they picked themselves up and the lights went out again. Crashes, screams, shouts and hellish howls echoed in the dark.

CHAPTER 57

Parked cars lined the road up to Mother Penny's church. Women in long white dresses, white head wraps and tennis shoes marched into the church carrying tambourines and drums— the few, white-suited men came empty-handed. Dave had to park about two hundred yards from the church. Monica led him and Gem at a merry clip; her precious drum hung over her shoulders.

Spectators consisted of primarily men, who crowded the open church windows; the burning candles fluttered, but stayed alight. Bev and his brother, Carl, sat left and right on the pulpit, pounding the large bass drums. They had stacked the seats against the walls. Monica and the rattle drum corps hung their drums around their necks and played in the cleared area. The hundred or so white-dressed faithful sang and danced in the middle.

Gem sat by a window, stomping her foot to the drums, and her mother closed her eyes on the floor as if she had left the world. Her head swiveled side to side, drenched in sweat and the drumsticks blurred in her hands. Gem had seen people caught in the spiritual zone in their old church, but the people before her… she searched for the right word and blurted it.

"Hijacked, yes, their spirits were hijacked from their bodies," Gem said.

Gem's tambourine rattled in her hands. The infectious drumming reached her, and she jumped to her feet dancing.

Mother Penny led the chorus.

"We are free, we are born again. Born, born, born again. Thank God, we are born again. Well, I am born of the water, the spirit and the blood. Thank God, we are born again. I am so glad Jesus set me free. Satan had me bound, but Jesus set me free. Singing glory hallelujah, Jesus set me free. He broke the bonds of prison for me. Jesus set me free, the stone of Babylon, she got to be removed. The stone of Babylon, she got to be removed. Send down the rain, send down the gospel rain. The Blessed Holy Ghost comes down and falls on Zion…"

The women caught in the spirit rocked on their feet, until their knees buckled and their semi-conscious bodies fell, squirming on the floor. Ushers pinned their dress tails together and fanned them to keep them cool. The white-clad intoxicated congregation traveled back to when their unique spirits were untainted by slavery and scarred by wanton hatred. They stomped, swirled and danced as they did when alone and free in the world. Gem realized that drums and dances were her ancestors' constant companions, caressing their spirits and souls without boundaries or fears.

Hallie's bedroom copied her chaotic mindset. While she buried her head under the pillows, clothes and small articles swirled around her room as if they spun away into a whirlpool.

Prince Dinek landed silently on his lion at Mother Penny's backyard, yards from Hallie's dark bedroom window. From his vantage point, he stared at the pulpit inside the church. The lion's eyes glowed red and pulsed as if the drums had invoked something in them. Gem glanced through the window, straight at Prince Dinek and his lion. Without glaring, she shifted her eyes away.

"I do not thing the child can see us in the dark from the lighted church, but we are going invisible to be on the safe side," Prince Dinek said to his lion.

Gem slung another quick eye, and invisibility did not shield the prince nor his pet from her eyes.

"You're trying to hide from me, but not from these eyes. I'll inform Mother Penny," Gem whispered.

A lamp burned on the night table in Mother Penny's bedroom. The cross hung over the bed as steady as a lead ballast, although objects vibrated from the bass drums and stomping. The cross glowed dimly, bobbed on the string and swung as if a wind had blown through the locked room. It swayed, glowed and upended on the line tensionless. The lamp dimmed, and the objects developed an eerily transparent hue.

The swirling objects in Hallie's room fell on her. She shot into a sitting position on the bed, and her anxious eyes searched the room. After a minute, she dropped on her back on the bed, wiggled and curled on her side.

Gem moved to another head-height window on her tiptoes. Prince Dinek stood in the dark, his lion stood at his side and he pointed. The lion leaped at the house and disappeared through the solid wall. Gem ran to Mother Penny and pulled her dress to get her attention. The song lyrics flowed from Mother Penny's mouth like water into a fountain.

Mother Penny's consciousness had left the Earth, Gem figured. Her right foot rose and dropped in the same spot in time, duumm, like the big drums. She tugged Mother Penny's dress until the thread gave at the waist but could not get her attention. To Gem, the congregation had fallen unconscious on their feet in glory. 'Where was the tall dreadlocks girl?' She asked herself. *What's her name… what's her name, again? Elli, Ali, oh, yes Hallie. She lives in the church but did not attend service, but si yah.* She turned left and right and darted through the side door into Mother Penny's workroom. She ran from the kitchen into the passage, silvery and glowing as extreme moonlight. The lion, tall as a cow, stared her down six yards ahead with flaming eyes.

"Jesus Christ," Gem gushed.

Gem tried to back away, but her feet propelled her forward towards the lion. It ogled her at the door, turned as Hallie's room door swung open and entered. The massive tail twirled in the passage. Gem reached the door as the lion's tail moved inside the surreal lighted room. Hallie levitated and spun around the room amongst clothes and objects. Her eyes were white as if she had died days ago. The lion reared on its hind legs, and a mighty paw cocked to strike. Gem grabbed its tail, pulled and screamed.

"No, help, wake up, Hallie, wake up," Gem bellowed.

The lion turned on her. Sitira erupted through the floor into the lion's midsection. It jumped over Gem and passed through the wall outside. Gem ran to the window as Prince Dinek's finger zapped the lion.

Sitira expelled as a black fog, exploded into misty bits and scattered violently into nowhere. Prince Dinek and the lion returned to invisibility and melted into the shadows as if they feared discovery. However, Gem could see them, and she ran back into the church.

Chapter 58

Hellish, cacophonous darkness blanketed the Moreland Hill Towers' mezzanine. The foundation of the rocking building tore, screeched, settled and dimmed lights brightened and held steady. A dungeon replaced the greater mezzanine, and macabre torturer's instruments hung on the walls. Bloody people squirmed and screamed on the torture racks.

"Will someone wake me?" a man yelled.

"Not in here, fellow. They can wake me the fuck outside. I'm outta here." a suited gent said.

The fountain fired a deluge of blood and drenched the occupants. An absolute panic ensued as people dashed toward the entrances but met angry poltergeists entering from Hell.

The doors slammed sealed as the fiendish denizens fanned out and tore into people.

"We're gonna die. Oh, my God. We're gonna die," a woman screamed.

A mean wraith screamed back in her face.

"You have hit the nail with a large hammer,"

It rotated a finger around the screaming woman's head. Her head turned 360 degrees a few times, and when it settled, her eyes gazed down at her backside. A hellish scream of terror escaped her.

"Run," the ghost screamed.

She ran a few steps, keeled over under the feet of the panicked hordes and they trampled her to a pulp.

Bodies littered the mezzanine floor from one end to the other. Shrieking ghosts and human screams echoed off the walls. The reverberating echo chamber had people covering their ears in agony.

Paco a Cuban Ghost stomped a foot on a shrieking man's protruded belly on the floor.

"Pappi, you got the earplugs?" Paco asked the man.

He stomped repeatedly, and on the third try, his foot paused midair as if he'd remembered something. Paco pulled a waterlogged address book from his back pocket and bounced to a terrified man hiding behind a column.

"Pappi, you got the phone?"

The man shook his head, drooling fear incoherently and his eyes rolled back as his knees wobbled. Paco kicked him across the room and rushed toward a woman.

"I've got a phone. I've got a phone," she screamed.

She fumbled in her pocketbook for what seemed an eternity. Paco grabbed the bag, fished out the phone, flipped his address book open and a dead doctor fish fell out. Paco dialed a number.

"Mami, Mami," Paco said.

"Who's this?" the responder asked.

"It's Paco, Mami, and I'm finally on my way to Miami."

"What sick joke is this? Paco left Cuba in 92 on a raft. Get the fuck off my phone."

"Mami, it's me. I got a storm delayed, me in Jamaican waters, but I'm on my way."

"Where the hell have you been hiding since 92?"

"At the sea bottom, Mami."

The call cut, and the dial tone resounded.

Paco stared at the phone in his hand, with an incredulous expression of disappointment covered his face. Why did they resurrect him if he can't go home to his Mami? He ran out the door back into the water, dejected.

A heavyset female ghost chased a man, swung a mace and backed him against a wall.

"Please don't hurt me, please."

She shied the mace, and the man cringed.

"Fooled you, didn't I? Give me five," the ghost said.

She held her hand up, and the man reciprocated. The ghost rammed the mace handle into his right eye.

A uniformed officer fired into a kind face specter, tossed his empty weapon at it and backed away. The human-like ghost had ten bullet holes in its upper torso, and it approached the officer, exhibiting a Sunday school teacher's empathy.

"Why do we resort to guns, guns, guns, bam, bam, bam? Do we ever give reason a chance?"

The man cowered against the wall.

"Who said I wouldn't let you go if you plead for your life?"

"Please let me go, please," he begged.

"You can go."

He glanced at the closed doors.

"Yes, the door will open for you."

He ran for the exit.

"Protected man coming through, give him free passage," the ghost bellowed.

Another ghost used a boat paddle and slapped a woman across the room.

"What's up with the protected man thing?" one ghost yelled.

"Watch," Kind Face said.

An exit door opened, and strong hands pulled the man through. Two dozen riot police rushed through the door.

The exit door slammed shut and sealed. Kind Face grinned.

"Listen up, Hell spawns. It's gonna be a long night in here," Kind Face declared.

The police shot at people and ghosts randomly. Paddle Ghost's paddle batted back bullets into four riot officers, and the others took cover.

An older woman screamed around a corner into Bloody Eye Detective from Tilly's penthouse, his badge hanging on his chest.

"Thank God, help me, help me, sir."

She trembled in his arms. The detective held her hand and stuck her finger in his injured eye socket.

"Do you think I survived a bullet through my eyes into my brain?"

Realization dawned on her terror-filled face. She screamed, and the ghost yelled back in her face. She floated away, light as an inflated balloon into flying wraiths, and they passed through her, ripping her to pieces.

The Hell spawns killed everyone in the mezzanine and scattered through the building. They rode the elevators, slammed doors and invoked terrified screams from every floor.

A young dapper scammer ghost leaned against an apartment door in the corridor. His left hand held his shiny belt buckle in his low riding jeans.

He had no idea his partner killed and robbed him on the day of his biggest haul. The way he carried himself said he would prefer death to five years in a cold-ass North Dakota prison, though. Four bloody ghosts blasted from an apartment, broke the door in the middle and it swung from one hinge. They gathered around Dapper Ghost, howling and frothing at the mouth stunk of alcohol.

"I've got it covered on this floor, get outta here," Dapper said.

The ghosts stumbled away down the hall.

"I hate it when fucking scammers can't hold their liquor," Dapper said.

A young woman slept in the fetal position in the apartment bedroom, her back toward the door. Dapper crept in, lifted the covers, peeked under, grinned and rubbed his palms in anticipation, but first, he took one of the two phones off the night table and left the room.

Dapper Ghost leaned back against the door in the hallway and placed a foot against it. He held the phone to his ear, and his free hand grabbed his crotch. Inside the bedroom, the other phone rang until it vibrated to the floor. The sleeping girl opened her eyes, glanced up and went back to sleep. Dapper Ghost crashed through the door, and the girl jumped out of bed. He grabbed her flimsy nightdress and pulled her to him.

"Eeek, eeek, eeek," escaped from her lips.

"Didn't you hear the phone ringing?" Dapper asked.

He shook her head several times. She mumbled something and bit her tongue.

"I'm going back outside to call you again."

He shoved her back on the bed, and she bounced a couple of times.

Dapper retook his position against the door, grinning into the phone.

"Yes, ma'am, I'm the prize director for the lottery. I was going through our records, ma'am, and I saw where you have uncollected winning tickets…"

He leered into the phone, pumped and blew smoke from a joint as an extended "Eeeeeeek" emanated from the phone in his hand.

Chapter 59

The vibrations of the beating drums and the stomping feet vibrated objects on the shelves in Mother Penny's bedroom. Vials shook, fell and rolled, but none dropped to the floor. The cross swung like a thing animated, and the grooves glowed red. A whooshing breeze blew the door open, and Songeeta levitated inside the room. She caressed the cross as if she had missed it, and flames flared in her eyes.

She dropped Sanga's diary wrapped in the goatskin on the bed, took the cross, stopped at the door and turned. The cross sailed, reattached itself to the string and it bathed her back in a spectrum glow as she exited the room.

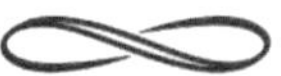

The Rolling Calf stood under the mango tree in the dark watching Prince Dinek maneuvered behind the house, focusing on the new pulsating light in the bedroom window. The Prince would have died the moment he arrived behind the house, but Songeeta had forbidden it. A tilt in the ground placed the window above his reach. He stood on the lion's back and peeked through. The cross glowed as it swung back and forth through the curtain, out of reach. Prince Dinek spoke to the lion in Twi, and it grew taller.

He opened the window, inserted his upper body and reached for the cross. His face lodged in Songeeta's bosom, and he recoiled taking her through the window. They fell, rolled few feet down the decline and the lion attacked. Songeeta's hand darted, caught it by the mane and hoisted it above her head. Flames raced along her arm and devoured the lion from its head. The fire consumed it at tremendous speed, and after the head, the body did not make it to the ground. Prince Dinek scrambled to his feet. Songeeta reeled him back to face her and kissed him. His arms pushed her off him until they became withered, dried and blackened before breaking off. She tossed his carcass against the wall; the window slammed shut, and Songeeta ambled away around the house in her slow casual gait.

Gem had failed to get anyone's attention. She danced and played the tambourine close to Mother Penny to hide her fears. She missed a step, and her left hand froze midair over the tambourine.

Her mouth gaped, and her widened eyes locked on Songeeta entering the church through the front door. Gem shifted her eyes to Dave singing and dancing across the room. A church remained a church. She wanted to smile, but how could she after seeing the woman? Her parents were moving closer to Mother Penny's church soon popped into her head, to replace the thing disguised as a woman, a beautiful woman too.

Gem glanced at Songeeta, closed her eyes, tightened them and danced over to Mother Penny, who had not changed position, and her right foot stomped the same spot, "Huuummmph." The same sound came from her mouth. The congregation repeated Mother Penny's "Huuummmph" in unison as they stomped their feet.

Gem searched outside for the lion man or any other monster, but not what the cute Black girl had underneath her skin. She did not understand how something so hideous dared to attend a church. It did not take much imagination to believe the thing disguised as a woman could stunt a child's growth. She imagined herself at forty and not taller than a nine-year-old; what an ugly picture.

"Wait, what happened to Hallie? Did she awaken? Boy, they've got a duppy woman living here. How come she wasn't even scared of stalking a monster lion?" Gem opened her eyes and mouth in wonderment. "Rahtid, Hallie can defy gravity. Every person in Moreland Hill has powers. Boy, it's gonna be adventurous living in Moreland Hill. Yes, they're moving from Bath Mountain, and no one told her." Gem said.

Gem peeked in Songeeta's general direction, but she had moved into the congregation. Her mother and father beat the drum and sang halfway between Heaven and Earth.

Gem tiptoed and glimpsed Songeeta as she bounced out the door. Even from the rear, Songeeta appeared as a monster. Gem would never inform her parents about the woman monster thing, ghosts or anything unearthly. When the chance arose, she would update Mother Penny, though. She feared her parents might ask Mother Penny to take back her sight. Savvy kids were aware of how parents panic over the most minor things. The ghosts did not scare her, but the evil lion-man did and how could a hell-beast like that disguise itself as a beautiful woman? She thought *Men must be careful out there, women too* and her body shuddered.

Gem told herself not to dwell on it or her again, lest she failed to add another inch to her height. Songeeta glanced back and locked Gem's eyes. "Laad Gad, I've peered too far into Hell," Gem said to herself.

Songeeta hurried around the house, through the wall and into Mother Penny's bedroom. The cross floated to her and she stuck it in her bosom. She glanced at Hallie's door down the hall and disseminated an energy wave from her eyes.

Hallie rotated above her bed in slow motion. The invisible energy wave hit her, as she fell across the bed and her head hung over the edge.

"Hey, where did a lion come from in my room?" She mumbled like a drunk, her eyes still closed.

Her eyes popped open after a couple of beats. She rolled to her feet and scrambled to the door.

"Grandma, did you zing me?"

She hurried into the hall, shuddered, sneezed and heard Mother Penny leading the robust singing in the church. Hallie frowned, shook her head and stumbled back into her bedroom.

"Ghosts and things run around here as if we ran a blasted playground between Heaven and Hell. A broken-hearted ho in the making can't even mope in smelly peace," Hallie blurted out.

A whiff of her armpit twisted her face further.

Chapter 60

The landscape around the towers had transformed, and thick unnatural black fog cloaked both buildings' foundations as if they moved to a high, rocky, nightmarish cliff. Giant bats circled the spires, and the moon ran behind ominous clouds, leaving the towers in darkness. Waves crashed against the cliff and sprayed white foam in the air.

Darkness from some foul dimension or Hell covered a square mile around the towers in every direction, and the two towers were the epicenter. Lights from the unaffected areas surrounded the possessed zone.

Fiery hellholes and bottomless pits pockmarked the lawns and streets. The swamps reclaimed a section, and reptiles slithered from macabre muddy hellholes in the dark. Local ghosts, Tainos, Spaniards, British soldiers and slaves roamed the dark streets. Dead bodies littered their wake.

Near the towers, people hung from rope vines, screaming in agony. The recently departed police officers conducted traffic checks, pulled terrified motorists from vehicles and bludgeoned them. The ghosts roamed up to the solid dark wall partition, dividing the lighted zone from the dark.

Songeeta flew like a dark nocturnal bird and landed on the bright side of the divide. The darkness crept towards her, eating away at the light. She used her arms to brace the shadow wall back and held it at bay from expanding. She mumbled in a low growl, eased back and the dark wall crept a foot forward. She placed a shoulder against it and braced as she chanted in an indefinite tongue. She released the tension, the void stood still, she observed it for a few moments and hurried away.

A rumble developed deep beneath a hotel's front lawn. The unsteady ground formed a cone-like mound. Ghosteater, a tattered demonic creature's blood-red eyes popped above ground in brown rags and had a gaping, bloody, scowled mouth, jagged, razor-sharp fangs, as well as talons for fingers. As it erupted from the hole, hellfire shot into the air, and it sealed. Four fiery balls streaked from its rag toward the sea.

Legends claimed whenever the living experienced a ghost infestation, Ghosteater would rise to cleanse the Earth. It hovered, and its eyes flashed like blinking lights above the fray. The ghosts scattered as Ghosteater's long, black tongue darted and lassoed a ghoul around the torso. It transformed the thing into light energy and slurped, making a hollow sound. The specters and people scattered in every direction from the Ghosteater, many of them rushed the divide, but it repelled them.

Mother Penny greeted the last few departing members at the church door. Monica and her family hung back in the aisle. Mother Penny beamed at them; Monica hugged her, and Dave shook her hand.

"What is your opinion, Dave?" Mother Penny asked.

"It was a unique experience, Mother Penny, but it grew on me."

"I understand. You may consider a change of address," Mother Penny said.

"We're experiencing a fair amount of hostility back home," Dave added.

"My son is moving from next door. The house will go on the market," Mother Penny said.

"It's a nice house. We'll check it out this weekend, Ma'am," Monica said.

"Moreland Hill, here we come," Gem whispered.

"How do you maintain the church without tithes?" Dave asked.

"I could not have done it without the generous people of Moreland Hill. Gem, how are your eyes?"

"They're fine, Ma'am, and my vision has expanded far and wide."

Mother Penny read the secret message and winked at Gem.

"Dave and Monica, could you lend me Gem for a second?"

Mother Penny did not wait for an answer as she led Gem into her office. Monica stepped out in the fresh night air and inhaled a mouthful.

Mother Penny had Gem perched on a chair in her office.

"The lion man was mean, and he could not hide from my eyes, even when he went invisible."

"I do not believe he will revisit here ever again. Gem, you gained some powers when the powers fixed your eyes. It will go away," Mother Penny said.

"I love it, Mother Penny. No one has mentioned Heaven has Black angels. I had to witness one for myself."

"When you move here, we will talk some more. Your parents are waiting," Mother Penny said.

"Check your skirt waist, I tore it trying to get your attention, but you were off the planet," Gem replied.

"I went home for a bit there, didn't I, dear?"

She and Gem giggled.

A crazy hurricane had visited Hallie's bedroom and left in a hurry. She balled in bed, her back to the door. Mother Penny knocked and barged in, but Hallie remained as she were.

"He told me he loves me," Hallie said.

"No man has ever said I hate you to a woman before he gets in her drawers," Mother Penny offered.

"So, a broken heart is the sum of it?" Hallie asked.

"Men do not romance trees in the forest. If you add the zeros, it gets no different or better. And you are giving away the handle for the blade."

"What do you mean, grandmother?"

"The blade is in your hands. You call the shots."

"They were all lies, Grandma, everything he said to me."

"If men did not lie to women and use the primal directive to procreate, it would have been extinct, exterminated and more extinction."

Mother Penny tapped Hallie's shoulder.

"You should watch a documentary on male animal species and their shenanigans to procreate. It's written in their DNA."

"You're saying he has a right to cheat on me?"

"Life is harsh and cruel, period. He hides his nectar under rocks and hard places. You're not the first to find out it's not so easy to ride off into the sunset, you and your first love."

Hallie turned her head, and her red eyes cut her grandmother.

"It's happened to many people, and you shouldn't let your first living experience define your future. You are not an ordinary Jane."

Mother Penny stood and turned at the door.

"Beware also of people smashing the glasses to gather the pieces. Find out what Faith, Irene and your boy are doing and take it out on Tilly. She's wrecking the damn town."

Mother Penny marched out, and the door slammed behind her.

Hallie jumped to a sitting position.

"Damn, she must be keeping it real. It sounds like you're disappointed in me, Grandmother."

Mother Penny's voice carried into the room.

"Tilly is wrecking the damn town, a prelude of what she had planned for Jamaica I said. And I did not touch your door," Mother Penny said.

"I guess I have a possessed door?"

"A lion scared your door. It's profoundly sad when friends and doors turn against a person."

"What lion friends?"

Chapter 61

Tilly relaxed in her macabre throne, perched high on a spiral staircase inside the hellish renovated Moreland Hill Tower. She wore a royal crimson high-collared gown, and Lonesome sat at her feet in regal mauve. Twenty helper ghosts growled at the foot of the stairs.

"Disperse to the streets and raise Hell," Tilly commanded.

The ghosts rushed away, and Tilly grinned at Lonesome.

"Boy, you remind me so much of your great-grandfather."

"Tell me about him?" Lonesome asked.

Tilly held her thumb and index finger less than an inch apart.

"Well, I was this away from devouring him when he ran," Tilly offered.

"Smart man," Lonesome said.

"What do you think of my army? By tomorrow, the politicians around here will grovel at my feet."

"Are you going into politics?"

"Before the week is over, I will run this Island, but, for now, I am going clubbing."

"Are you gonna leave me here?"

"Do you want to behold the things I do to men to keep my beauty?"

"I'm dead tired on my feet anyway," Lonesome said.

Tilly slapped his shoulder.

"You will be fine."

Chapter 62

Hallie sat on her bed, wrapped in a towel, drying her dreads. Sitira appeared and leaned on the door frame; her weather-beaten straw hat sat crooked on her head. She puffed on her unlit pipe and gave Hallie a cynical eye.

"What do you want, Miss Sitira? Are you coming back from Mo-Bay? And who told you to cut off the Gulf Marshal's hand?"

"Fingers, my girl, there is a difference. Yu lucky, a de little four eyes pickney save you," Sitira said.

"What are you talking about?" Hallie asked.

"The lion was gonna kill you, and de pickney bawl fe help and disturb me while I was loading the boy's high-grade Ganja in my pipe. You should back check my girl."

Hallie's eyes went white, and she jumped to her feet.

"Lord God, this is serious, mon."

"The African hit me with a dispersal spell. I found some of my missing parts near Little London," Sitira said.

"Something else entered the house, something powerful."

Hallie pulled on black pants.

"You should use wild-basil, fresh-cut and rat-ears bush wash your hair. A dem mi used to use, and mine is still full bodied to this day," Sitira said.

Sitira lifted her mane, showing it as proof to Hallie.

"I'm sending you on an errand to Bath Mountain," Hallie said.

Sitira nodded her head.

"Fly to Hay Hill Corner and fetch dead Loris' machete for me. Mi buried it pon de right bank, under a big greengage mango tree," Hallie said.

"My gal, yu a go butcher?"

"I'm expecting you back here in ten minutes or less."

"It's more than forty miles away," Sitira added.

"Slow and old," Hallie replied.

"Busted heart, Miss. I haven't aged a day since I died," Sitira shot back.

"Fetch the machete for me and go home and rest."

"Mi nuh have nuttin fe do wid neither Heaven nor Hell. Yu four eyes, broken heart wreck."

"Levitate the machete outta the bank. A dat yu fe go do," Hallie instructed.

"But see here. Pickney Gal, are you telling an old duppy whore, how to do things?

And how does your room smell like inna mi coffin so?"

"Vacate my room, duppy woman," Hallie said.

Sitira spiraled away in a white mist, and her ha-ha-ha echoed.

"Keep your duppy friends outta mi house at late hours," Mother Penny shouted.

"You wait till she comes back with de duppy machete. You'll see something," Hallie said.

Pots and pans banged for an answer.

"Yu going to have nightmares if you eat dis late," Mother Penny said.

"Yu think so?"

"Old funny woman."

"You sent a telegram. You should have used an email," Mother Penny continued.

"What's a gigabyte, Grandmother?"

"Go shove it up Tilly's butt. It sounds painful."

Hallie grinned ear to ear.

Chapter 63

Ranchie strutted from her apartment building in an elegant, black, strapped mini dress and as she strutted into the parking lot, ominous shadows darted about in the shadows.

An ear-splitting scream came from the dark end of the lot, and grotesque shadows raced inside the building.

The apartment corridors were empty, and the elevator pinged opened on the fifth floor. Fez, a balding man suffering from weight issues with a bad posture exited, wearing a neck brace. He hobbled away on crutches toward Queeny, a hot, younger woman, dressed for a night on the town

"Oh, my God. What happened to you?" Queeny gasped.

Fez grimaced in pain to gain sympathy and, somehow, his eyes appeared puffier.

"A moron on her phone tailgated me."

"My God. I'm sorry, Fez."

He piled on the sympathy-seeking grimaces, stepped off and stumbled on purpose. Queeny quickly reached out and steadied him.

"If I can be of any help, holla at me."

"Thanks, I'm coming from the hospital, the pain is still excruciating," Fez said.

A door banged and a blood-chilling scream followed.

"What the fuck?" Queeny asked.

She gawked over Fez's head. Her terrified eyes bulged, she kicked off her heels and raced back the way she came. Fez struggled to turn his neck, and instead, swung his body around as a terrified nude female ghost ran at him, roaring like a runaway train. Fez dropped his crutches and dashed down the hall. Silly things flash through a mind in grave danger, and Fez kept repeating.

"I should have checked if it were still a woman."

A refrain ran inside his head, but he figured he dared not slow to turn his head.

Fez zipped a few feet by his door, stopped and turned back, fumbling to open the door, as the ghost ducked behind him mumbling gibberish. Fez took her actions for aggression and bellowed to wake a cemetery. His keys fell, as he searched blindly for them. He fastened his eyes between the ghost's legs. The ghost tried to keep him in front, but Fez maneuvered away. The silliest thing ran through his mind. *I don't imagine I'm gonna live to tell what I'm seeing.*

He ripped the brace from around his neck in one swift motion. The ghost kept him in front, its eyes locked up the hall as the lights dimmed and the ghost screeched, "Save me, save me."

Ghosteater swooped, swiped at the specter and it pushed Fez forward. Ghosteater razor talons ripped Fez's stomach, and a pile of gut fell at his feet. The ghost bolted through the wall leaving Fez mesmerized by his intestines on his shoes and a horrific sound escaped his lips as he collapsed on the floor. Ghosteater hovered as Fez took his last breath and his soul rose from his corpse, bright as a star. Ghosteater pounced on the soul, and it squirmed between its talons. It overpowered the living flame and stuffed its gaping, red mouth. The socket's eye surveyed, a forked tongue darted, licking its lips as it blasted away.

Chemmie and his partner Juan Jingles, another tattooed punk, cooked crack in his apartment at the other end of Fez's floor. They stirred steaming pots on the stove and blasted loud music from the living room. Crack packages and some large caliber guns sat on the kitchen counter under a white Virgin Mary holding a black baby Jesus. Incense and votive candles burned around the kitchen in expensive candle holders.

A hot female, sand and seaweed covered spook, walked in quietly like a moth on wings and approached the men. Her head leaned inquisitively, as if her eyes were peeking around corners and the face turned into meanness, as she gawked into the boiling pots. The men aimed their guns, but the spook appeared to them as the beautiful woman she was when alive.

"Why blast such a hot woman in a hasty rush on a dry night?" Chemmie mumbled.

The spook smiled sweetly, but she had forgotten her teeth, except for four, back on the sea bed.

"Is it crack?"

"Bitch, are you blind?" Chemmie asked.

"I sailed from Haiti in a boat, and the men abused me until I had to jump to my death for relief. My crackhead brother could not make the trip," It said.

The ghost advanced on the men. They opened fire, and water, sand and a beer can pour from the bullet holes. The ghost's arms twirled like a dancer, froze and levitated both punks in horizontal positions. They hollered in fear as a pot of crack sailed and hovered over Chemmie's mouth. He tried to close his mouth, but invisible forces pried it back open. The pot emptied the boiling liquid in his mouth. Chemmie contorted, twitched and made an ugly sound as he crashed to the floor, dead.

"No, too easy." the ghost said.

The spook blew an arctic blast in the pot, force-fed the contents to Juan Jingles until he burped and shot to a sitting position. His eyes bulged and the right one popped loud as a balloon. He screamed before his left eye burst, and he twitched in silence until his head cracked open. Bloody bits stuck to the kitchen walls and fixtures.

"More pleasing," the ghost added.

Hot Spook picked up a magazine and fanned, plopped on the living room sofa and zapped the stereo into silence. It stretched out, the back of a hand resting on her forehead.

"Shit, I may be coming down with something," it said.

CHAPTER 64

Tilly moseyed onto a packed Addiss nightclub dance floor, a fresh wind on a still, hot night. Her red, one-piece mini left nothing to the imagination.

She deep kissed an awestruck hot chick. A tall, large hand lesbian grabbed Tilly's business and almost lifted her out of her shoes. Tilly winked at her, danced dirty on a dude's butt and patrons pushed spiked champagne glasses and bottles in her face. She gulped from flutes and bottles as the tall lesbian lifted her, and Tilly locked her legs around the woman's waist. She kissed Tilly until eternity, and another purple-haired woman poured rainbow pills into a champagne bottle and placed it in her hand. Tilly gulped the spiked champagne and jumped from the tall lesbian's arms.

"Mr. DJ- spin some dancehall music," Tilly said.

The DJ spun the latest hits, and Tilly outdanced the house. The lesbians' fraternity formed a tight circle around Tilly.

"Sorry, girls, I am an iron and fire-rod type woman," Tilly said.

She led two big, rough men, Clive and Nelson, to a side table.

"What a fucking waste," a woman said.

The tall lesbian gulped her champagne from the bottle. Her jealous eyes fastened on Tilly, and she flashed the men a finger as a last envious act. Tilly plopped on Clive's lap and placed her feet on Nelson's, gulping from her bottle.

Nelson handed a package to Tilly.

"What is this?"

"It's cool people's high."

"Can I do it in here?"

"Oh, yeah."

"Are you guys the police?"

"Hell no," Clive said.

"I do not want to go to jail."

They grinned in Tilly's face as she pointed to an exit.

"What is behind the door?" Tilly asked.

"An alley."

"It's always comfortable outside, and the sky is my roof."

"Let's go," Nelson said.

A dark cloud slid over the moon, and ominous shadows covered Clive as he kissed Tilly against a wall. Nelson had a hand deep inside her bosom. Tilly lifted both men by their lapels and transformed into an ugly, skeletal, bald, seven-foot-tall Hell creature. The men bellowed in fear, and Tilly blew arctic breath into their faces and exposed their life-force as warm golden halo radiating around their heads. Flames streamed from Tilly's mouth, fed on the men's halos and flew back into her nostrils. She absorbed their essences until the burned carcasses crumbled into her hands. The bodies broke into black dust at her feet. She inhaled and savored as if she'd experienced a sexual moment.

Her two shoulder blades showed stumps and scars as if a sharp instrument had hacked off her wings. She reverted to her human persona, dressed in a low-cut red evening dress, pulled it up enough to hide her aroused nipples as she hurried away in the dark.

Chapter 65

Hallie stood under a tree in the darkness, dressed in black and the gleaming machete in her hand emitted a ghoulish glow. She stuck the weapon under her hood and hurried away.

Two spaced-out, pale-yellow street lamps fought the darkness in the alley like stubborn fighters not giving ground. Rats and roaches foraged in the glow between the next lamppost a hundred yards away and a swath of darkness between the two. Powerful headlights drove the rodents and insects scurrying into crevices. A car stopped, two men hurried to the trunk, fetched a wrapped body and slung it in the trash.

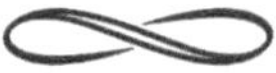

Hallie ran and skipped between the bumper-to-bumper traffic on Norman Manley Boulevard.

The evil phenomenon had ground the town's transportation to a crawl, and nerves were on edge. Emergency vehicles wailed in the streets, going nowhere.

A fire truck tried to enter the dark zone, but hit an iron wall and the crew abandoned the vehicle.

Beeps and honks from angry motorists filled the night.

"What's going on? Why have the police blocked off the street?" a motorist asked.

"Total blackout, they say."

"It's a fire. It was on the news," another said.

Police officers directed traffic on the chaotic streets. Two men who dumped the body in in the alley whistled at Hallie from their car.

"Yow, girl, come ride wid wi nuh?"

Hallie gave the men an eye and whipped her head away. She missed a step, and her expression changed to malice. She turned and scrutinized the men. The driver flung his door open, the passenger followed him and they ran to the nearest police officer.

"Officer, we should not have done it. We raped and killed a girl and dumped her body in a trash can in Bread Lane," the older man said.

"We deserve the gallows, Sir, for what we did to the poor girl. We'll show you where we dumped her body, Sir," the second man said. "And it's not our first kill, either."

The police officers appeared lost for words and were unsure if the men were mischief-makers.

"Cuff them, Officer. The victim is Jennie Johnson, the missing schoolgirl," Hallie said.

The men assumed the position, and the officers cuffed them.

Hallie raced into an alley in a foul mood and cast a giant white shadow against the buildings from a naked lamppost bulb.

The clenched fists, chiseled jaw and the long, purposeful strides said tons to any observers.

Chapter 66

Thirty people attended a beach party a hundred yards from the possessed zone and had split into discussion groups after a few drinks. A woman stomped sand off her slippers and gazed about several times, uncomfortable about the mysterious phenomenon up the road.

"A friend called and said she heard strange, unnatural sounds and screams outside her hotel room, but something cut the call," the woman said.

"An apartment fire, they say," a man said.

A gentle wave licked the shore, and moonlight spread a zillion diamonds on the water, too light to sink.

The fixtures overturned coming from the street side, and overturned furniture crashed as if runaway animals ran through them. A woman screamed, and it gurgled inside her throat.

"Correr."

"Correr."

"Mas Rapido."

"Mas Rapido Tortuga," the ghosts cried.

Dishes and pans crashed, and drinks spilled. People jumped to their feet and locked their eyes in the direction of the commotions. The old Spanish galleon crew Tilly had murdered centuries ago charged through the party set in the nude, dove into the water and the Ghosteater followed.

People scattered for their lives, but those that destiny selected from the womb as stragglers and fodders or for others to learn lessons from their actions. Missed a step, gawked too long, and the charging Ghosteater skewered a young couple each on a talon. It held them high like a fork and waited for their souls to exit their bodies.

Back in the dark zone, the ethereal army crashed through glass windows and doors. They invaded hotels and apartments, thick as marauding bugs. Screams, shouts and yells overpowered the night as terrified people fled for their lives.

A lingerie-clad woman jumped from a fourth-floor balcony into a hotel pool. Her heavier male companion jumped, and she screamed at his trajectory. He crashed on the concrete, shattered his legs, and two ghosts jumped from the balcony at him as he riddled in pain on his back. She vacated the pool and raced away over a hedge grow.

Roy and Bev, a young couple, ran while screaming along the hotel corridor from modern and ancient specters.

The Ghosteater flew from an apartment, and in an instant, the hunters became the prey.

An old British seventeenth-century army corporal caught Roy and jumped into his arms for protection from the Ghosteater. Roy tried to dump him, but the corporal clung to his neck.

"Run through the wall, bloke. Run through the bloody wall," The ghost said.

"You run into the fucking wall and take me with you," Roy said.

"I cannot concentrate. You, me, the bloody same, different, innit?"

Another ghost hid behind Bev in terror. Ghosteater impaled them both, lifted them on a taloned.

"Bloke I am riding your back, you can run through the wall, do it." The corporal said.

A second ghost hid behind Bev in terror. Ghosteater impaled them both, lifted them on a taloned hand, slurped the spirit and licked its lips, waiting for Bev's soul. Roy took aim and charged through the wall, carrying the corporal clinging to his neck.

Fire thundered in Chemmie's kitchen and engulfed the block. The west wing collapsed, and the flames leaped into the night.

Apparitions raced from the burning building, and the relentless Ghosteater pursued. A policewoman led a group of people in the Ghosteater's wake.

"Let's go. It's safe behind the thing, but don't get too close," she said.

"Suppose it turns?" a man asked.

"Wait and shake its hand," a woman answered sarcastically.

Chapter 67

Lonesome sat on Tilly's throne, a lonely king waiting on his queen and subjects. He sprawled, changed to a stiff-backed posture, leaned forward and placed his elbows on the armrest.

"Take him to the pit," he commanded.

Greg's image flashed across his mind. He had drifted from his memory, and it was not on him. Tilly must have taken away his empathy.

Ghosts rushed through the throne room's doors and locked them. *From whom were they running?* They tried to climb the stairs to the throne, but an invisible wall stopped them.

"She protected me. She loves me. Maybe the ghosts will obey me my commands?" Lonesome asked himself.

He took back his position on the throne.

"Dance for me, my subjects," Lonesome said.

The ghosts danced the tango, quadrille, swing, ballroom, belly, ska, dancehall and hip-hop. Many were human-like as if they'd died yesterday, and others were skeleton bones covered in period rags. Lonesome pointed out the putrid, rotting flesh ghosts.

"Go hunt and kill people."

The tattered-flesh ghosts shuffled away and left the hot women ghosts; his mind drifted, and he caught himself unashamed. Someone and a specter must have had a thing somewhere, sometime?

He ambled over to a window and gazed out on Negril. The darkness circled a mile around the towers, but the remaining sections had lights. Businesses flourished as usual, and Tilly was out there having fun. He remembered his hotel was situated north of the towers.

"I hoped the ghosts ran into the bitches who'd ridiculed Greg and me. They should pay."

He turned to the ghosts.

"Fly over to the Buccaneer Palace and bring me some young, hot tourist women."

The undead army hurried away.

"Wait a minute." He pointed out the six most attractive ghosts. "I want you to stay here and guard the palace."

The others raced through the walls, and Lonesome leered at the sexy women ghosts.

Chapter 68

Ranchie arrived at Club Addiss four miles from the dark zone to vociferous adulations as she joined the throng on the dance floor. She danced over to the bar, shouting above the music, "Jerry, run the Crystal until I say stop."

Inebriated patrons exploded joyously. Ranchie whined and bumped across the dance floor, exalted to her core. She considered it her farewell party and tomorrow, she'd fly to Europe. When she called Gustav, the delight in the man's voice cracked her LCD screen. Unbeknownst to her friends, they were in the middle of her farewell celebration.

After thirty minutes of entertainment, Ranchie paid her bill and bolted. She ran into a warm, pleasant night and Ronah and Shelia, two co-workers, outside.

"How's the crowd?" Ronah asked.

"It has played out and dropped flat."

"Let's hit Hurricane Alley. Rich man's money is burning their pocket," Shelia said.

"I'm as mellow as a full moon. I'm doing someone I fancy for nothing tonight, wet as the ocean," Ronah said and giggled.

"Is free sex legal?" Shelia asked.

"Damn. Mellow has lost its way," Ranchie said.

"Crazy is more like it," Shelia said.

"You're telling me. Even if I wanted to, I can't do it for fun sometimes?" Ronah asked.

"Do banks add freebies to accounts?" Ranchie asked.

"I do my child's father for pure joy. I'm not a machine. And I'm taking charge and nailing a man without mercy tonight," Ronah added.

"My freebie was a deacon and my mom's husband. I seduced him and said he raped me," Ranchie confessed

"You're joking, right, Ranchie?" Ronah asked.

"I'm not laughing."

"Why did you do it?" Shelia asked.

"I did it because I could, but I didn't figure pregnancy in the equation."

"Where is he now?"

"He ran away."

"Jesus Christ, don't your conscience prick you?" Shelia asked.

"No, it doesn't. I never grew one," Ranchie said.

"You're a fool. Didn't you know your mother has powers," Ronah said.

"I didn't care."

Ronah and Shelia gawked at Ranchie in disgust.

"Are you riding or what?" Ranchie asked.

"You go ahead, Ranchie. I'm a whore, not an evil motherfucker. When your judgment comes, mi nuh want deh near yu," Shelia said.

Ronah hopped into the car and Ranchie sped away; her laughter hung in the hot night air.

Chapter 69

Hallie approached Tilly's victims' remains gingerly in the dimly lit alley. The dull thump of the music from inside the club rattled a piece of metal on the roof. She unshielded her supernatural machete, stirred the ashes, sniffed the air and tramped away.

Her mind raced over to Steve and took a seat. What was he doing, and in the company of whom? Iced water ran through her veins, dumping on her soul and freezing it. She lost focus and stumbled at the edge of the abyss.

A scraggy, homeless man jumped from the dark, wielding a stick and swung. She blocked him, and her blade sliced through the man's weapon.

He lunged at her, the broken piece in his hand. She sidestepped, and the man crashed into the wall. Hallie used the blade's flat, slapped the man and dazed him, but a second man sprung from the shadows, tackled, and pinned her to the ground.

"Get off me," Hallie shouted.

"Shut yu mouth, gal, before mi cut yu."

He pried the machete from her hand, and she didn't resist. It flamed and consumed his body in seconds.

"It wasn't your old, everyday blade," Hallie scoffed, looking at his remains.

The machete jumped back in her hand. She slapped the first man on his head against the wall, knocking him unconscious.

"If I don't clean Steve from my mind and focus, someone will kill me. How could I let crazy people jump me?" Hallie said aloud.

Two officers, male and female, patrolled the alley on foot. They stopped under a pale bulb of a hole-in-the-wall joint.

"Maragh, let's check out what's going on inside here," the man said.

"Hell no. I'm not going in there."

"Are you scared of nudity, Maragh?"

"Fuck you, gwan if yu want," Maragh said.

"Hold my gun."

He handed his AR-15 to her and dived through the dimly lit door. Maragh strode away as Hallie hurried by the club.

"Young lady, what're you doing out here this late?" the female officer asked.

A running Hallie ignored her.

"Stop. I'm talking to you."

Hallie ducked around an old car under a tree.

"Homeless men and a cop, damn. I'm a dumb broken old relic at sixteen," Hallie said.

"You, behind the car. I hope you're not going into that dump to prostitute yourself."

The policewoman's flashlight beam circled the car but found no one.

CHAPTER 70

Club Hurricane was an upscale joint; it masked a laid-back ambiance and sophisticated clientele, but the relaxed setting disguised a raw, deadly underbelly. The debauchery usually ran as frequently as spilled drinks.

Tilly leaned against the bar, having a drink in the company of two fortyish men, Dean and Wings, fixtures around Negril's night scene. The drop-dead beautiful, fresh, strange woman puzzled them, and try as they may, they failed to place her accent. It sounded ancient and country, but positively Jamaican. When Dean was about ten, he used to run errands for a sweet old white lady named Miss Minnie. She lived in a large old house near the Prospect Estate. Tilly had the same distinct old-world accent mixed up in Jamaican rhythms and rum as Miss Minnie did.

Tilly perched on a stool, her legs crossed and her mini riding high. Dean tucked his eyes under her skirt without pretense.

Tilly's eyes lit up.

"If you plan a visit, we are open to visitors," Tilly said.

"How soon is soon enough?" Dean asked.

Tilly pulled him to her and kissed him before turning to Wings.

"Boy, will you grab something with those large hands?"

"My car is out back," Wings said.

"Get me something to drink and come show me what you offer."

"Bartender, a bottle of white rum, please."

Wings led Tilly onto the dance floor. What an excellent woman, and he did not have to drug her. It dullened some of the excitement, but he wasn't gonna pull his hair out over it.

Chapter 71

Mother Penny's psyche felt cleansed and rejuvenated after the service. She had cleaned up the kitchen, headed towards her bedroom and stopped in between like a brainstorm hit her. Hallie's power could take care of the she-devil without a doubt; nothing to worry about there. She had welded those incredible powers and had confidence in their abilities. However, she still felt something slightly off and riding her like one of those compelling feelings that forced people to glance over their shoulders.

She gathered herself, entered her bedroom and jumped back in fright as if she had hit a dangerous mystical wall. She moved forward tentatively, sniffing around the room. Sanga's opened diary sat on the bed; the cross was missing, and the empty string swung back and forth. The legend said the journal had filtered through her family from one generation to another and stayed permanently from the day Sanga and Tilly had disappeared.

In fact, folklore claimed her church stood on the spot where the cabin of her great-great-grandmother, Sanga's last wife, once stood. How many greats should she use? The lovesick child had a handle on everything modern. She was also the fifth healer named Penny in the family and the last. Mother Penny smiled and hoped the tall girl did not call her kid Sashamika or a similar crap. She had zapped Ranchie the morning on her way to Montego Bay sixteen years ago. If the girl had walked over semen that morning, she would have gotten pregnant. Poor Charles, Mother Penny sighed in retrospect, how one thing always leads to another.

They had never hidden their trade paraphernalia from the family, but only the chosen amongst them could access the powers. The diary's pages flipped in her hand and stopped on a newly written page. As she read, her eyes bulged and a hand shot to her mouth.

"Oh, my God, no"

Mother Penny dug for a slender object wrapped in white cloth from a drawer and ran from the room in deep distress.

A half-hour later, a cab pulled up at the Addiss Night Club, and Mother Penny bolted through the club's door, the fear of death plastered on her face. She charged onto the dance floor, peeking into faces and two large security men accosted her. A glare from her backed them off.

"Has anyone seen Ranchie?" Mother Penny bellowed.

The booming music drowned her voice. She stabbed a mean finger at the DJ booth, and the music screeched to a stop.

"Has anyone seen Ranchie? And I don't want to ask again."

"I believe she went to the Hurricane Alley, Ma'am," Shelia said.

Chapter 72

Wings kissed Tilly against Dean's car, parked away from the others in the dark. Dean lit a joint and blew smoke in the air. Tilly transformed into the Hell monster, hoisted the men, and they bellowed, kicking the air.

"Hello, Tilly Whitelock."

Tilly spoke in a deep, demonic voice. "I have been expecting you, Hallie."

"You've erred. You should've run back to Hell and hide."

Tilly laughed.

"Are you coming clean before you die, Sanga's little grand bitch? He scattered his dust on yonder wind ages ago to spite me."

"The wind will not weep for Tilly, and you've defecated on my town," Hallie said.

Tilly tied the men into an energy mesh and dumped them beside the car.

"I'll be right back, fellows."

Tilly turned, shooting crimson fire.

Hallie transformed into pure white energy and returned Tilly's flame twice as hot. Tilly generated a whirlwind and dispersed the fire.

"Young pup," Tilly said.

"Tilly Whitelock, you're a dinosaur."

Hallie generated a wide swath of white holy fire, engulfed Tilly and slammed her against a wall. The beast growled and shot crimson flames back at Hallie.

Hallie's white energy changed Tilly's crimson flames to pure white, drove it back as a living thing in her face and knocked her flat on the pavement. Tilly's painful howls had the dead trembling in their graves for miles. She ascended like a rocket, and Hallie zoomed after her as pure white energy. Tilly turned mid-air and flew back at Hallie in an ugly, monstrous, fiery apparition. The young white lighter held her ground and wrapped Tilly in white-hot holy flames. Tilly roared in agony as Hallie's powers overwhelmed her, and she tried to fly away. Hallie reeled her back like a monster howling on a line and teetered. Tilly thrashed across the sky in anguish.

Hallie rose above her, pouring fire into her mouth until a furnace burned inside Tilly. They dropped back on the concrete, cracked it and Hallie's power beat Tilly to her knees. The white flames spread in Tilly's mouth as broad as Hell.

Chapter 73

Chaos reigned inside the Moreland Hill Towers, and the glowing ghosts broke out into flames, ran into each other and slammed into walls. The building creaked and rocked, and Lonesome's throne vibrated as if it were about to break apart. He grabbed the armrests, riding a runaway roller coaster as the six nude female ghosts he ogled scattered in flames.

The ghosts on the streets caught fire, and the street lamps relit. Ghosteater zipped back and forth, frustrated, sniffed around bushes, found nothing and blasted away in a puff.

Tilly howled on her knees in the parking lot as Hallie's white flames bubbled like a caldron inside her mouth. The fire stream died as if Hallie's power had run dry. She clenched and unclenched her fists, but they fired blanks. Tilly recovered first, reverted to her human persona and sneered at a shocked Hallie.

"A Neutralizer has unknowingly entered the fray, wench. Do you even know about them yet?"

The ghosts in the dark zone had disappeared as if they had gone into the next dimension. After a few seconds, they reappeared meaner than when they left. The Ghosteater's rags exploded and popped as it returned. The specters bolted for cover, and a short, stocky ghost dove underground. The Ghosteater dove after it and popped back up, juggling a squirming ghost on its talons. The lights dimmed, and the streets twisted back to Hell's backyard.

Tilly fly kicked Hallie and slammed her against a wall.

"Your Foreseer slept on the job. How come she did not destroy the Neutralizer? Oh, well, let us not disappoint them," Tilly said.

Tilly slammed Hallie to the ground. Hallie leaped, jabbed her a left, stepped and landed a nasty right uppercut. Tilly backed away, evaded a sidekick and grabbed Hallie's foot.

Hallie head-butted her from the ground like a Jack-in-the-box. They tussled against the wall, and she straddled Tilly's shoulders, held a fistful of hair and hammered Tilly's face.

Tilly raced backward and slammed her against the wall, knocking the wind out of her. She pounded Hallie against the wall and bloodied her face. Hallie got a double headbutt in, pulled her machete and slashed a deep gash across Tilly's face. It oozed black matter instead of blood, and the relentless assault backed Tilly up.

As a gash closed, the netherworld weapon opened a new one, and Hallie jumped high, hacked for the kill, and Tilly caught the blade between her palms over her head. They tugged for the machete into a stalemate.

Chapter 74

Ranchie and Ronah had arrived in the club during the fight and danced across Club Hurricane's dance floor, guzzling from champagne bottles held high above their heads. A cheering gallery made a ring around them. Ranchie danced the circle, pouring champagne into glasses from two large bottles until they ran out. Six bottles of champagne sat in the center of the floor in a large ice tub. Ranchie picked up two fresh bottles, not knowing or caring that her daughter fought for her life yards away. Mother Penny barged through the patrons and accosted her. Ranchie met her aggressively.

"You couldn't be searching for me, woman," Ranchie declared.

"You have got to go now, Ranchie," Mother Penny demanded.

Ranchie stared at her scornfully.

"You came in here spewing your Christian bullshit? Leave me alone."

"Listen, Ranchie—"

"I don't want to. I'm a whore. Deal with it."

Ranchie wheeled away and mocked Mother Penny, twerking.

Tilly pulled the machete away from Hallie, cornered her and swung. Hallie ducked and lifted a massive rock, and Tilly chopped it in two.

"Say goodbye before you even arrive, dear."

"What's going on here?" Officer Maragh asked from behind the fighters.

Tilly turned in one swift motion and flung the machete at the officer.

"No," Hallie shouted.

The glowing blade stopped inches from Maragh's midsection and hung suspended. Her gun fell from her hand, her knees gave way and she fell into a bungle from shock.

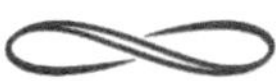

Mother Penny chased and placed a hand on Ranchie's shoulder from behind inside the club.

"Woman, leave me the fuck alone," Ranchie snapped.

"Please, your daughter's life is in danger."

"Pissing her out doesn't make her my child. Your husband never paid me for the one-day stand, either."

"Ranchie, please."

"Fuck you."

Ranchie wheeled away. Mother Penny pulled the knife Sanga had used to skin Tilly, from the cloth. She rammed it between Ranchie's shoulders, placed an arm around her neck, and stabbed her rapidly in her bosom. Ranchie's last scream stuck in her throat as she collapsed at Mother Penny's feet, jerked a few times and died.

The screaming patrons raced for the exits, and the doors slammed shut. Mother Penny waved her knife over Ranchie's body and turned it into spiraled dust.

"Heathens. Those who have eyes had seen, and those who have mouths shall speaketh not."

Mother Penny turned away from her petrified audience, and the doors banged open. She stopped at the door and turned.

"Did I mention how genitals will rot and drop? If I heard a whisper of what happened here tonight?"

A woman whimpered, and a man grabbed his business.

Tilly had beaten Hallie by a long arm, snatched Maragh's fallen rifle and fired point-blank. Hallie flipped away under fire, crashed into the wall and her blade flew back into her hand.

Tilly fired, and Hallie used the blade to block the bullets. Her power surged back, transforming her arms into pure white light. The machete shot holy fire and twisted the gun barrel in Tilly's hand as she reverted to the beast.

The white flames streamed into Tilly's mouth as if Hallie wanted to empty the source. Tilly expelled crimson fire and crashed Hallie against the wall. She pounced like a dragon, poured red flames into Hallie's eyes and Hallie screamed and thrashed on the ground in pain. Songeeta appeared behind Tilly, holding two eggs in her hands unseen by the fighters.

"Child, it's impossible to defeat me." Tilly boasted.

Tilly laughed as she poured crimson fire over Hallie's head oblivious of Songeeta.

"Misses Tilly, I brought back your eggs," Songeeta shouted.

Tilly turned, her mouth opened and froze for a beat.

"Sanga," Tilly yelled.

Songeeta flung the eggs in Tilly's face as she transformed into a piercing light and streaked into Tilly's opened mouth.

"Nooooo," Tilly hollered.

Tilly's stomach glowed translucent red flames from the inverted cross. The occult writings peeled from the shaft and dispersed inside Tilly's stomach. Hallie rose in pure white energy. The grooves and letters raced through Tilly's translucent body as if driven by a ten-horse-powered pump.

Tilly wallowed, screamed and peeled paint from the nearby buildings.

The plus sign from the cross appeared on Tilly's forehead, red like an opened wound and Hallie poured holy fire in the opening. Red flames turned white, raced through Tilly's stomach and liquefied. Tilly rose, wobbled and dropped back to her knees.

Hallie concentrated her holy fire assault on the opening in Tilly's forehead. Tilly pushed her hand through her stomach wall, pulled the hot cross out and tossed it along the ground.

Sitira appeared, picked up the cross, flung it like a flying spear into Tilly's forehead and buried it up to the arms. Sitira used the machete and nailed the cross home in Tilly's head to the hilt. Hallie's holy fire hammered her forehead until the last bit of cross disappeared inside her brain. Tilly screamed on her knees and held her face skyward. Hallie and Sitira covered their ears from the sonic sound as time stood still and silenced the agonizing screams.

Tilly's shrieks beamed from her mouth like a soundless streaming vapor, and she exploded into a million fiery bits. The cross dropped at Hallie's feet, and a crimson whirlwind gathered Tilly and Songeeta's marble-sized remains and burrowed into the earth.

Wings and Dean squirmed as the restraint holding them disappeared. Hallie gave the men dirty eyes. "Miss Sitira, they're yours," Hallie said.

Sitira chopped the men into bits gleefully and left bloody pieces on the ground.

Officer Maragh moaned and stirred. Hallie helped her to her feet.

"Who're you?"

"I'm Mother Penny's granddaughter, and you can stop blaming yourself for not conceiving."

A surprised Maragh backed away.

"It has nothing to do with the abortion you had back in your teens. It's your husband and his zero sperm count."

"Yu Obeah, right?" Maragh asked.

"Hell no, Obeah hides when I'm in town. Did strange things happen here tonight?"

The damaged gun flew into Maragh's hands, repaired.

"Not from where I am."

"Bring your husband to Mother Penny's church. Tell him it's for you. He won't know we fixed him," Hallie said.

"Are you sure I'm not damaged?"

"You're ready to go, but your flowers need pollination."

Maragh held her stomach and smiled joyfully for the first time in ages.

"How old are you?"

"Officer Maragh, you still think I was here?"

Hallie transformed into white energy, reverted to herself and hurried away. Maragh stared after her in total shock, and her knees could not cope. She leaned against the wall for support.

"Yu should be glad I never went off to Heaven, eh? Who woulda help you defeat de whichy?" Sitira asked.

"Sitira, you're not going near Heaven, but thanks," Hallie replied.

Sitira nickered like a horse.

"Did the police si me chop de boys dem, Hallie?"

"Wat, yu fraid a jail?"

"Tell her it was I who stopped the machete from impaling her. Hey, did you sense a presence while you were fighting?" Sitira asked.

"You sensed it too? It felt like a curious little boy's eyes were on us."

"Hallie, you have a shadow stalker. You're kinda sexy anyway," Sitira said.

"Duppy woman, are you blind? I'm a fifteen on the ten-point sexiness scale."

"Sexiness a spillover, eh?"

Hallie bumped her fist.

Sitira glanced about curiously.

"Who could it be? It felt like when the boys used to watch us bathe in the river back in the days."

"I didn't even know the river ran there when you were alive."

"I used to enjoy their eyes, mon."

"Get away from beside me, yu sick ass ghost," Hallie said.

"Call me ghost again if you think yu bac…"

Tilly's spell on the Moreland Hill Towers and Negril broke. The ghosts burned in the streets, flaming as if someone had set controlled fires in certain spots. The building shuddered as the throne crumbled and caught fire. Lonesome ran, but the living flames cornered him and burned him into black ash. Out in the streets, the nightmare facade lifted, and in seconds, the landscape reverted to normal, except for the blackened apartment buildings and the bodies.

Chapter 75

A night later, Steve had parked his car under a large Poinciana tree, and fallen petals made a cluster on the hood and windscreen. The vehicle vibrated as if the shocks were alive as Steve, Irene and Faith tangled limbs into limbs in a contorted tango.

Hallie crept up to the car in the dark and knocked on the window. Bustles and shuffles ensued inside. Hallie yanked the door open, her fists clenched, and her face calmed as a mirror.

A perturbed Mother Penny watched Hallie rage from the shadows.

"Please do not do it. Please, Hallie," Mother Penny said."

"Hallie, it's not what you think," Steve said.

"Irene, catch you and Faith in school tomorrow. Have a lovely night, Steve," Hallie said.

She slammed the door and strolled away. Mother Penny sighed, a happy woman.

"Yes, you are my girl."

The second night after Tilly's death, Hallie and Mother Penny visited the buried gold. The Sentinels' ghosts stumbled about aimlessly, and many of them had lost their weapons.

"What're we gonna do about them, grandmother?"

"Their shift has ended."

Hallie fired a portal, the ghosts dived in the rotating portal, and it disappeared, popping like an elephant walking on dry wood.

"Are we going to leave it out here?" Mother Penny asked.

"I don't want to keep coming out here and get cuts and bruises."

"Well damn, Missis Queen Ma'am. Pull twelve bars, we have the architect to advance and a rent-a-dread Orange Bay house to buy. Gem and her lovely parents need a home."

"Let's take it all home tonight, Grandma. I'm through dancing mosquitoes and the bugs' tango."

"Beneath the church will do."

"Uncle Jeno's chest is lofty. His head gonna touch dust in Saturn's rings soon," Hallie said.

"If it will get him away from next door, it's good."

Hallie worked her arms like a conductor, and tons of gold rose from the hole in the ground, spinning inside a white energy field.

"Grandmother, help me make it invisible."

"My power is not strong enough," Mother Penny said.

"Flip the cross around your neck and grab my hand," Hallie replied.

Mother Penny pulled the glowing cross from under her shirt, upturned it on the string around her neck and it glowed. She held Hallie's hand, as they teleported into the sphere, sat on the gold bars and the sphere went invisible.

"I hope Sitira nuh steal and sell the bars, one at a time."

"Sitira's grave is under the house, Grandma, not the church. We have over three hundred million dollars in gold bars."

"Do you expect an old, poor ass Mother to comprehend such figures? What did the thieving chatamouth duppy gal tell yu?"

"I'm losing my concentration, Grandma."

CHAPTER 76

Hallie sat at a window seat on a speeding bus, sleeping on Mother Penny's shoulder on a bright sunny morning. Mother Penny clutched a heavy tote bag on her lap and adjusted the weight as her eyes roamed the lush Jamaican countryside. Hallie watched Wings and Dean in her mind's eye dropping drugs in women's drinks, kidnapping and raping them. Mother Penny spotted Hallie on her shoulder.

"Evil things."

Hallie cuddled up to her.

An hour later, Mother Penny and Hallie carried the bag between them in the upscale shopping center at Montego Bay Freeport. They located Obie's Gold and Diamond store and sat on a bench waiting for the store to open. Obie, a fifty-year-old greedy, beady, callous man, shuffled up to a rear service door and slipped in like a fugitive in his own business place. It took him fifteen minutes to open the front door. Mother Penny and Hallie entered ahead of his staff.

Tourists from the two giant cruise ships docked in the harbor waded through the shopping center in their colorful vacation-best like reef fishes.

Hallie and Mother Penny were the only two customers in Obie's shop. If Obie had smarts, he would ask why his employees were not at work yet, and cruise ships were in the harbor.

Mother Penny opened the bag on the counter. Obie's eyes brightened like nuclear furnaces, and they could hardly conceal his intentions.

"Come to my office, please."

Mother Penny sat across from Obie. Hallie stood beside Mother Penny.

"Who sent you here?"

"Are we in the wrong place?" Mother Penny asked.

"No, you're not."

"Gold was 1,233 US dollars an ounce this morning. I am selling you mine at one thousand an ounce," Mother Penny said.

"I'm thinking more in the range—"

"My grandmother hates to repeat herself."

Obie placed a gold bar on a scale.

Mother Penny and Hallie exited Obie's store, arm in arm, as tourists flooded through the door. Obie spied on the women through the window while he spoke on his phone. In his greed, he failed to realize neither customers nor his staff had entered his store while the two women did their business.

"Yeah, the wrapped-head woman in white and the girl? Okay. Take your twenty percent and bring back my money. Hey, Piece-a-man, make sure they take you to where they got the Spanish gold from before you dust them."

He listened and changed the phone to his left ear.

"Yeah, I suspect they've many more where these came from, mon."

Hallie and Mother Penny window-shopped, and the visitors admired her traditional dress and asked to take selfies.

A sweet, middle-aged, upper-class woman wrapped Hallie's long dreads around her neck as her husband snapped away. Their eyes said they had never socialized or spoken to Black people—unless they counted on TV.

Mother Penny and Hallie said their goodbyes, escaped the photo ops and walked the quieter shops.

"It will be a five thousand seat temple, healing center, and shelter for abused women and children," Mother Penny said.

"A school, two hundred beds and we're going viral too."

"What are we going to do with pennies?"

Hallie laughed and glanced back at the two men trailing them. Piece-a-man came up to about five feet short, thus his alias. On gigs, he usually shot his victims before they got any ideas.

"Grandmother, if we cure cancer, diabetes and AIDS, the large pharmaceutical companies will come for us."

"Yes, finally, evil people are coming to die," Sitira said.

"What're you doing here, Miss Sitira?" Mother Penny asked.

"Watching your backs."

"We can watch our backs," Mother Penny said.

"I don't want to repeat what the tall guy following you is planning for an old tree trunk like you, but poor Hallie deserves better."

"We got them covered."

"Yes, and nothing for me. I need to do those two murderers, please."

"Okay, they have murdered enough. Take them back to the gold buyer and do your thing before him. If he remains in business, we should not have any more problems where he was concerned," Mother Penny said.

When Sitira did not answer, Hallie turned and saw the two men pitched backward as though someone invisible had pulled them by their hands back the way they had come.

"I'm not doing the college thingy, Grandma."

"With your penchant for expensive things, you will need decent jobs."

Hallie eyed Mother Penny.

"One fine day, you will sweat away your holy fire abilities and become an ugly, old Obeah Mother," Mother Penny said.

"I can abstain," Hallie replied.

"Do not even try. You are going to college. I said the same thing to my mom."

Mother Penny glanced at Hallie and smiled mysteriously.

"Your bloodline enhanced your brain, and hotness travels below your belt. Let me say this in your peer's language. You're gonna be one hot-ass love fe dweet, bitch."

"Grandmother."

"Promise me you will abstain until you graduate college."

"I promise."

"My husband is coming home after sixteen long years in the wilderness."

"Where is he, and why the taboo and mystery?"

"He bought his ticket yesterday."

"Did you talk to him?"

"Child, do I have a phone?"

Hallie grinned. "Do you still…"

"I am only fifty-three, and you have my permission to read my mind."

Hallie gawked at Mother Penny and opened her mouth in shock.

"Where do I start, Grandmother?"

Hallie's knees weakened, and she dropped her butt on a bench. Mother Penny sat next to her.

"Oh, Lord, where do I begin? You're a shameless, horny, old woman Grandma. Our family is the epitome of shame and scandal. You killed Ranchie, and your husband is my father. Do you think I'm a boy, Grandma?"

"Your duppy friend denied the two she took away to the butcher shop the chance to sort out the gender question for you."

"Whew, you're a bad woman. Dear Lord, we're living Junkanoo. My half-nephew is my half-brother, Jesus, mercy."

"Ranchie's Neutralizer abilities awoke that afternoon. Her stubbornness would have killed you."

Mother Penny shook her head in regret. *If Ranchie had only listened and walked away.*

"These new happenings could traumatize a child. Come, the phone shops are this way."

"We cannot use Tilly's gold for personal things. The pain will drive us mad. I told you, your Grandfather, Rhygin, went that route."

"I'm too young to deal with such details, but, my Lord, imagine an old lady having those things on her mind?"

"But si yah. Did I ever wake up dead one morning?" Mother Penny asked.

"I can't believe you."

"Where is the 'my-phone' shop? Mother Penny said.

"Grandma, they're called iPhones. You want me to laugh, and I changed my mind. I'm getting an Android instead."

"I refuse to ask." Mother Penny handed Hallie a handkerchief. "Wipe your nose."

"I don't have a cold."

"I said, wipe your nose," Mother Penny demanded.

Hallie rubbed her nose and bloodied the handkerchief.

"Can I say damn, Grandmother?"

"I have said worse… for new show off panties from the pennies."

"Who were you showing off to?" Hallie asked.

"Who's the adult around here?"

"Questions for answers again, but a decent job is gonna be a priority. Because I love expensive things," Hallie said.

"Mathematics and science are the future. But if you can cope with a two-day headache, you can get a computer or a tablet from the gold."

"How severe, Grandma?"

"You will wet yourself several times a day. A car will send you to the emergency room for a month."

"Suppose I abstain forever?" Hallie asked.

"You can try, but the urge to procreate will drive you crazy by your mid-twenties."

"The next Gunzey Healer in the family will be my son or daughter?" Hallie asked.

"Or your grandchild. If I am lucky, I should get at least seven years out of you."

"I can make quick money sprinting. I've been working on it," Hallie said.

"What is sprinting, and can you sprint?"

"Well, they have these tracks and things called blocks. Sprinters usually blast out of them and zoom to the finish line."

"So, what happens if Long Legs Susan is ahead?" Mother Penny asked.

"Long legs and speed are not synonymous, Grandmother. Shelly-Ann should jump in your head?"

"If you use your powers to win a race, medics will cart you away before the world," Mother Penny said.

"I'm gonna burn the tracks at Champs next year, and I'm using my middle name, Elaine."

Mother Penny threw an arm around Hallie's shoulder.

"When your father comes home, I do not want you to waste our time on fatherhood things in the first few weeks. You should pick up a book and hold your corner," Mother Penny said.

"Nasty old woman."

"Also, I want you to secretly use one of your healing apps and hit his backside as you lay eyes on him…"

Hallie giggled: "An app, grandma?"

"Listen to me, child. He has poor circulation, bad cholesterol, diabetes and a weak heart from eating unhealthy foreign food."

"Are you sure you got it all, Grandmother?"

"Yu getting fresh yu nuh pickney. Use yu damn imagination."

"I'm gonna drop my Grandmother's company and pick some obscene, dangerous peers. I'll have a better chance of hitting Heaven," Hallie said.

Mother Penny smiled at her.

"Yu tink mi did dun, nuh? So, what did the duppy gal tell you?" Mother Penny asked.

Hallie grinned at her.

"You're forgetting, I read your mind and saw your once-a-month thingy while I'm at school, and I'm not naming my daughter Penny."

"Why did I tell you to do something so silly?"

"You left home intentionally and gave Ranchie room to seduce your husband, so your gunzey grandchild could be born," Hallie said.

"Blame the cross, but you sounded a little disappointed you had to come through the birth process."

"But why not a neighborhood boy?" Hallie asked.

"The cross didn't show me a boy. It showed me, my husband."

"I bet you didn't see him running, huh? And a man from St. Mary, Grandmother?"

"I didn't look far enough around the corners, but a life lesson is there for you. For every action, be prepared for the reaction," Mother Penny said.

Hallie glanced at her in reverence, for those were valuable lessons taught casually.

"Mr. St. Mary served his purpose. I could not let a man from Moreland Hill laugh at my husband's back when he returned."

"You know you could've managed it better," Hallie said.

"Child, no one ever equates the fuzzy, white-haired smart guy and me."

"Do you mean Einstein?"

"The people of Moreland Hill's hard-earned money is not wasted on your school fees," Mother Penny said.

Hallie smiled at her grandmother. She met her eyes, and the mutual respect would endure until the end of time as they entered the phone store.

"I popped a Mac computer in my dad's head for me. The PC at school ran XP."

"As there is a God, I'm not going to ask what you are talking about," Mother Penny uttered.

Hallie grinned at her.

"Mary playing the fool to ketch Tom," Hallie grumbled.

The End